1ᵒᵒ ᵍᵉᵒ
6.19

The Illegal Gardener

Sara Alexi is the author of the Greek Village Series.
She divides her time between England and a small
village in Greece.

http://facebook.com/authorsaraalexi

Sara Alexi

THE ILLEGAL GARDENER

oneiro

Published by Oneiro Press 2012

ISBN-13: 978-1479190218

ISBN-10: 1479190217

For Sophia

Chapter 1

Aaman forces his hands deeper into his pockets, pinning his arms to his sides for warmth, tucking his chin to his chest and wonders if he will eat today. His toes curl for some relief from his pinching trainers. Closing his eyes he allows himself to drift for a moment, the bright moon not dispelling his need for sleep.

He looks up as the grumble of a tractor jerks him awake. The tractor hauls a flat back of crates, ready for the casual labourers to fill them. As it passes Aaman's head sinks to his chest again.

The flick of a light in the pharmacy opposite lays a rug of orange across the road. There are muffled noises within, buried in the depths of tinctures and bandages. Aaman rocks onto his heels and back, snorting warm air down his jumper, the heat giving him a momentary sense of civilisation.

The baker and his wife, next to the pharmacy, begin their work before Aaman arrives in the square, and the strong smell of bread gives him a time check. Each morning the oven door opens at the same hour so the day's staple can be presented to the trickle of

3

locals for breakfast, although it will be some time before the first of them appears.

A cockerel crows, its raucous call irritating a dog into barking. Their cries echo around the village above the noise of the wind machines that have been switched on to keep the oranges from freezing on the trees. When it hits below zero, it sounds like helicopters surround the village.

There is one such machine mounted on a pylon next to the building where Aaman sleeps, so cold at night, only warm by day at this time of year. Last night was three below zero. Cold and noisy, he wishes the seasons would hasten.

The kiosk's fluorescents stammer their way to life beside him, but the awning blocks his view. Protective metal shutters clang as they are taken down from the front of the drinks fridges, and glasses chink as crates of empty bottles are stowed away. The kiosk lady never speaks to him. Day after day they share this space, the village square, with its dried-up fountain and a lone palm tree surrounded by a circular bench. Aaman presumes she has seen illegal immigrants like him come and go for years. He is faceless to her.

A bitter aroma drifts from the kiosk; her daily flask of coffee that readies her for her shift. Aaman, unwillingly, recalls morning cups of tea with his father and mother after morning prayers, full of buffalo milk, heavy and rich and warm, chasing the cold away in winter.

The rumble of another tractor draws him back to the present, and he stands tall as it shudders to a halt. There is a chance; he is the only one here so far today. But the farmer has not stopped for workers, instead he greets the kiosk lady by name, chats for a while and leaves with a pack of cigarettes, his other hand helping to bring the conversation to its amusing end. He chuckles as he climbs back onto the tractor's metal seat, pulling his coat under his bottom to fight the cold.

The smell of bread percolates through the neck of Aaman's jumper, where he has buried his nose. He didn't eat the day before. No work, no food. A deathly cycle. No work, no food, no energy, no work, no food until, until what? Shuffling from foot to foot creates warmth and keeps his mind distracted from his stomach. He glimpses a movement behind the palm tree.

"Hi." It is Mahmout.

"Hello." Aaman doesn't sound friendly, it is not his intention. He is not here to make friends even if Mahmout is the only other Pakistani looking for work in this village. Aaman is from the North, the Punjab, a small village close to Sialkot. Mahmout is from the south, a world apart. Friends are irrelevant to Aaman's quest. Mahmout is grinning, as always.

Mahmout slumps, yawning, onto the circular bench. The temperature inches above zero and the wind fans in the orchards come to a stop, allowing the waking movements of the village to be heard in the ensuing silence. A woman chastises, a door slams. Dogs dotted across the village bark randomly and another cockerel crows. Soon the sun will be high enough to heat the day, making work a sweaty, mouth-drying job.

Two tall men walk up and stand next to them. Aaman judges their height and manner and decides they are Russian illegals. Their dialogue confirms this. They do not acknowledge Aaman or Mahmout. Tall and strong, they stand with authority, knowing they will get work first. Their clothes look shop-bought, not passed on as Aaman's and Mahmout's do. They look like they have had a good night's sleep.

Mahmout will also get work before him. Aaman is short, like a child. He was so thrilled, at the age of five, when he was given the job of fetching the jugs of water home. The jugs were heavy and for a long time it was a struggle. He saw it as following his brother, the beginning of manhood. He got up early and relished the chance day after day to prove his worth. It took nearly two years before the jugs were no longer a struggle. He was proud the day he noticed that. His mother was proud of him too, and his father ruffled his hair.

Aaman's father has two bullocks for ploughing, which he keeps at the back of the house in the village near Sialkot. Like his brother Giaan before him, Aaman would bring them grass and water. It was a peaceful household. The only time anyone raised a voice in his family was once when Giaan argued with their father. He said honour and status come from hard work, not from turbans. His father, who has worn a turban all his life, believed turbans said much more than that. They denoted his position in life, his point of view, his outlook. Soon after that, Giaan went to work at the factory, leaving Aaman and his father to till the soil. Aaman felt very alone.

He worked alongside his father and his grandfather in the fields until, at the age of eight, he tried for a job in the factory where Giaan worked, making footballs. Aaman thought he was a man, and he worked for a week with no pay to show his ability. He spent time in the storage room where roll after roll of cotton was stored, and in the laminating room where the layers of cotton were coated with liquid vinyl, another layer of cotton smoothed on top, layer after layer to the thickness of leather.

At first his brother worked in the noisy cutting rooms where the booming rhythm of the stamping machines stipulated the speed his die cut the hexagons. Aaman was impressed by the rate at which the men in this room worked, the floor thick with hexagons. Giaan later progressed to the printing rooms which were much quieter than the cutting rooms with their echoing presses. They were still, each man to his colour, each hexagon printed individually. Giaan screen printed the colour red.

That fateful factory.

The village cafe opens its doors, and two waiting men enter and sit on the hard wooden chairs, one on each side of the open dimly lit room, his own seat, his usual metal table. One lights a cigarette and the owner takes them unordered coffee, the routine of years. No one speaks.

A van pulls up. All the men stand stiffly on the edge of the pavement. Aaman takes his hands out of his pockets, tries to grow, letting his pride fill his chest. Mahmout fixes a grin on his face. The two Russians look assured, hands in pockets, no smiles. Serious.

The driver points to the Russians without hesitation and waves with his thumb for them to get in the back of the van. The Russians smile now. They will eat today.

Aaman didn't get the job at the factory where his brother worked, and not long after he stopped growing. His body stunted at ten years old, never to catch up with his pride or his conscientiousness, both large to compensate his diminutive stature. Eventually he managed to get a job at a carpet factory where no questions were asked of his age or ability. The hours were very long, and it was hard on his father and grandfather who were left to till unaided by youth.

Some teenagers come and stand at the bus stop opposite the square, backpacks ready for school. They call hellos to the kiosk lady then settle, nodding their heads to unheard beats. They don't see Aaman. A younger boy runs to join them; they smile and reach to tickle him, teasing and familiar, gentle.

One evening at the *chopal*, the evening meeting of the villagers, Aaman was tickled by one of the elders.

He was taken for a child even though he had turned sixteen. He snorts and pushes the thought away.

Another man shuffles onto the square, and it is only when he moves that Aaman realises the man was curled up in the opposite doorway, motionless until now. He is tall, but his bony frame shows despite his oversized coat and layers of thin jumpers. He is bearded and looks perhaps Middle Eastern. His eyes reflect his surprise and powerlessness at the nearness of his own death. His shoes have no soles, socks worn on his hands. He has no energy to move, to warm himself.

The children opposite chorus a 'Good morning' and smile as an old man shuffles by them, dressed in thick cotton trousers, jumper, solid boots and carrying a shepherd's crook which he raises in answer and hobbles on towards the cafe.

A woman pulls up in a car. The men ignore her. Aaman watches as she surveys them from the safety of her metal box, and wonders if she might be looking for a labourer so he takes his hands from his pockets. Mahmout seems to recognise her and smiles and waves in a vaguely hysterical manner. She lowers the window. Her jumper is thick and warm, and she wears a hat that covers her ears. Her cheeks glow and she looks healthy.

Aaman pulls himself to full height next to Mahmout. The woman looks him up and down. Mahmout grins widely and jabbers.

"Hello, you remember me? I help with water." Mahmout interrupts her silence, his accent makes his English difficult to understand. '

The woman seems to quickly tire of his chatter. She remembers him from the day before when he offered to carry a six-pack of water bottles from the kiosk to her car, a distance of about five metres. Aaman closes his mouth firmly as he hears the exchange. He will get a job based on his merits, not from ingratiating himself with petty tasks. He is a man who needs work, not a handout.

The woman seems inclined to talk to him even though she has met Mahmout before. Aaman is surprised. He has presumed her choice had been made for her. He draws himself up as she scans his face.

"Do you speak English?"

He nods, a little taken aback. She hesitates; Aaman tries to think of something to say in English.

"Yes," he flounders in a state of panic. But he is too late, he can see it in her face, her look of eager anticipation exchanged for closed decision.

"You are too small," she says and signals to Mahmout to get into the car.

Mahmout grins as he leaves, but Aaman knows that domestic labourers don't always get food, which is only assured on the larger building sites, and not even on those sometimes. The sun is up now and warm enough to remove his gloves and hat, which he places carefully on the bench, then sits and leans back against the palm tree. It is unlikely that anyone will come for workers this late.

Aaman falls into a half sleep, hope keeping one eye alert. The bakery's doors are open for business and there is an intermittent stream of customers. The kiosk and the corner shop both do a steady trade in cigarettes and the pharmacy unbolts its doors, the orange rug now dissolved by the sun.

The man with the sole-less shoes has wedged himself between a wall and a tree and remains motionless, soaking up the warmth.

With the prospect of finding work fading Aaman considers whether or not to walk all the way back to his home, if the place where he sleeps can be thought of as 'home.' It is a small storage barn made of mud bricks in the middle of an orange orchard. The farmer has put shelves all the way around from floor to ceiling, each just wide enough for a man to lie on. Most of the sixteen men who sleep there have had steady work picking oranges for a few weeks and have formed themselves into teams. Romanians, Albanians, Bulgarians working together.

It costs thirty cents a night to sleep on the shelves. No covers, only boards. The farmer makes 120 Euros a month and keeps his oranges safe from gypsies who come in the night with trucks to steal his crop. Some of the illegals who have been there longer have found themselves blankets from somewhere. Some stay for a while, others pass through, and nothing is safe to leave there. What you have you keep on you. Consequently no one has much more than a packet of cigarettes and each, down his trousers at night, a mobile phone, a tool for finding work.

Aaman drifts off in the warmth of the sun. The helicopter fan for the oranges abutting the sleeping barn was switched on at two in the morning last night and it was hard to sleep after that. A motorbike backfires by the kiosk and Aaman jolts awake again.

The cafe is now full of men smoking and sipping morning coffee. Snippets of subdued conversation quietly ricochet around the room. At the bakery there is a queue of four people. The bus has come and gone, taking the schoolchildren off for the day. Shutters are being opened all around the village, glints of sun reflect on gleaming glass.

Aaman recognises the red car. The woman who hired Mahmout earlier has taken her hat off to reveal dyed blonde hair. The world of the West. She glances over and makes fleeting eye contact but drives on. She also sees the bearded man who has wedged himself between the wall and the tree. She looks twice at him.

The woman stops outside the bakery. Aaman watches her inside where she talks and points. He looks away as she comes out and across the road toward him. She smiles and walks past him a few more steps to the man with the beard, who wakes with a start. She hands what she has bought from the bakery to the man and walks away without a word, climbs in her car and is gone.

Aaman stares at the bearded man in disgust, and at the sandwich he has been given. His gaze follows the route her car took, this Westerner with so much wealth she can just give it away. He waits to see if the bearded man will eat the sandwich or if his pride will dampen his hunger.

The man inspects the sandwich. A cat appears from nowhere, hopeful for discarded ham. He tears off a piece of sandwich, turns his face towards the wall and puts it in his mouth, repeating this process in quick succession until it is gone. Aaman stares blankly, watching him eat, until the bearded man looks up and makes eye contact, embarrassed. Aaman turns away.

The bearded man unwedges himself from between the wall and the tree trunk and scuttles away. His day is done. He has eaten.

Aaman shifts his position. This woman can afford to give her food away and he can't even make enough to feed himself. She has money for a car and the irrelevant, unnecessary vanity of hair dye, and he doesn't even have the thirty cents for tonight's sleep out of the frost. With little hope of work at this late hour, and his enthusiasm dampened, Aaman considers that he may as well start the long walk back to the barn, conserve his energy. Try again tomorrow.

The car pulls up, the door is flung open and, before Aaman has shifted his thoughts from his internal dialogue, she is standing in front of him.

"Who speaks English?"

Aaman quickly looks around to see another Russian-looking man has joined him, and although disoriented he embraces the opportunity and tries to smile.

"I speak English, Madam." Aaman waits for the Russian man to speak, for the battle, for the defeat.

The Russian is tall and strong but he shrugs, mute; he has no English. He admits defeat.

She smiles at Aaman and pulls the passenger door open and motions him in.

Aaman doesn't hesitate. He climbs into the car feeling like a king. She puts the car in gear and they move.

"What is your name?"

"Aaman."

"I am Juliet."

They drive in silence just around the corner and up a narrow private lane that needs weeding, an opportunity. The lane ends at a whitewashed stone farmhouse with faded blue shutters. The gates stand open onto a weed-filled gravel courtyard. Mahmout heaves a sack full of rubble around from the back of the house.

The car comes to a stop, Juliet springs out, and Aaman quickens his speed. He takes off his jacket, puts it on the ground and rolls up his sleeves. A good worker does not delay.

With a sweeping gesture she indicates the garden to the rear of the house. She hands him a rubble sack from a pile.

"Please clear this. Put the full sacks by the gate."

Aaman sees enough work to last weeks. He also sees Mahmout grinning at the lady. Aaman pulls a pair of seam-split leather working gloves from his back pocket. He will work harder than Mahmout.

The lady leaves them to go inside the house, her hair shining like gold in the sun. She turns, and Aaman realises he has been staring after her and quickly averts his gaze. She seems to be about to say something but changes her mind and goes inside. There has been no agreement about wages and Aaman does not feel it is his place to raise the subject. On a good day he has been paid twenty euros and been fed, on a bad day five euros and no food.

He still wonders if he will eat today.

A phone rings in the house.

Chapter 2

"Hello?"

"Juliet? Where are you?"

"Michelle?"

"Yes. You OK?"

"Yes, of course, I feel great!"

"Where are you?"

"In a village."

"In a village in Greece?"

"Yes."

"Thomas said Greece, but I thought I must have misunderstood. What are you doing there?"

"I live here."

"You live there?"

"I bought a house! It took ten days to complete. It needs work and the garden is unbelievable."

"Juliet, are you serious?"

"Apparently Albanian refugees had been renting it for ten years and, by the looks of the garden, they never threw anything away."

"Albanian refugees?"

"I've counted three mattresses out there so far and that's just what's visible!"

"Juliet? What on earth are you talking about? I had to call Thomas to find out where you were. He gave me this number and said you'd left the country. He said Terrance knew and that you had to 'get away.' I thought it was some elaborate joke. What's going on?"

Juliet laughs, briefly. "I'm in Greece and I am fine actually. Now that I'm here, I feel great. It is so beautiful." Her tongue drawls on the word beautiful as she looks around the undulating plastered stone walls and tiled floor. A small, green, shiny-backed beetle runs from under the faded sofa.

The uncared-for look of the cottage intoxicated Juliet. The traditional fireplaces whispering secrets of years gone by, the crude wooden cupboards in the kitchen telling of men with basic tools, old ways. Their chambers full of mismatched crockery, wooden bowls and tins even though human presence has been absent for some years. Piles of abandoned domestic artifacts and heaps of past lives crawl from corners. Outside, greenery climbs over unnatural shapes, hiding the debris of a disrespectful generation around a solitary old olive tree.

Juliet looks out of the little window in the back door to what will be the garden, the two men, hunched in the bright sunlight, beginning the care.

"I'm so glad to be here. I had just had enough. Mick, solicitors, Mother, enough of people and their ways. So I decided to take a break from people. Take myself to a place just for me."

"Hide away, more like ..."

"What?" Juliet looks at the receiver and curls her upper lip, surprising herself as she slams the phone

17

down. She grabs last night's wine bottle and pours a drink. The bottle clonks, echoes, as it slams back on concrete work surface. Juliet swallows in one and throws the glass in the stone sink. Curses and the glass breaking shatter the interior's silence, both dismissed in the wake of her stomping into action.

Opening from the still of the greying whitewashed sitting room, with its overfilled sofa and painted chairs, is a room that brims with the passing of time. A wooden dough pan is crammed with garden implements that have escaped a museum. Brass bed ends lean against a wall cupboard, which lies on its side on the floor, one door missing, the insides spilling, promising finds and treasures. A hook on the wall supports a donkey's bridle and a ring of several dozen large, old, rusted keys. The light streams though a cobwebbed window, picking up dust flecked in its rays that dance with Juliet's approach.

Her oversized washing-up gloves impede her anger as Juliet yanks the door to this room wide open. Wanting to see some immediate progress, Juliet pulls at the largest item in the room. The mouse-eaten, disintegrating mattress mounts its defence lung-threatening fluff and hand-gashing, rusted spring ends. Her self-righteousness gives her the power of twenty and she pulls and manoeuvres, twists and bends until the remains of the bedding sit wrapped in twine like a foot-bound animal, awaiting its fate by the gate.

Juliet flounders backwards as the mattress comes to rest, her energy exhausted. At the sun's insistence, she slumps against the wall of the old stone house. She becomes vaguely aware of the forgotten men working around the back. Tinkering sounds, hushed voices.

She sits, her focus on the patch of ground in front of her. Batteries, an odd shoe, half a plate, and blunted knives fight for space with plastic bags, empty unlabelled tins, and unidentifiable electrical circuit board pieces. The enormity of the mess begins to overwhelm her.

Contemplating her foolishness, she finds herself thankfully distracted by a pitiful sound. A small-framed cat meows its plight and, half afraid but desperate through curiosity, it sidles from under the shade of the old olive tree towards her.

"Hello kitty kitty."

The cat grows bolder at the gentle sound of Juliet's voice.

"Come on, then." Juliet now as much in need of the touch of soft, comforting fur as the cat is in need of a friend.

The cat fights the battle of fear until it succumbs to the pleasure of the ruffling and stroking of Juliet's hand.

"Hello, you cute little thing. Where have you come from?" The cat's presence gives Juliet a new energy, a slight sense of power. The cat winds its way through Juliet's legs, its black and white fur leaving traces on her grey, faded jeans.

The phone rings again inside. Juliet reluctantly shuffles to her feet, marches inside and pours herself some water before picking it up.

"Sorry."

"Michelle?"

"Yes, sorry, I didn't mean anything by it. But you can see, can't you? It does seem a little bit—well, come on Juliet—moving out there on your own is a bit crazy for most people."

"But I am not most people. You know, better than anyone, that I have been stifled, suffocated, smothered, for goodness' sake, all but strangled by that man for so long. So now I'm doing it my way. Besides, what did you expect I would do? I have a job I can do anywhere. Was I expected to stay in that poky flat and just hang around waiting for a man to replace Mick?"

"I was never for Mick, as well you know. Those that were just thought he might settle down, calm down your wild ways. You were pretty wild, you know. And it seems you still are. I mean, you've just left the country, bought a place abroad ..."

"And it's fantastic," Juliet says. She picks at some fluff hanging from the edge of the sofa, then stuffs it back into the hole it came out of.

"Are you expecting to get more translation work out there, or do you think because you speak the language you will just fit in and get a job? I mean, we had a great time when we went. It was hilarious, but it was only two weeks and it was, well, ages ago."

"Nothing's changed Michelle, I still feel the same about this country the way I did back then." She looks out at the sunshine.

"I know it really caught you, else you wouldn't have spent all these years learning Greek, but there's more than language that separates cultures. Who are you going to spend your time with? How will you get by? What about the boys, at least?"

"The boys are fine. Thomas is talking of coming over next spring with Cherie. Terrance sees it all as a big adventure. Anyway, Terrance is so wrapped up in his mission to save the world through his study of 'waste management' that what anyone else does doesn't really matter to him. I need time out for me. If you're not going to support me in that then perhaps this isn't a good time for us to be in contact." Juliet looks up to the faded paint of the wooden ceiling.

"Stop it, Juliet. Of course I know what you need. But did you think I wouldn't be surprised at this sudden move? Come on, you knew I would be, and you know everyone else will be. But isn't that what you wanted though, to shock people, push them away?"

"I wasn't thinking about anyone else for a change," Juliet says.

"Look, Mick was bad news and you stayed for the twins, so you have done what you thought was right. But Mick just put off the inevitable. You've got to dig a bit deeper if you're looking for any amount of contentment."

21

Juliet, whilst listening with the phone tucked against her shoulder, runs a finger along her arm. Her mood plummets down a familiar black spiral. The thin, translucent skin puckers like a plastic sheet, gathered where the scarring gives way to healthy skin. When her fingers reach her thumb, with force of will, she pulls herself out of the void, takes hold of the phone and bounds off the sofa.

"I am digging deeper. I have hired help who are digging the garden as we speak. So you should be pleased that I won't be alone." The cat has wandered indoors; Juliet wafts her hand at it and makes hissing noises.

"What are you doing?" Michelle asks.

"There's a cat, got to go. Bye." Grabbing the opportunity, she replaces the phone. Michelle dismissed, Juliet shushes the cat through the light-filled door into the garden, The Mess.

The cat, surprised and apparently deeply offended that he is not given a hero's welcome to the cool sanctuary of the house, hesitates before he disappears over the wall. Juliet expected the cat to only go out as far as the garden. She tuts her indignity after the fickle creature.

Juliet can see over the wall into next door's garden. It is large, more like a small field, and is filled with neat rows of tended vegetables in heaped rich soil. A one storey house with a crumbling tiled roof is beyond the last row, and behind that, an olive tree-covered hill fades into the pale blue sky. Not a cloud, not a breath of air. Calm, sleepy.

On impulse, and completely forgetting her two workers in the back garden, Juliet leaves the rusted gate creaking on dry hinges as she marches down the weed-edged lane towards the village centre.

The lane gives way to the road, which is a short distance from the square. A dog crosses her path, collarless and dirty, cowering at her approach. She feels power and empathy. A cockerel crows in the distance, out of sync with the hour. The day's heat demands submission of all.

The *kafenios*, full of retired farmers, masculine domains that fringe the square, hum with murmurs of tongues that drift with the aroma of strong coffee. The conversations ebb and flow as Juliet passes. Nothing changes quickly here and Juliet's face, a relatively new one, is worthy of comment.

As she nears the door of the corner shop and with the necessity to speak approaching Juliet notices the insecurities rising within her. The demons of not being heard, the goblins of not being understood, the imps of not being considered important, and the fight between them confuse her thinking into a shade of panic.

The cool cavern of the village shop is a cornucopia of practicality. Goat bells hang next to hairnets. Bottles of bleach jostle with jars of fresh honey, local eggs sit in a brown paper bag nest on the counter top. The shop owner rises from amongst cartons of cigarettes and bundled shepherd's crooks and wishes Juliet "Good Welcome."

Juliet swims in delight at hearing her Greek spoken by a native.

"Thank you." She feels rusty. Her hard fought-for business translating documents has increased her love of the language over the last two years, although speaking out loud still feels unfamiliar, but exciting. Juliet shuffles her feet and structures her sentence before breathing it to life.

"I would like some box of match and a stamps please." She can hear her mistakes but it is too late to retract them. She knows what she should be saying but her tongue is unpractised. It's like being back in night class all those years ago after that spontaneous holiday with Michelle. That moment of warmth, sea, and friendly people who made eye contact and then slowed down time to make room for her. It was the visit that shifted her soul from its plinth never to feel settled again. It was the beginning of the end for her and Mick.

The shopkeeper frowns briefly. Matches appear with a strip of stamps torn from a large sheet. The exchange goes well. Juliet gains strength. She envisages her next sentence written on paper and then gives it life. The shopkeeper holds her breath anticipating an unintelligible request.

"I need a box of bleach, something for wood to wash, to be good, and that which is metal and you use it to wash pans that have been baked in the oven." Juliet is thoroughly aware that, although a competent academic translator, her conversational skills lack fluency.

After another brief frown, the woman behind the counter reacts as if she has been given a jump start. She is either relieved that there will be no English to struggle with, impressed by Juliet's moderate abilities or flattered by the importance of her mother tongue. Whichever it is, she is roused to be as helpful as possible, pulling one item out after another until it is ascertained that 'that which is metal' is a pan scrub and that it is polish that will 'wash wood and make it good.'

The very language transports Juliet to the world she has imagined is Greece, lazy days and soft-spoken people, quick tempers and forgiving natures, friendly faces and open houses, welcoming families, and always one extra place for the latecomer, a place she sought after and studied for all these years.

She quickly learns the new words for polish and pan scrub and stores them away.

After the items are gathered, Juliet adds a goat bell which she likes the sound of for the front door and a wooden carved stamp, which the lady says is for impressing a mark on the dough for the traditional Easter bread.

The shopkeeper is curious. Surely Juliet is not alone? She busies herself displaying candles to sell for Easter. Where is her family, her parents? Her father is dead; oh she is sorry, and so young. Sometimes we grow strong from these things. Not close to her mother! Oh dear, well, it happens. Where are her children? Where is her husband? Ah she is sorry; she too has a daughter who is divorced. When

25

was that? Oh so recently. Is she OK? Was it her choice? Oh good, it is better if the women decide these things. What will she do now? How can she work through the Internet? No please don't explain it, it doesn't really matter. Does she have friends here in the village? No! Well, now she has one. Marina. She pats her house-coated bosom and smiles.

Juliet skips out of the shop having dealt Goliath a mighty blow. The language is real, her ability to speak fluently is returning quickly. She has the power to be understood, to survive. She dances three steps before quickly returning for her stamps and matches and another enthusiastic departure.

On the lane to her house she meets the cat, who winds between her legs and trots to keep up.

"OK, I cannot stop you walking with me or hanging around, but let's be clear, cat, you do not come in the house."

Halfway up the lane, she remembers she has the workmen at her house and she has left all the doors open. Hurrying the rest of the way, she has visions of her laptop, her work gone, and her passport along with it.

The cat chases her.

Chapter 3

The front door is wide open. Bugs buzz in and out of the shade and cool. Juliet rushes in to see her laptop safely on the sofa, her handbag hanging, untouched, from the kitchen chair. The house has the chill and stillness of a church after the heat of the sun. She peeps out of the back door where the two men are still working. She smiles, she relaxes. *This is Greece*.

Watching the two men bent over, up to their knees in weeds and rubbish, she estimates, judging by the amount they have done, that the garden will be clear within a couple of weeks. Then the slow process of digging the rich dense red soil will begin, turning it over piece by piece, taking out the stones. Maybe she will need to add something to make the soil more manageable, drain better, before the fun of planting trees and flowers, sowing grass seed and deciding which vegetables will go where.

Mahmout stops and turns to smile at Juliet.

"Madam appears happy."

Juliet snaps out of her daydream and looks at him blankly.

"I am thinking Madam is happy to see two such good workers making her home very lovely?"

Juliet is shocked and resents the intrusion into her thoughts. She bought the house for the silence it offers, the escape from people, a place where she can choose to be quiet. But here is a man taking that quiet away, demanding answers to unimportant questions. Juliet frowns. Using workmen has its drawbacks. She weighs the choice between answering him politely and self-preservation.

"Get on with it." She returns inside through the back door, eager to make a distance. Flopping on the sofa, the cat looks up at her.

"Out!" She scrambles to her feet and chases the cat through the front door. However, once the sun touches her skin, she is reluctant to return indoors. Her movements slow in the warmth, and she turns her face to the sun, allowing herself to be still. The sound of goat bells comes from a nearby hill, a farmer calling to slow them down as the hollow clonking of the bells speeds up, a slope maybe.

After some time passes, minutes, or maybe hours, it doesn't matter, Juliet looks over her arms to see if she is tanning. She notices a big weed by the toe of her sandal. Lazily she pulls at the weed; it pulls away like a knife from melted butter. She pulls the one next to it, which is followed by another and then another. Energised by progress she begins to pull weeds as quickly as the roots will allow. Some come away with a slight tug. With others, she digs her fingers into the soil to claw away around the tap root, snapping the hair-fine roots as they come free. She waves a lazy buzzing insect away, her nails filled with soil.

After a few minutes, Juliet finds her gardening gloves and wheels the wheelbarrow near where she is working. There is a traditional adze in the wheelbarrow. The more stubborn weeds come up swiftly and smoothly using the adze, and the wheelbarrow fills. Juliet works until sweat drips from her brow and her gloves feel too hot and sticky. The adze is heavy with the clinging red earth.

Pulling the gloves off, she returns indoors, sighing in the comparative cool. She selects a tall, thin, hand-blown glass and fills it with chilled water from the fridge. The water and the cool revive her, and she continues to drink, then rolls the cold glass across her forehead whilst she wanders to the bedroom. Here, unseen through the gauze curtains, she watches the men working at the back.

The grinning one is not grinning now; he is squatting and picking at little things which he puts in a rubble sack. The smaller one is pulling large items from the abundant bindweed and manhandling them around the corner towards the gate. He has found an old padded chair with wooden arms. He stops and looks at the house, up to the roof. Juliet tries to follow his gaze but he is looking beyond where she can see. He pulls the cushions off the chair and takes them around the corner. He returns and jumps on what remains of the chair and piles the pieces of wood just the other side of the bedroom window.

He was looking to see if there is a chimney!

Juliet moves to pull the curtain aside and open the window to talk to the men but thinks better of revealing herself. She puts the glass of water down and returns through the kitchen to the back door.

"Yes, any wood you find, please pile it up by that window."

"Oh yes madam, we will do a good job," the Grinning One calls.

Juliet cannot bring herself to look at the grinning, squatting man, he reminds her of a toad with his wide mouth. His sycophantic ways are annoying, not pleasing. She returns indoors, back to her bedroom where she shuts the door, her sanctuary, to watch.

As the sun slides its way to its zenith, the Small One has cleared a bigger area than Juliet would have supposed possible in the time he has been working. The Grinning One is still sitting on his haunches, his rubble bag nearly full, a small area of ground before him pristine.

They talk, the language strange to her ears. She listens for the patterns and cadences which mingle with the heat. The Grinning One talks the most, the Small One answering occasionally. It reminds her that she has some translation work due. Still hot, she drinks some more water before she sets down the glass and returns to the papers in the sitting room, picking the soil from under her nails as she reads.

The murmur of the men ceases and nothing is heard except the scratching noises of their work floating through the back door, the occasional dog barking in the village and the goat bells, now far away. Juliet is lost in her translation, reading and writing. A couple of hours pass.

Thirst awakens Juliet from her work. Her glass needs retrieving from the bedroom. It is cooler in the bedroom, an older part of the house with thick walls of massive stones piled carefully together over a century ago. When she first moved in, there was an earthquake. Juliet ran on liquid legs to the gate, the pomegranate trees rustling, the ground quivering. But the house stood sure, unperturbed by nature's power.

She can see the men still working. The Small One has taken his jumper off. Juliet is surprised it has taken him so long; she is wearing the lightest clothes she has. Retracing her steps to fill her glass in the kitchen, Juliet finds the cat curled up in her seat on the sofa. She picks it up by the scruff of the neck and takes it at arm's length out of the back door.

She is tempted to drop it to see how easily it will land on all four feet but at the last moment puts it down gently and strokes its head before nudging it away from the door with her foot.

The Mess has definitely decreased in size. There are at least ten rubble sacks by the back wall, and the Small One is pulling up armfuls of bindweed to reveal what is hidden underneath. Juliet steps into the forceful heat of the mid-afternoon sun. Both men look up from their work. The Small One seems to be staring. Avoiding his gaze, Juliet begins to turn away.

"Please?"

31

Juliet pretends she hasn't heard and takes a drink of water as she steps back indoors.

"Please?"

Louder this time. Juliet turns sharply, chin in the air.

"What now?" She meets the Small One's gaze.

"Water."

Juliet drops her chin and looks at her glass. After the briefest of pauses she finds she is embarrassed by her own thoughtlessness. She hesitates as the number of glasses of water she has drunk during the course of the morning comes to mind, unbidden. Frowning briefly, she raises her head and looks the Small One in the eye.

"Of course."

Juliet wonders whether they will want glasses or if they will drink from the bottle. She finds two glasses she doesn't use (she feels the glass is too thick), pinches them together between finger and thumb and takes them and a water bottle to the waiting men. She doesn't give them to the men but instead puts them down on the windowsill and walks past the men around the end of the house to see how much of The Mess is piled by the gate. There is an unexpectedly high pile. The cat is there digging a hole in the gravel to relieve itself by one of the rubble sacks.

Juliet flaps her hand at the cat and decides she needs to find someone who will take The Mess away. Turning from the gate, she notices that one of the men has jumped over the garden wall into the next door plot.

Orange groves surround Juliet's house on two sides at the back, the fence between, high, but pleasantly unnoticeable, a wire mesh rusted into camouflage, a lacework of holes giving footholds to creepers and vines, a canvas for grasses to weave. The patio and the drive are edged by a whitewashed wall that overlooks the tended field and neighbour beyond, but the fourth side is flanked by a piece of disused land with an old stone barn, its roof slowly falling in. It is over the old stone wall to this land that the man has gone.

She sees only the man's leg and foot, the last of him to disappear from view. She has no idea which of the men it is. Nor does it matter, it is a liberty, and for what? Juliet feels her chest swell in indignation and is on the point of calling out loudly to ask what he thinks he is doing when realisation saves her the embarrassment.

She has surprised herself during the morning and feels uncomfortable. Twice it has been completely out of her frame of reference to consider the basic human needs of another. It is not the way she sees herself. She has been—is—a mother. The needs of the twins were her priority for so long. But now she overlooks the obvious needs of another for water and basic facilities. She was a good mother and wonders why she would be missing the skills that were her pride for all those years.

The young twins seem a lifetime away. *They'll be twenty-four this year.* The same age she was when she had them. Thomas now content and nearly married, Terrance just finishing a Master of Science degree and ready to rule the world. At twenty-four, Juliet had already been married a year.

Michelle, such a good friend for all those years, phoned her about Mick on several occasions. She was her usual tentative and sensitive self with each call. But the bottom line to these conversations, and Juliet could hear it loud and clear no matter how Michelle dressed it, was that she thought the match was a bad idea. Juliet was determined that Mick was to be her happy ever after. Michelle's stance drove a wedge into their friendship, at least in the early days of her marriage.

Now Juliet can no longer see Mick with her eyes from back then. All the traits that seemed so spontaneous and rebellious now make him appear shirking of responsibility and lacking in intelligence. He seemed so free and without a care, seizing each day and squeezing out the fun. But when the boys came, the spontaneous pint in the pub became predictable. The carefree taking the day off work irresponsible as his pay was docked or, as in more than one case, he was sacked and their budget tightened even more until he was taken on again.

However, she can still picture the way his dark hair curled behind his ears, the pout of his upper lip when he looked at her. The way his eyelashes made his blue eyes look permanently eye-lined. His accent was a tentacle from the old country, her childhood home, early memories of simplicity and safety. In those early days, he made her feel as if the world couldn't breathe without her.

The boys were a product of their spontaneous delight. But within months of changing nappies, preparing food, burping, and bedtimes, it was Juliet who felt she couldn't breathe under Mick's gaze. He became at first demanding, then critical, then dismissive. The boys took her focus, her own needs lost in mounds of washing and meals to make. Homemaker and mother for two years, with never a moment off. Until Mick's mother came over from Ireland, and Juliet took the holiday to Greece that ignited her passion for this country and its language. The holiday she took, not with Mick, but with Michelle, the first time she had seen her since school. In fact, it had been the last time too.

The holiday was fantastic. Juliet laughed until she ached. They were kids again without a care in the world. But towards the end, Michelle began to suggest that Juliet should leave Mick. Somehow it grew to an argument that encompassed the events of their childhood and forced Juliet to look at things she had buried. The argument became the sole topic of conversation and it continued from the hotel to the airport, finishing with Juliet storming off once they reached home ground.

Twenty-two years Michelle has been calling her, keeping that relationship alive, but not once apologising.

Lost in these thoughts, Juliet is startled by the Grinning One coming round the corner.

"Is madam pleased so far? You must excuse my bad English. Here, in this country, it is difficult to learn English." He is grinning between his words and his head is never still.

Juliet is well aware that he is trying to ingratiate himself because he needs the work, but she is also aware that his ingratiation technique is stopping him from doing this work.

"Yes, I understand, you do not need to speak English to do this work." She points in the direction she wants him to return to his labour.

He grins. She turns away towards the house.

"It will be beautiful when we are finished, madam, have no fear, no fear at all," he calls after her.

Juliet leaves them alone for half an hour before asking them if they would like an iced coffee. They are both very pleased. She takes the thick glasses she gave them for water by their bases and carries them into the kitchen where she puts them in the sink and washes them with hot water and soap. The iced coffee fills them to the brim and she presents them on a tray. She wonders if she is overcompensating.

After the coffee, Juliet resumes her translation work. Low volume music comes from the back garden. Bollywood music, tinny, from a mobile phone perhaps. She smiles and stands up and puts her arms out to her sides and wiggles her hips, images of colourful saris and nose rings and hennaed hands completing the transformation in her mind. As she wiggles, she gathers her notes and takes them all into the bedroom and lays them on the desk before the window. The music will be a little closer and therefore louder working here.

The music seems so happy to Juliet, and after a short while she stares out of the window, watching the men work. The Grinning One has a serious face now. He works slowly and is talking quietly to the other one. He looks cross. The Small One stops his hauling of the larger pieces and stretches and then rubs his stomach and pulls a face. Juliet wonders if he has a stomach ache.

Returning to her work, she feels fidgety until homing in on the sensation of hunger. At the same moment she recalls the Small One's face whilst rubbing his stomach and realises he must be hungry too. She feels happy to have thought of this and goes outside to ask them.

"Are you hungry?"

The look on their faces as they meet her eye makes her feel foolish for asking in the first place. She doesn't wait for an answer but returns indoors and lays out two plates with bread, tinned sardines, a salad of fresh tomatoes and cucumber and a couple of apples apiece. She has emptied the fridge; there is no more to offer. Juliet wonders when she can shop for food if she is going to have someone helping in the garden. She shouldn't leave them alone even if the house is locked.

Not sure where to lay out the food, Juliet hovers with a plate in each hand between the kitchen table, repainted and transformed from when she moved in, and the cheap folding table on the porch. After putting the food on the porch table, she covers each plate with some kitchen paper to keep any flies away. She checks the front garden and over the wall for the cat. There is no sign of him.

Juliet tries the tap on the porch. It doesn't work. She considers getting them a bowl of water for their hands but then decides that would be ridiculous.

"Come and eat." She beckons them to the kitchen and shows them the sink and a new bar of soap she has just unwrapped. They both wash their hands thoroughly and Juliet lays out a hand towel each on the edge of the sink. The men seem to feel awkward about the towels. The Small One gently wipes his hands before replacing the towel carefully and the Grinning One uses the same towel. Juliet indicates the front door, where the food can be seen on the table beyond, the paper covering being caught by the slightest of afternoon breezes.

Whilst they eat Juliet tries to be discreet, but her curiosity is heightened. What she keeps expecting isn't how events unfold. They used a towel between them, as if a towel is something other people have but not them, but then they didn't thank her for the towels, which if it was an unusual or special event she would have expected. Nor did they thank her for the cold coffees earlier, or the water. They wanted the drinks, but they accepted them like it was their right.

She imagines they will dig in to the food in an appreciative fashion. She looks forward to seeing them eat with gusto. So much of their behaviour has left her at a loss. Their responses unexpected, their manners are so different. What she will enjoy when they eat is seeing expected behaviour. She needs some normality, something familiar.

But they both stand beside the table and talk whilst looking at the food, indicating what they are clearly discussing. Juliet feels sure she hasn't put any foods that they wouldn't eat on their plates. No pork for Muslims, no beef for Hindus. She is unsure which they might be, but as she has neither in the house, she is at a loss to explain their hesitation.

Eventually they sit and eat slowly, selecting what they choose with care and attention whilst making quiet conversation. They savour everything that is on their plates, using the bread as a scoop. There is a pause to talk a little and sit a little before they change plates and begin on the fruit. The Grinning One pushes his shoes off the back of his heel with his other foot. He picks up some gravel that has made its way onto the patio and throws it to scare the cat away. Juliet's lips tighten.

When they have finished, they do not sit. They stand and walk around the house to begin working again.

Juliet collects the dishes. The Grinning One's plates are empty but the Small One has left an apple. He has balanced it on the peel of the first apple to leave the bruised side uppermost. It has been carefully placed so as not to roll, the imperfection on display. Juliet feels affronted. Is her food not good enough? She would eat the apple in that condition. It wouldn't occur to her that it was anything but edible. Is it a comment? Has she offended them by offering imperfect produce? Are they in a position to choose?

Juliet stacks the dishes in the sink, but leaves the apple plate on the side to contemplate.

Having started so early and lunched so late, the working day is nearly at an end. Juliet, stationed behind the gauze curtain in the bedroom, sees the taller one again squatting on the ground, filling another rubble sack. The other has worked his way through to the back of the garden and has cleared a track, causing a division. He is pulling something from the ground. It looks like weeds, but he is taking great care not to harm it. After a struggle and many pauses to release the plant in places, he pulls free a tendril, green and leafy, over ten feet long. Juliet is curious. He has left it and walked out of view, and she anticipates his return. He comes back into view with a post which he hammers into the ground with the adze that he must have taken from the wheelbarrow.

The post reverberates with each blow, the solid 'thunk' echoes off the back wall of the house, movement in several places in the undergrowth, tiny creatures running for safety. His muscles flex and relax. With no self-awareness, concentration distorts his mouth, creasing his eyes.

Once the pole is up, he shakes it to check its firmness and then winds the green tendril around it to keep it off the ground.

He doesn't stop to admire his work. He moves on to more pulling and freeing; he lifts a decomposing plank and smiles. He takes out a rotting shoe, followed by another, and another. He pauses to take a rubble sack and then fills the sack with the endless haul of rotting shoes he has found. The sun masks some of his movements with glare. He leans down with a different movement, and Juliet sees the cat's tail in The Mess. He seems to stroke the cat before returning to his cache of footwear. After the sack is full, he stops. He stretches; he looks up, his mind broken free of the work. He walks towards the window and retrieves his thin, grey, shapeless jumper. As he puts it on, Juliet sees the split under each arm and down the V at the front. With this detail just the other side of the gauze and the window, Juliet moves away, snaps into action and looks for her handbag so she can pay them.

She finds her purse on the sofa. The Small One is at the front patio walking towards the wheelbarrow.

At the back is the other man.

"A very good day's work, Madam. Very good indeed. Aaman is my very best friend and we work so hard together, like a team of six. So much done today, but much to do ..." He grins, waiting for the following day's invite.

Juliet is still considering what she should pay them. She has heard the rate is anything between

41

twenty euros and thirty-five euros for hard, unskilled work.

"Thank you for today's work. I will not need you tomorrow." Juliet hands him twenty-five euros, which he pockets uncounted whilst searching her face. She doesn't wait for any more of his reaction, but walks away, around the end of the house, leaving him slowly rolling down his sleeves.

The Small One is by the wheelbarrow, cleaning mud off the adze.

"Thank you for your work. What is your name again?"

Juliet notices that they are the same height.

"You are welcome. I am Aaman. At the back, a grape tree, not a weed. Tomorrow?"

"Ah, it is a grape vine. Yes, tomorrow, eight o'clock, here. OK?"

"One or two peoples?"

"One, you."

Juliet gives him twenty-five euros. He takes it without acknowledgement and puts it in his shirt pocket uncounted.

His very best friend appears from around the corner.

Chapter 4

The gate is thick with paint, the top layer the colour of mustard. Mustard over a darker brown, over yellow. The strata are exposed where time and weather has flaked pieces away. Aaman is at the gate at five minutes to eight. Mahmout tried to talk him out of coming. He said the woman obviously needs their help so if they stick together they would both get paid.

When Mahmout came from the back of the house the previous day, his face was angry and. he spoke some words Aaman didn't like to hear. Mahmout believed he had ingratiated himself and worked hard enough to deserve work the following day. Aaman doesn't see life in those terms. In his world, no one deserves anything. Life is a privilege and what comes your way a blessing. Mahmout has become Western in his thinking. Aaman doesn't seek his company.

He stands for a moment by the gate. It is already warm. A bird sings from the garden. The wind machines were not switched on last night, and he feels rested, his shoulders limp, his limbs gangly. He also feels an ease that, with his pay from the day before, he has secured his bed for the week at the mud brick barn. He has faith that his work with this lady will also last a day or two at the least. He has hope. He can hear many birds singing now. The cat is at his feet and he bends to stroke it. It purrs and jumps through the gate towards the approaching lady.

"Good morning."

"Good morning, ma'am."

"Please do not call me ma'am. I am not the Queen. Call me Juliet." The cat winds around her legs as she opens the gate.

Aaman immediately takes off his jacket and leaves the lady to begin his work. The lady, Juliet, goes back indoors.

He works for a while and, as his activities and the sun begin to make him hot, he senses movement by the house and turns to see the lady putting a bottle of water and an iced coffee on the windowsill. He continues his labour until she is gone.

It is not buffalo milk coffee, but it is good. A slight breeze lifts his flopping fringe. It is more peaceful without Mahmout's constant talk and the ground is beginning to take shape. He decides which piece to clear next and wonders if he should clear each area more thoroughly as he goes or move all the big debris first and then clear the whole area more exhaustively. A lizard darts.

A rumbling from across the valley catches his attention. He has heard the same rumble in Pakistan. The sky is dark grey in the distance, the wispy clouds in the blue overhead tell him the wind direction will bring the grey towards him. It will rain within the hour.

The rain comes in teasing, intermittent, warm dips. A deep grumble directly overhead causes the clouds to heave. The ground responds with a breath of ozone before the sky unloads its weight in a torrential sudden roar.

Aaman runs for the back doorstep to stand, looking out at his work, the covering growth bowing under the weight of the downpour. The light green foliage has turned to deep emerald, the darker hollows to black. There is a whiteness to the light, like moonlight.

"Come in, you will get soaked."

They stand in the kitchen. Juliet looks out at the rain. Aaman looks round the kitchen.

"Inside needs work too?"

"Yes, I need a woman to come and help me clean and organise. Do you have a wife here who could come?"

"Not here." Aaman does not wish talk to this lady about his wife. Saabira is back in Pakistan, waiting. He was nineteen when he married her. They had met twice before her hands were hennaed and she entered *maayun*. She was so timid, like a trembling jasmine. The thirteen years since passed with many sorrows, but Aaman feels proud of his relationship with his wife. He has been gentle, conscientious. He waited for her to come to him. Now she adores him; she treats him like a prince. It is her belief in him that has brought him to these foreign lands.

45

"For inside work I will do it, I do woman's work." Aaman's frown is sudden and deep, he drops his head, his hands twisting on themselves, the tension growing visible across his shoulders. He is not proud of his words. The rain is increasing its pace, cool air blows in from the open back door. Looking up, he is surprised when his eyes meet hers. He has not stood this close to her before, nor looked her so boldly in the eye. Saabira is the same height as him; he is a man at home. He feels himself grow, empowered, as he meets his employer's eyes on the same level as his own. A man not a child.

"Would you really want to do inside work?"

"Ma'am, Juliet, I am your house boy."

Her lower lip raises into her upper lip, between her eyes creases; she pushes her hands into the front pockets of her jeans, lowering her gaze to the floor.

"Oookay..." She drawls the letters out slowly and looks back up. Aaman wonders if he has chosen the right title for the job he is trying to secure. He searches his memory for another English phrase to express himself. He feels gratitude toward Saabira who taught him the English he knows, but also much frustration in drawing all he learnt to the surface. He decides to take a risk by constructing a sentence of which he is not sure, such little practice.

"I am your man, all jobs for the house." He meets her gaze, level with his own. By the look in her eyes, he feels sure he has used the right words. He pushes his shoulders back to breathe in the cool moist air filtering through the house. The rain continues to pound. He looks past her and sees the cat sitting on the sofa in an indentation beside some fluttering papers.

Juliet follows his gaze.

"Off." She darts across the room, shooing the cat. Aaman steps forward and picks the cat up, takes it to the front door, puts it down gently and closes the door. He feels disquieted as Juliet steps away, as if the door is no longer her own. She looks away from him; Aaman shifts uncomfortably. He feels unwelcome, but she says she wants to put the house in order.

"The kitchen. Mice. I bought the place just as it stood." She leads the way and opens a cupboard door. Old plates and cups are stacked in dust and mouse droppings. She begins to take things out and put them in the sink. Aaman sees the work to be done and gently eases his way between her and the cupboard and takes over the job. She begins in another cupboard, but Aaman quickly realises that if she helps, she will take his work. Also, she will get in the way. She stands with some pots; he moves to her and takes them from her, looking her in the eye, unblinking. He is aware that such eye contact is challenging but he needs the work to last, he needs her to need him. She stares back for a moment, shifts her weight, tightens her lips and retreats to the sofa. Aaman feels ashamed of his behaviour. He fears he is becoming like Mahmout.

He cleans each cupboard and the contents. The floor now has dust and mouse droppings on it.

Aaman is aware that she is watching from the sofa. Saabira does not sit during the day and would have found other work around the house. . He finds a broom and sweeps, then mops. Saabira sweeps the house many times a day, and keeps it very clean. She took the work from his mother when they returned to live with them just as he tried to relieve his father of some of the work in the fields.

But the village was dying. The young no longer wanted to work the land. Everyone in the village had a son, even a daughter in the city working. With their help gone, the family needed to employ labour when harvest time came. The children in the cities sent money home to help. Saabira felt that this was not the answer; she saw this was a trap. The more people who left the village, the more workers the village needed to employ at harvest time. The price of the labour was so high, it needed to be subsidised by the children working in the cities to make the whole system, how had she put it, 'economically viable'. She saw it as a cycle that would only make them unhappy because families were forced to be apart.

It was Saabira who first said they needed a harvesting machine. Aaman suggested it at the *chopal* one evening and it was discussed by the men of the village. The discussion went on for weeks and it was clear a new machine could never be bought. They were many, many thousands of rupees, but there was a big trade for secondhand machines. Someone said a New Holland was the best. The useful working life of these secondhand machines had expired, which is why the cost was so cheap to the importers. The importers then sold them to the farmers. The farmers sold them on to other farmers when they could afford better. It was possible to buy one collectively.

Aaman begins to clear the ashes from the fireplace. A daily job, but one which has not been done for weeks. He looks over to see Juliet flicking through some papers, her feet crossed up on the arm of the sofa. A Western pose.

The villagers found that they could afford one if they divided the price by the amount of land each owns. The larger families could find the money without much struggle. They worked out how much time each would take at harvesting, and this let them know there would be much time left when the machine would sit idle. They invited a nearby village where there are many cousins to become part owners. Now the divided price became manageable for all but the poorest families. Aaman's is one of the poorest families.

The fireplace is clean and re-laid. He begins on the windows. Juliet jumps when she hears the first squeaking of newspaper against the panes. She gathers her papers, disappears into another room and shuts the door. Aaman continues with the room to himself.

Saabira suggested that Aaman get a better job in Sialkot to raise his share of the machine, but Aaman knew, as he was unskilled, he would find it hard to secure a position that was any better than the one he had previously. With the pay he could expect, raising his share would take a lifetime. They thought through all the cousins they could borrow from, but the cousins had one by one left and lost themselves in cities. He asked himself, 'What would my brother have done?' His chest swells, even after all this time, at the thought of his brother. Tears prick his eyes.

"Do you want water?"

Aaman didn't see her come back in the room. She looks out onto the grey weather, the gravel drive saturated to the point of puddles. The bright orange-red flowers of the pomegranate trees against the whitewashed wall a sharp contrast to the charcoal sky.

"Yes."

Aaman sweeps the sitting room floor. He lifts the rugs, takes them onto the covered porch and bangs them against the garden wall. The dust settles quickly in the damp air.

When he returns, there is a glass of water on the table and the room is empty.

Aaman drinks the water down in one and refills the glass from the bottle in the kitchen. He surveys the room; the bathroom door is open. He arms himself with a cloth and enters.

It was Saabira who suggested Aaman go abroad to earn their share. She had such belief. His mother did not approve. His father remained silent. His grandfather and grandmother gave him their blessing, whatever he decided. Aaman worked all day for many days with nothing else on his mind.

Saabira so confident, so sure of him, Aaman began to believe he could do it.

Normally the fee for such a journey was six hundred thousand rupees. But they wanted to raise money, not spend it. Saabira thought of a way.

The bathroom now clean, Aaman looks out at the weather. The skies have lifted, the rain stopped.

The air smells full of energy and freshness in the garden. The ground is muddy, but Aaman begins his outdoor task once again.

Saabira did much research and she could see a way for Aaman to use each country's authorities to aid his journey down to the rich countries of the West. There was a man in the next village who was travelling to visit relatives near the Iranian border. He already had two passengers, her distant cousins, who would travel with Aaman.

The three of them would cross the border at night and then begin a very long walk to Kerman. If they could make it beyond Kerman, it would be a victory because when they were picked up by the authorities, they would be taken to the capital, Tehran. They needed to get past Kerman before being picked up, or they would be taken back to the Pakistani border. The Iranian authorities, although not particularly friendly, would hold them in very unsavoury places for some days before they could confirm that they were illegal and assist them out of the country. The nearest country was Iraq but the authorities knew taking them there would only result in their return, so they would willingly take them to the Turkish border.

The rain starts again. Aaman returns inside. Juliet is on the sofa.

"It's raining."

Juliet is prepared. She gives him a brush and a tin of paint and points to the kitchen wall. There is a sheet covering the surfaces and newspaper on the floor. She leaves the room.

Aaman brings the stepladder in from outside. The newspaper grows soggy where he plants the feet of the ladder. He opens the paint and begins.

Once in Turkey, they would head for Ankara. The authorities would probably give them a lift to the capital. They too knew the direction of travel, and if they took them back to Iran they would simply be brought by the Iranian authorities back to the Turkish border. So the Turkish authorities would take them to Ankara. There they would be held in warehouses with many other illegals. They could be held here for up to two years before being deported, but not to worry, Saabira said, because they would be used by the government as underpaid labour in tourism and local industry. At this point, it would be good to bribe to get to work sooner and to get a job of choice. When out labouring, it would be easy to make contacts and escape the authorities to make their way to the border crossing to Greece. From there, they would need to bribe again or they could go into Bulgaria and then down to Greece where the border was, in some places, even unmarked. In

Greece, it would be possible to make money and go to Italy. In Italy, it would be possible to make even more money and go to Spain. In Spain, it would be easy to get papers to work legally before maybe even flying home. She was told all this by a man who came to the village offering to escort people for a fee. But Aaman was clever. He did not need an escort.

Saabira made it sound so heroic, Aaman grew in stature with every word she spoke, every plan they made. He would return tall and wealthy.

The paint splats on Aaman's trousers, and he looks around the room to ensure he is alone before using the tap and cloth to wipe it off.

Saabira estimated the journey to the first country where he could make money would take maybe four months if he was lucky. He would then need another ten months, travelling and earning, to make the money they needed. He would be back within two years, just in time for when the village planned to buy the machine. She would be so proud of him.

The painting is a very satisfactory job. The grey walls cover well in the white, and the progress is quick. At the end of the first wall, he wonders if he should continue on to the next. He turns to ask Juliet, but the room is still empty.

He made the journey to Greece in five months. He was very lucky. The longest part of the journey was the walk through the hills in Iran. When he arrived in Greece, he made arrangements and finally rang Saabira on her neighbour's mobile phone. She acted as if she had expected his great achievement. He didn't talk of the horrors he had seen and the hardship he had suffered. He didn't mention that the way into Greece was patrolled very tightly, his skirmish with patrol dogs, or that he had been beaten and robbed in Bulgaria. He felt so grateful for his life as he talked to Saabira that day that he didn't want to talk of hardships.

Aaman starts on the next wall. The rain has stopped again but the progress he is making is very satisfactory, and he is not a man to leave jobs unfinished. The cat is curled at the bottom of the ladder on the newspaper.

Juliet comes into the kitchen. Aaman carries on his work. Her tongue clicks off the roof of her mouth, and she takes a breath as if she is about to speak, but then the softest of exhalations tells him she has decided not to.

She clatters about the kitchen before announcing food.

Aaman climbs down the ladder and washes his hands well, removing all traces of paint. The food is on the kitchen table, and he hesitates not knowing whether he should take it outside onto the folding table at the front now that the rain had stopped. He pulls out a chair and sits in the kitchen. He looks over to Juliet on the sofa, who is stroking the cat and feeding it bits of bread.

"How long have you been here?"

Aaman is startled and tries to think in English. "Sorry?"

"How long have you been in Greece?"

"Ten months."

"Is there work?"

"No."

"Will you stay?"

"Maybe I move on. Papers are easy in Spain."

"To make you legal, you mean?"

"Yes, legal means more work, better pay."

There is a pause.

"I didn't ask you to paint the second wall."

"It was a necessity."

Juliet leaves the room. Aaman feels that she is tense. He washes the pots. He finishes the wall. On impulse he nips outside and snaps off some of the twigs bearing the pomegranate flowers and arranges them in a jar on the kitchen table. He stands to admire his work before cleaning the brushes and going back into the garden. After a while, Juliet wanders out to see the progress.

As he picks among the debris, he asks her, very quietly, if she has any old clothes, especially shoes, that would fit him. "For work."

Juliet spends an hour searching through the clothes she brought with her. She has brought some scruffs for painting or gardening and some old trainers. She also has a pair of walking shoes that she has never really worn and she decides that Aaman's need is greater than her own.

Considering his pride, she wraps the items in a good towel and places them inside a large brown bag. He will walk through the village as he leaves and he will not want his secondhand clothes to be seen, she imagines.

As he puts on his jacket to leave, Juliet hands him the bag. She expects a single word of thanks at least and smiles in anticipation.

He does not smile. He walks with the bag back to the patio and, squatting, opens it. He takes out the white t-shirts on top and declares them too small without unfolding them. He pulls out some unisex jeans that Juliet thought she might use for painting. He nods as if they pass the first test and then searches along each seam. He finds a worn area the size of his thumbnail in the crotch. He displays it to Juliet, shaking his head manfully, tutting.

Juliet is speechless. Each action he performs so carefully is so far from her comprehension that she is left without even a question to ask, just a deep, sickening confusion that spirals her away from the scene.

He finds the shoes at the bottom, admires the walking shoes at arm's length, but then turns them over to inspect the sole. He undoes the laces with small movements and slow progress and puts them on, re-laces them equally as neatly and then stands and walks.

"No, no, no, too tight." He takes them off with little care and glances at the trainers, picks them up, looks at the soles and then drops them after noticing that the laces have lost their plastic ends. Before standing he brushes down his trousers where the shoes have been resting.

Juliet thrusts his pay at him.

"Just go," she says and turns on her heels. Juliet feels as if her guts have been pulled from her stomach and spread across the patio for ravens to pick over. He is generally neat, so why has he left everything strewn so carelessly? The t-shirts, shoes, jeans, and bag are littered across the patio. She kicks them together with one foot and breathes as deeply as she can to freeze the surging, oscillating lump of emotion that rises, constricting her throat and forcing unwanted tears to streak her cheeks anew. The paper bag scuttles on a breeze, so Juliet gives up the effort and flops indoors to the sofa. The cat nuzzles for attention, sticking her hair to her wet face. Juliet's dam bursts, sending shudders across her shoulders and limpness to her limbs.

Chapter 5

The sharp metallic sound stabs through the layers. Levered out of the depths, dreams falling away, she rouses herself to make sense of it. The sound continues. Juliet tries to work out where she is. She opens her eyes to the exposed beams and, with a rush of pleasure, remembers she is in her little stone cottage under blue Mediterranean skies.

She kicks back the sheets and jumps into her jeans. The metallic noise continues intermittently. Someone is tapping on the gate. Images of the bearded postman on his motorbike bring excitement at the thought of letters from Thomas or maybe even Terrance. Pulling on her t-shirt, Juliet bounds out of the bedroom, strokes the cat who is curled on the sofa and heads to the gate. The sun dazzles her.

The puddles have all sunk into the drive, and the air is warm. There is not a cloud in the sky. A bird sings, a gecko basks on a stone by the gate. The cat has joined her, and he stops to sprawl on his back on the gravel, paws flopped over, eyes closed.

Juliet looks past him. Her step falters and stops as the glare gives way to focus. Her bounce melts.

"I wasn't expecting you today." She is ready to turn away.

"Juliet?"

She is shocked at the sound of her name on his tongue. Loud, sure, confident.

"Go away." Her briskness overcompensates for too many years of no voice. She turns and re-enters the house. The metallic tapping resumes for a while and then stops. It is quiet for a long time. She makes some coffee, the aroma filling the room, promising relaxation, satisfaction. The sun coming in the kitchen through the back door invites her outside. The Mess is looking less like A Mess and more like an unruly garden. It makes Juliet smile. There is still much to be unburied and disposed of, but it is better. Many full rubble sacks line the back wall like melting candles sagging on their bases.

She balances her coffee on the window ledge to lift one of the sacks. She hugs it and braces her back to bend from the knees. It is so heavy it is immovable. Her back jars at the lack of give. Slightly annoyed that this is a job beyond her strength, she scuffs it with her sandal. Picking up her coffee and leaving the sack, Juliet wanders round the end of the house to see how much is now piled by the gate.

Aaman still stands there. He says nothing, just stands on the other side of the gate. The cat is meowing to be stroked, and Aaman bends to caress him. As he strokes the cat, Juliet notices how flaky the paint is at the bottom of the gate. It needs painting.

She moves slowly, with indecision. The cat comes to her. She picks it up and walks to the gate. Aaman reaches through the rusted metal gate bars and strokes the cat. One stroke on its head and then a longer stroke the length of its body. His hand stops as the very tips of his fingers accidentally touch her arm. Her t-shirt is short-sleeved, the skin of her arm is puckered thin, translucent blue in places. He looks at her quizzically.

"It's a burn."

He nods his head in recognition, as if he understands, as if burns are familiar, a softness in his manner.

"Come on then, you're here now, you might as well come in. I can't move the rubble sacks by myself."

Aaman takes off his jacket and strides his way to the back garden, long sure steps.

"I will find someone to haul the sacks away." Juliet goes inside.

It takes him just a few minutes to move the sacks to the front gate whilst Juliet is on the phone finding a man with a lorry to take the debris away. After finding a man who can come today, Juliet looks for Aaman. She leaves the house by the back door and finds him cleaning off a rake.

"Aaman, will you move the sacks to the ..." She stops in her tracks as she sees the sacks have gone. She marches to the end of the house and sees them by the gate.

"I put them by the gate."

"Aaman, we need to talk."

"Yes ma'am, Juliet?"

"You are here to do a job. It isn't that you are not doing this job, it's just ... well ... I expect that I have to tell you when to do things. Don't get me wrong. It is not bad that you do them before I ask it. I mean, things need to be done and I cannot stand over you every minute of the day, otherwise I may as well do it myself. But I think it is better if I tell you first then you can do it. Someone has to oversee what's happening, else we won't know where we are. It's better that I tell you. So I know what you are doing, when you are doing it. Do you understand?"

"Yes." Aaman waits. Juliet says no more. "No. Ma'am, Juliet, I don't understand. Are the bags in the wrong place?"

"This is my home!"

"Yes. Your home?" Aaman eyes dart here and there searching for understanding.

"I know what I want!" Her voice becomes louder. Aaman takes a step back. "I can make my own choices." The cat comes to her legs and pushes his head against her. She doesn't pay him any attention.

"Yes." Aaman begins to rock, ever so slightly backwards and forwards. His head is nodding side to side, a familiar Pakistani movement. He is drowning.

"Have you any idea what it is like for me to have you come here and do this?" She is now shouting.

"To do this? What 'this'? Clear the garden?" With tears ready to spill, Aaman leaps on the chance to get an explanation and the words come overlapping the end of her sentence and they sound loud and strong and aggressive.

"Exactly! You haven't a clue, or maybe you have and it is a game." Tears flow down her cheeks.

Aaman remembers tears flowing down Saabira's cheeks. He could not forget. She was so strong for so long and then, days after she lay still, she began to weep and she didn't stop for days. He held her for hours, his mother held her, even his grandmother sat and patted her hand. But no-one could bring back what had gone. His grandmother said he was lucky not to lose Saabira too and that he must be thankful for his blessings. Aaman was thankful. He was so, so grateful that he had Saabira.

"No, no game, it's very serious." Aaman sees her react, and realises he must expand on what he is saying.

"How you feel, it is no game, it is very serious. You are not happy, this is serious." Aaman can see another wave of emotion taking hold of Juliet. Almost imperceptibly her head moves back, her chest rises like a wave until she comes crashing down in tears, all self-consciousness lost.

"Stop it, just stop it," between breaths and tears. Her hands brought up, splayed, tense, creating a wall between them.

"Stopping is not the problem, but please tell me what it is that you wish me to be stopping. I am trying to be a good worker but I can see I have not pleased you. Please tell me how I can do better."

Juliet has made half a step backwards and with the distance she grows calm.

"Forget it." Juliet wipes her face on her arm, turns to go back indoors.

"Sorry, but no. I need to be stopping."

Juliet's eyes are shining, pupils dilated, her arm muscles sprung tight as her fists clench. Aaman's darting eyes rest on her burns. She turns her body to hide the scarred arm from him. Aaman looks back to her face, her eyes staring, indignation.

"What?" It is more of a hiss then a word.

Aaman wavers. Saabira shouted at him. She needed to shout. She shouted blame, she shouted unfairness, she shouted for release. He needed to be strong, allow her to shout, to hear what she said but most importantly, he found, was to let her know that he heard her.

"I said no, I cannot be forgetting it. You are not happy. It is my fault. I cannot forget. Tell me what I must be stopping."

Juliet turns as if she wishes to go inside, away from him, away from this emotional scene. She wipes her eyes again. She begins to step away. Aaman sees his opportunity for several days work leaving with her, and he is also drawn to her distress, to Saabira.

He steps to the side and reaches out and touches the arm she tries to hide. He calms himself.

"Tell me. Much in life is pain. I wish to be no pain for you, only good work. I need this work. Tell me so I can have work and you can have a good worker."

The touch of his fingers on her thinned skin draws her attention. She looks at his hand on her skin, brown against blue white, and he responds by carefully taking it away.

He waits.

She sighs, she is settling, in her calmness she seems more controlled. Aaman can see that this is all very tiring for her. She sits on the doorstep. Aaman looks around him and pulls forward a large empty paint tin and sits down, quietly, respectfully. Knees together, neatly. Like he did when he was a child. Juliet alters the way she speaks to him.

"Yesterday I didn't like what you did. You overstepped the mark." She uses small hand gestures to demonstrate overstepping a mark.

"What does it mean, 'overstep the mark'?"

"It means to do more than you should."

Aaman's brows furrow. It makes no sense to him. He is here to do as much as he can. Being a worker is not enough. He wants to be an exceptional help to her. He is planning to seek out jobs before being asked, and to do them with speed and care. Aaman wants to become so useful that he will have a job for a long time. He wants to be indispensable.

"Look, when I went to chase the cat out yesterday, you picked it up and put it out and closed the door. My door. Not your door, my door. It is not your place to put the cat out in my house and close my door."

Aaman lifts his brow. He can feel his eyes widen in surprise.

64

"It wasn't helpfully?"

"If it had been just that event. But you gave me such a look when I was going to do some of the cupboards in the kitchen that I felt I should not be in my own kitchen, that I was a nuisance in my own home."

Aaman searches for words, but Juliet has not finished.

"And what was all that with the clothes? If you don't mind me saying, you are in no position to be quite so proud. The first job you get mixing concrete, and you'll be glad of any shoes going. Just look at the shoes of someone who has mixed concrete for a day and you'll see they are hanging together by a thread, or the soles have fallen off, trousers disintegrate in the dust where it has splashed. You wear clothes you expect to throw away when you work as a concrete mixer! I have seen it, here in the village. I offered you something for nothing, and you didn't even have the manners or the sense to just take it and say thank you."

Aaman looks down and begins to pick paint off his upturned seat. His surety and calm are disturbed, which fuels her momentum.

"And I didn't ask you to clean the fireplace out, although I was quite pleased when I saw it was done, but I definitely did not ask you to clean my bathroom. That is my bathroom, I keep personal things in there and I would like to think that some places in my own house are just for me. I felt your actions were comments about my life. I don't know why or how, but I just sensed it. I almost felt you were saying I was sitting down all day when I could be cleaning my house. To be honest, I've had enough of being judged and being told what to do in my life, someone taking over, playing the boss. So although you probably didn't mean anything by all these things, it just felt too much." She begins crying again, no noise, just long streaks of shine down to her chin. In the space between words the sun dries them to white lines.

Aaman understands part of what she is saying. He doesn't need to understand all the words to grasp the meaning, to understand the feelings. He has seen many women who were suppressed in Pakistan; they all had the same look. A look of no hope and the need to be heard. He had much sympathy for them. When he was told he would be marrying Saabira, he made up his mind that he was not going to be the sort of husband who has a sad wife. He kept his promise in all respects, but sometimes life takes its own route. He could not save Saabira from the sadness that made him sad too.

Aaman continues to sit in silence, his learning from the past mingling with his needs of the day.

"I haven't anything more to say," Juliet concludes.

Aaman considers what she requires. Misunderstandings are best resolved with honesty. His father taught him that. When both sides can clearly understand the other's point of view then they can work together to achieve harmony. He adjusts his weight on his bucket seat.

"I am proud. I am stubborn. I need to do the work well. Not just for the money. Can I say?" He looks at Juliet for permission. She nods.

"My brother. He was big, he was strong. We loaded wood into the cart for the fire. We raced. He was always stronger and quicker. I was always trying to be as him. But I am smaller. I need to do everything good, to be more than I look. To not need any help. To race my brother. Difficult to say in English. Maybe it is not a good thing." He drops his head and picks some more paint off his seat.

Juliet sits listening; he wonders if he should have said so much.

"OK. Right then. Well that's how it is then. Best get on with it." She slaps her thighs as she stands.

He takes his cue and stands at the same time. He turns to go back to work and Juliet goes into the kitchen. She returns with a glass of water and walks up to Aaman and hands it to him. He takes the water and his fingers enclose her scarred fingers briefly as the glass is exchanged. She smiles like his mother used to.

He watches her back fade into the darkened interior as she enters through the back door. He misses Saabira. He drinks the water in one and puts the glass on the windowsill.

The land has been cleared down to ground level, so Aaman begins to dig pieces of rag and plastic and batteries out of the topsoil. He thinks of Juliet. He had in his mind a very clear image of Western women, blonde, beautiful, rich, immoral, and happy.

This woman doesn't fit half of his picture. How can she be unhappy with such a big house and so much money? Aaman presumes from what she has said that she has been married and that he was not a very considerate husband. But it seems that he is gone now so where is the problem? Western women don't mind changing husbands, so if she is lonely, why doesn't she just get another Western husband?

The image of her salt-lined cheeks brings him sadness. She was like Saabira in her tears. What must her husband have done to her for her to fight so hard for her independence? These things never come easily, so the struggle may have been very hard or very long, or both. It is always sad when a marriage is lost, but if she wanted her freedom then she has that now.

And yet she seems lonely.

He pulls at a bit of black rubber which turns into a bicycle inner tube as it comes out of the ground. In the hole that is left is a playing card - the seven of diamonds. Aaman picks up the card, which seems so well preserved and yet useless on its own. He throws it into the rubble sack.

He struggles to fully comprehend what Juliet was talking about. She said she needed to be the boss. But as she is the boss, this didn't make sense. He wonders if she would rather do the garden by herself but cannot because she lacks the strength. Craving independence is very frustrating if being small makes it impossible. He knows. But at the same time he has the feeling that she does not wish to be alone,

68

not completely. That is what confuses him. It feels like she is pushing and pulling. She wants him there, but she doesn't want him there. She wants him to do the work, but she doesn't want him do the work. Aaman wonders if she is afraid of him being there. That is not good.

He makes the decision to be gentler in his steps in the Western woman's house. She needs someone to tread softly no matter what the work requires. He must put his pride in doing well secondary. If she does not ask him to finish a job, then he must leave it undone if by leaving it undone is better for Juliet. He will tread as carefully with Juliet as he did with Saabira.

"Food."

Aaman takes his time to wash well. There is hot water here, and soap. He scrubs his nails with the little brush and uses soap all the way up to his elbows. He quickly wipes over his face but feels it is not right to take advantage and have a full wash here.

Feeling fresher, Aaman walks out onto the patio and relaxes. The consequent shock of finding that Juliet has laid the table for two people to eat may be exaggerated by this fact.

He looks over the table with no hurry. Goat's yoghurt, fresh bread made with olive oil, stuffed vine leaves, butter beans in a tomato and oregano sauce, and a salad of cucumber, tomato, and olives. He reflects that he would be happier to eat alone, but he appreciates her gesture in eating with him and is a little surprised that she wants to close the gap to that degree.

The same food, at the same table, the two cultures, the two statuses. It is not immediately comfortable. The cat circles for scraps.

Aaman does not offer conversation, nor does Juliet. They sit in silence and eat slowly, in Aaman's case carefully, listening to the birds all around, the cockerel who still doesn't know the time, and the goat and sheep bells as a herd moves from meadow to stall.

It is only when they have finished eating and they watch the cat washing itself on the sun-soaked step that they both realise they are both enjoying the silence of each other's company. The cat stops licking and curls up, adding to the unity of the stillness. The three of them balance between their expectations and the difficulty of making themselves understood.

Chapter 6

Juliet is up and dressed, ready to work alongside Aaman in the garden. With two of them working side by side it will be a quicker job. It might even be fun.

The cat slides off the sofa as Juliet opens the front door to greet the day. There is no post in the box hanging on the gate which she leaves open for Aaman's arrival.

As she clicks the kettle on, the phone rings.

"Hi Mum!"

"Terrance, did you get your essay in on time?" Juliet asks.

"Yes, no worries. Just wondered if you were coming home soon or what."

"Come home to where, love?"

"I don't know, just home."

"Darling, I don't have a home there anymore." Images of the home where they all lived together for so many years spin in her thoughts. The moments of laughter, cups of tea, the coziness of them all together, the Englishness of it all.

"So that's it, you've gone?"

"You and Thomas helped me plan this. We searched maps together to decide on the location.

You and Thomas divided all the household stuff out between you when I whittled my belongings down to two bags. Why are you …?" Juliet looks at the clock. "It's six in the morning where you are. Why are you even up so early?"

"Mum, just come home. It's Easter in a week."

"OK, Terrance what is it?" Juliet pushes her hair off her face before putting her hand on her hip. She looks at the floor, taps her toe, waiting for the whole story. It feels like a familiar action, a practised patience.

"Look, there's been a bit of a cock up."

Juliet sighs and sits down. These words tell her this has something to do with money. Thomas is amazing with money, but then again he is earning. Terrance, on the other hand, the dreamer, never has it under control.

"The job I had at the university bar? Well I was studying one evening and I sort of got so carried away with it that I forgot to go. Well, that idiot James from the first year was there, at the bar I mean, so he took my shift and must have done some super grovelling because, well, basically, he took my job."

"And?" This sounds so familiar.

"And, well, I was looking for another job, but I had ages before I needed to pay the rent and I had a bit in the bank. But, wouldn't you know it, last week Jim finally said he had fixed my car but he wanted two hundred quid. So really, if it wasn't for Jim, I would have my rent money. But the landlord says he is coming round at the end of the week, he kind of threatened, saying he had a load of students who want this room and if ..."

Juliet cuts him short. "Do you have a job now?"

"I have even heard he can get really heavy, Mum. Someone said he chased a student out through the ground floor window with a stick once."

"Terrance. Do you have a job now?"

"At least it was the ground floor. Yes, in a student sandwich shop. I talked the manager into opening more hours and giving me a job, but he won't pay me till the end of the month."

"You have the gift of the Blarney stone, Terrance. I'm not sure you deserve it!"

"The end of the month, Mum. Are you even taking me seriously? What'll I do about the rent?"

"OK, listen. Is the sandwich shop enough to pay the rent?"

"No. I'm on my way to a job cleaning the floors of the local co-op before the shop opens."

"Ahh, so that's why you're out of bed so early."

"Come on. This is not funny. What am I going to do? They're not going to pay me till the end of the week and all I have is a bag of rice and half a bottle of ketchup."

"And a car and a mug for a mum."

"The best mum in the world, you mean. You couldn't see your way to lending me a bit in advance of my jobs, could you?"

"It had to be something like this to get you out of bed so early."

"Mum, can you? Please?"

"Last time, Terrance?" The cat has jumped on Juliet's knee; she strokes it and kisses its head.

"Absolutely!"

"I'll transfer it online, and it'll be cleared in three days. Is that OK?"

"Fantastic. Thanks, Mum, you are the best."

"Apart from that, how's your life?"

"It's great. I've hooked up with a girl called Emma. She's doing a Ph.D. in Waste Management. She took a look at my dissertation and said it was really good. She's going to Peru on some work experience exchange or something. I do miss you though, Mum."

"Yes, but you are fine really?"

"Yup. Brilliant! No worries. Got to go. Time to scrub floors for a living. Thanks for the money, Mum. You are a saint. Love you."

"Love you too." But the line is already dead. Immediate desolation freezes the room. It is a familiar feeling for Juliet.

It was exciting when the boys first went to university. She was backwards and forwards to them, across the country. The joke was they had chosen universities at the opposite ends of the UK just to be awkward.

That was the time when Juliet decided to take her love of the Greek language, which she had begun to learn all that time ago with Michelle when they went on holiday, to a new level.

She applied, and was accepted, to do it as a degree at the local technical college, full time but based on home studies. She and the boys were all students together and qualified together. That was a great three years.

Juliet realised, retrospectively, that the fervour that fired her studies was a wall to divert her attention from the divorce that she and Mick started as soon as the boys were studying. Mick even said that her chasing around the country after them was trying to compensate for the separation. 'Guilty conscience,' he called it. 'Desperate to get far away', Juliet would retaliate.

Juliet was determined that they wouldn't feel rejected or squeezed out by her and Mick's alienation. The most important thing for Juliet was for her boys to know that her love continued even if her marriage didn't. So she chased around and studied hard until they all stood in cap and gown receiving their rolled parchments, each in a different little bit of England.

Thomas got a job in the town where he had studied for his degree and he said he had no plans to move back near her. Then Terrance enrolled to continue his studies for another two years with his M.A., and it was Juliet who began to feel abandoned.

When the divorce came through, the house went on the market, all was amicably split (even if Mick was grumpy and sarcastic), and Juliet moved into a poky flat round the corner from the family home and finished her degree. She had no idea where she was meant to go after that.

She was saved by an offer from her tutor to do some translation work. It began with one piece he just didn't have the energy for and grew from there. Juliet channeled her energies into making it her career. She fell lucky and found she had a niche market.

Her work grew, her confidence to be alone grew, and when Terrance announced that he would probably stay on after his next year to do a Ph.D., Juliet gathered the courage to be selfish and consider the move to the warmer climate where her soul had lodged and remained unmoved for ten years.

The sound of a horn brings Juliet to the present. She glances at the clock. Aaman is over an hour late. The horn belongs to a truck promised the day before. "But, never mind, it is here today," the driver smiles. It takes them half an hour to load the rubbish and Juliet gloats at the space left behind as it drives away.

Aaman is an hour and a half late.

Juliet sits with a coffee, the cat, and a good book but soon accepts she is kidding herself and she is killing time waiting for Aaman.

He is two and three quarter hours late.

Feeling empty, she looks in the fridge. It too is empty. Thoughts search for why Aaman is late, re-running events of the previous day. Things said. Things unsaid. Intuition knows he is not coming. That snaps her into a decision and she arms herself with shopping bags and purse and heads to the car.

A farmer's market is held in the next village twice a week. In amongst the stalls, the perfume of fresh vegetables is delicate, hovering like the smell of rain. Juliet pushes thoughts of Aaman and Terrance aside as she strolls along. She tries to recapture the impression the market had on her on her first visit, the envelopment of a foreign culture, the excitement of the unusual. The expectancy of everything and anything. The limitless possibilities.

Passing the first array of fruit, she is beckoned with barked 'hellos!' and bellowed promises of the best ware. There is noise everywhere as the sellers compete for customers. Juliet cheers as the callers' sounds merge with people near her chatting in the relative cool of the shade under the stalls' canvas covers. Clusters of people, clothed in the colours of summer, catching up with each other, passing pleasantries, rehearsed clichés, and niceties block the path of her progress. No one hurries. The fruit stalls heave with the abundance of the season. Red, yellow, and orange compete with the vegetables in purple, white, sand, and green. This is a time for vegetables and neighbours, sustenance of body and spirit. Juliet's soul lifts itself from its resting place and soars with wings amidst the songs of exchange.

She stops to look at apples when another stall holder calls, "Hey, pretty lady. You come buy from me, for you very cheap price. Where you from? America? I have a brother in Boston. England? I have a cousin in Birmingham."

Juliet is hooked. He is smiling at her, a cheeky smile inviting her to collude, to suspend disbelief and enjoy the ride.

She accepts.

"I'm from England. I was born in a town called Bradford."

"Ah Bradford, I have uncle in Bradford."

"Sure, does he have a vegetable stall there?"

"No, he works in a vegetable shop. It is posh in Bradford."

Juliet laughs.

"Bradford posh, I don't think so."

He looks the length of her, self-satisfied that he has her attention.

"Tell me," he murmurs in a lecherous way, "tell me about your Bradford." He is only in his twenties, playing the role.

Juliet is flattered by the attention and enjoying the banter. Besides, she hasn't spoken to anyone face to face except Aaman for she isn't sure how many days.

"It is full of Victorian stone buildings that need a good wash, mills that have been revived for families to visit as 'an experience' at the weekend, and rows and rows of back-to-back houses."

His interest is quickened to learn a new English phrase. "What is this 'back-to-back houses'?"

"Long streets of stone houses where each one joins the next, a terrace of houses, and each house has another house built on the back facing the opposite way. It was a cheap way of building lots of houses for the workers of the mills, when they were working."

"Stone houses, very expensive."

"No, as cheap as it comes. It's full of Pakistanis. In some areas of Bradford, there are more Pakistani children than British children in the schools."

"Rich Pakistanis!"

"Ha, yes! I guess some of them are now." Juliet's childhood view of the Pakistanis shifts. Then they were poor migrants, today many are affluent Britons of many generations. "But there are still some that are poor."

"But not in England." He beams as he waves a parting gesture, more a flourish of finality as he has lost Juliet. She has wandered on, her mind balancing and adjusting her preconceived thoughts around the Pakistanis in England forty some years ago, when she was growing up, with the people of Asian origin who live there now. Aaman comes to mind. His situation, compared to the Pakistanis of Bradford, is absolutely desperate. Separated by such a distance from his wife and family with no notion of when or how he will return. No passport, no papers, no money, no permanent job. Just the clothes he stands in. The same clothes every day. Desperate. Her anger with him for not showing up dissolves. She hopes he is safe wherever he is.

With bags and bags of fresh fruit and vegetables, Juliet drives home. The cat is waiting and grows delirious as it smells fresh fish from the market.

Juliet chooses an old terracotta pot to be the cat's bowl. She empties some of the little fish into the dish and puts it on the floor next to the fridge. The cat lifts his head to her to be stroked before he hungrily eats.

A glass of water revives her after the heat of the day at the market. It was good to talk to Terrance. She decides to call Thomas.

"Mum? Hey, good to hear from you. Have you spoken to Terrance? He's got himself in a financial pickle again."

"Yes, I spoke to him; I am just transferring something to him now." Juliet picks up her laptop.

"Mug."

"I would do the same for you, in fact I remember a time when ..."

"So how is it out there Mum? Are you happy?"

"Yes, it's great, I've just been to the market. You must come, with Cheri, you would love it."

"We're thinking about it, it's just that getting time off together is proving tricky. Have you made any friends?"

"No, well yes, I think so. I've had a man here working for me from Pakistan. At first I think I was resenting him being here a bit but now I like it. He works really hard."

"You've made friends with a builder?"

"He's not really a builder more sort of a house boy ..."

Juliet pulls the phone away from her ear as Thomas bawls with laughter.

"House boy! You have made a friend and it is with your house boy. Mum, tell me you're kidding. Please!"

"Thomas. Stop it. Maybe house boy is the wrong term. He does all jobs that need doing around the house, from washing pots inside to moving rubble outside. He is very sweet, a little unsure of himself and sometimes a bit full of himself."

"And you've made friends with him because?" Thomas is hooting between words.

"There is no because, he is just working for me at the moment and we are getting to know each other."

Thomas finally manages to control himself and stops laughing.

"Mum, be careful." Juliet can see him wiping his laughter tears from his eyes. "There are plenty of people in the world that will take advantage of anyone who appears alone, lonely even. Why don't you come back here for a visit? You can stay with us. We've just rented a bigger flat so there's room if you don't mind the settee for a bed."

"You are sweet sometimes, when you're not being mean. When did you decide on a new flat?"

"Cheri got promoted so we are using the difference in pay to get somewhere bigger. It's not much bigger, but as least we have a sitting room now."

"Well done, Thomas, let me know if you need any help."

"Not me, Mum. I'll leave that up to Terrance. But seriously, if you want to come back for a holiday, just say so. But I'm afraid we don't have a house boy to run after you."

Thomas disappears into his own laughter again. Juliet hears him slapping his thigh and can picture him, knees curling to his chest rocking backwards the way he always did as a boy when he could no longer control himself. She smiles at the image, but with a touch of sadness from the loss.

The chortles subside.

"Mum, actually, I have to go, I have to pick Cheri up. Can we talk later?"

"Sure. You go and talk her into a visit here and let me know if you need anything."

After a reluctant goodbye, Juliet finishes the money transfer to Terrance and leans back on the sofa. The cat is at the door, and another cat is sniffing him nose to nose. They head bump and the new cat falls to the floor, rolling onto its back, wafting its paws in an invitation to play. The original cat licks its paws and ignores its new friend.

Wondering if her attitude to Aaman is reasonable, Juliet cuts herself some bread. She intends to eat the rest of the yogurt, the rice-stuffed vine leaves, and the olives she bought at the market. Aaman is a paid employee but he is also a person. She expects him to be subservient, or at least to say thank you when she offers him things. But is that because she grew up in Bradford all those years ago which led her to accept that as normal? Maybe what she offers now is as it should be, no thanks necessary. *Bloody Mick.* Mick treated her with such disrespect for so long and took everything she did totally for granted that she no longer knows the reasonable way to act or what to expect.

Thomas didn't help. But then, what does Thomas know?

The phone rings.

"Hi Juliet. How's it going? Did you get rid of the cat?"

"Michelle, hi! Wow, loads of phone calls today. No, the cat has now taken up permanent residence. I gave it fish today."

"Does the cat have a name now?"

"No, I don't want to get that friendly. If I name it, I claim it, and I don't want to claim anyone, or for that matter, be claimed by anyone."

"Hmm, that sounds mysterious. What's up?"

"How have we managed to stay friends all these years? I mean, we hardly ever see each other, and I'm so lax at calling you so, seriously, I don't mean to be rude, but why do you still call me?"

"Because you don't fool me with your hard man act, 'Jules'. You keep forgetting how long we've known each other. You act all tough. But why would someone who is tough and sure of themselves let someone like Mick under their skin? He was a cry for help if anything ever was. But I understand. I knew your mum when we were kids, and if anyone deserves someone to stand up for them, it's you."

There is a loud silence. Juliet had clearly been asking a rhetorical question.

"Have you hung up again, Juliet?"

"No." Juliet strokes her scarred arm, her thin skin ripples at her touch.

"Well, don't. Come on, tell me how things are shaping up."

There is a long, deliberating pause.

"The garden is looking better. There are tiny buds that will ripen into bursting red fruit on the pomegranate tree."

"Yes, you said you had some men digging away. Have they moved your three mattresses yet or will you be sleeping under the stars?"

"I have found one man to help. He cleared the garden. Really quickly actually. He was so determined, strong. He's one of those people who doesn't let anything stand in his way and just gets on with the job."

"Wow, does he have a brother for me? He could help with my garden."

"Ha ha, no. Find your own house boy."

"House boy. Ooo Juliet, that sounds like fun!"

"Well, I had to shape him up a bit at the start, you know how it is, but he is working out just fine." Juliet is laughing. "But seriously, he's been great. When it rained, obviously he couldn't work outside, so he came in and cleaned out the old kitchen cupboards that had been just left. He laid the fire, even cleaned my bathroom without me asking."

"Wow, he sounds like a treasure."

"He also seems like a pretty nice guy too. Quiet, a bit shy perhaps, compassionate, but he has his pride, sometimes too much."

"I like men who are proud, a little bit arrogant, that whole masculine, caveman thing. So is anything brewing or can I come over and grab him for myself?"

"He's an illegal Pakistani immigrant."

"So?"

"So he's married."

"Ahh, so if he wasn't married, would anything be brewing?"

"Michelle, sometimes you think the whole world thinks like you."

"Let me get this straight. You have a strong, determined guy who gets on with life, who, even though he does your house work without being asked, maintains his pride, and you don't know if something would be brewing if he wasn't married. I must deduce you have heatstroke, Juliet."

"He is shorter than me."

"Good reason, that and the married thing. Stay clear."

"Have you got anything to actually say to me or have you just rung to annoy me?"

"Just to annoy you."

The silence that follows indicates neither of them knows what to say.

"So is he there now?"

"No, he didn't show up today."

"Why?"

"I'm not sure. Yesterday I kind of let rip at him. I felt he was in my way or something, but we made up and in the end it was nice. But I think I must have done something more than I thought. Anyway, he's not here."

"Ahh. That sounds a shame. Why did you let rip again?"

"I don't really want to talk about it. OK?"

"Are you expecting him tomorrow?"

"I don't know. I'll just have to wait and see if he turns up. If he doesn't, I was wondering if I should go to the village square and see if he is waiting for work there. I don't know what I would say to him."

"How about, 'Please come home, you are the best house boy I have ever had.'" Michelle seems to find it as funny as Thomas did. Juliet smiles, laughs a little even.

Their conversation draws to a natural conclusion. Juliet finds the wine in the kitchen and pours herself a glass.

As if timed for maximum effect, the bottle is empty. The next town's supermarket will be closed by now. Juliet looks through the glass at her sitting room encased in emerald. The peeling paint and years of wear are unnoticeable through her meridian telescope, but Juliet is not cheered up. She picks at the label. It looks familiar. Marina comes to mind, and there in her mental background of cigarette cartons and shepherd crooks, she sees the wine bottle label, a row of them, top shelf, by the plastic flowers.

Invigorated, Juliet pulls on her trainers and sets off, even though it is late, to the corner shop.

Chapter 7

"And, thank goodness, she has not met anyone new. I did not want her to meet American boy. I have no problem with American boys but if she married an American boy she would live in America! So now she is home, where a daughter belongs. I can pray for her to meet a nice boy, just like I pray for her big sister to meet a nice boy." Marina, with a nod, breaks off her conversation with a lady dressed in black, who smells of sheep dung and who nods in return and leaves. The waiting dog outside yelps with joy at being reunited with his dung-smelling mistress, and the pair head out of the village towards the hills.

"Hello, Tzuliet." Marina struggles with the pronunciation.

"Hello, Marina. Could I have a bottle of that wine, please? The one on the top shelf next to the flowers."

Marina comes from behind the counter, her weight impeding at the beginning but helping the momentum as she gets going. She waddles toward the entrance and starts to take beer bottles out of a crate by the door, bending from the hips.

"Oh, are you busy? Shall I come back?" Juliet is not sure what to make of Marina's actions.

"Why you come back? I am getting your wine now." She continues to unload the crate, one bottle following the next until it is empty. She pauses for breath. After turning the crate over, she pushes it with her foot behind the counter and, using the counter-top as support, steps onto the crate to reach the wine.

"Oh, I would have been happy to have got it for you."

Marina waves a dismissal. After the exertion of reaching the wine, she sits down and puts her feet up on the crate. "You will be going to church tonight?"

Juliet is about to ask why but the decorated candles around the shop tell her that Terrance's talk of English Easter has confused her. It is Saturday, midnight Mass. Tomorrow is Greek Easter. She becomes alert.

"Yes, of course." Juliet chooses the least decorated candle within arm's reach.

An ember spits out from the fireplace. It is the call to action Juliet needs to raise herself from the comfort of the wine, cat, and comfy chair. She flicks the rug by its edge to bounce the ember back onto the fire.

Once up on her feet, the spectacle of the midnight Mass calls her to the village square in front of the church. She makes a quick search for her candle. It is a Barbie candle complete in its box with a Barbie badge, pink ribbons, and a Barbie plastic drip catcher. Juliet strips the candle of its adornment, gives the ribbons to the cat to play with, stuffs her feet into her permanently laced-up trainers, grabs her coat and sets off.

Closing her gate behind her, she can see her neighbours down the lane, the elderly walking at a somber pace, the young ones running around in excitement. Juliet keeps her distance but is pleased to be able to observe. The excitement of the new culture takes her into a world of undiscovered possibilities. She is alone and grinning.

As the lane end joins the main street of the village, people migrate from all directions towards the church. Each person carries an unlit candle ready for the moment of resurrection, the light of Christ. Each carries a hope for the year to come, following the end of Lent. Each wishes for the health of their family, with a bit of happiness thrown in, the lit candle carried all the way home as something to wish upon.

As Juliet nears the church, the street fills from every direction until they reach the square as one, brought together by an alliance of belief.

The church is full to overflowing, the wide, approaching steps a dense amalgamation of families, friends, and farming staff. A tingle of expectancy oscillates through the waiting throng. People coming and going, some have obviously been there for the duration, shifting from foot to foot. The microphoned singing drone of the *'psaltis'* - cantor - sends the words and prayers reverberating in the church entrance, echoing off buildings, seeking out every street and lane, and seeping into every corner of the surrounding orange groves. Rising and lowering, the nasal intone increases tempo and urgency until, finally, finally, Christ has arisen. *Kali Anastasi*, Good Resurrection.

The collective energy in the square increases. Children run around and are pulled to attention, and then the hush as the first light appears from the church doorway. Candle to candle, the light of Christ passes to the waiting crowd and the murmur, 'Christ is risen' on the giving and 'He surely is' on the receiving. The flame passes from neighbour to friend, to child, to worker. The flickering candles fan outward from the door, each candle lights two or more behind it, the square pinpricked with dancing light, the beginnings of a ripple effect which will spread out through the village.

Juliet is offered a light with the words, '*Christos Anesti*,' Christ is risen.

'*Alithos Anesti*,' - In truth he is risen, Juliet responds.

For the elderly people of the village, there is reverence, quiet excitement, the end of forty days of fasting. The days without meat are over. The candles must be carried all the way home without blowing out to give luck for the year to come. Above the door, on the frame, the smoke from the candle will be used to make the sign of the cross, a blackened smear renewing last year's cross. The children know that behind these doors of their respective homes a feast awaits them, and they are pulling on coats, ready for food and the game of cracking eggs that have been dyed red. There may even be a present or two.

There is life everywhere, young and old brimming with joy. Latecomers hurry with their candles, greeted by all; early leavers are flecks of twinkling light in the distance. The village is united.

Juliet thrills in her participation and cups her candle to ensure it stays lit. She wants the luck and would like to renew the cross on her house, simply because it is hers and she can if she wants to. She positions herself back from the main throng so she can watch without being drawn in. She is on the outer edge of the crowd, but senses someone behind her. She turns and wishes them a Good Resurrection, holding her candle out to offer a light.

Juliet looks in the dark for a candle at waist height, but there is no candle. Instead, there are hands in pockets. She looks to the face of this non-believer. It is Aaman.

"Oh, hello. Isn't it amazing?" Juliet looks over the sea of candles, which now flicker their way home, dispersing slowly to each corner of the village, a bobbing orange glow surrounded by laughter, colourful plasma coursing through the veins of the village from the heart.

"It is interesting."

"Have you been in the church to see? Come on, let's go over where it's a bit more central. We'll be able to look in from over there."

Juliet pulls at Aaman's sleeve. He yields easily, and they wiggle their way through the crowd. The people are thinning out now, but there is a dense clump around the church door and there are many still inside, talking, praying, kissing icons. But a few feet away from the door, the square has empty patches. There's a woman with her arm around a beautiful little girl, who in turn, holds the hand of an energetic little boy a year or two older.

"Where is your father now?" the woman rhetorically asks as the boy breaks free. "Spiro, stop running with that candle. You will fall."

"*Nai, Mama.*" Yes, Mum.

"I am going to go and look for him. Stay here, Spiro. Be good and stay with Vasso." Vasso begins to cry. The mother bends her knees. Her skirt is too tight, so she pulls it down as it rides up before wiping her daughter's eyes and giving her a hug.

"I won't be a minute, Vasso. Spiro will look after you. There are so many people in the church, you wouldn't like it. I won't be a minute, I will just get Baba, OK." Vasso nods and her shiny, well-brushed, waist-length curls bob. Spiro runs back and dutifully holds her hand, but as soon as his mother's back is turned, he is running again, round and round, through the crowds.

Juliet peers into the church at the gold gleaming above the throng of people, on the walls, and hanging from the ceiling. Whispered prayers merge alongside laughter and back slapping. The church seems to belong to the people rather than the people belonging to the church. They are so tightly packed, they shuffle as one, as if boiling, centres of calm and edges that break away in little flurries. Some shuffle to be nearer the altar. Others form a queue up to a glass case that contains a painted icon. A lady at the front of the queue genuflects before the glass, crosses herself and then kisses it. She crosses herself three times before stepping aside for the next person to repeat giving the honour. Some of them with lifeless eyes perform the ritual and once complete, they break away unaffected. Others have tears in their eyes and reach for lace-edged handkerchiefs.

Some women wear tight dresses and short skirts, their makeup heavily applied, the heels high. There is no subtlety in the adornment. Juliet reflects that there is something very sacrilegious in their sense of occasion. The men are in suits, leather jackets, or shirts, but all wear loafers. They smoke outside.

A brush past Juliet's legs brings her back to consciousness. Spiro runs around her and Aaman and they smile. He then, suddenly, stands still behind his sister, little Vasso. Spiro's candle catches Juliet's attention.

Everything changes. Anticipation slows time. Horror brings action. Juliet jumps towards Spiro. The mother runs. Vasso screams. The candle flares. People shout. Vasso's hair burns. Tip to crown. Fizzing, spitting. Aaman pushes. Juliet staggers. Aaman lays his hand on the girl's head, in one motion runs his hands down the hair, taking the oxygen, removing the burning, killing the fear. Juliet breathes again.

As fast as it happened, it is finished. The mother encloses her toddler in her arms and inspects the outer layer of hair that is singed away. Spiro is left alone with his inner conscience; no words could be louder. The crowd's momentary tension dispels. Vasso is offered a sweet. One old lady, the same height as Spiro, takes hold of his arm, speaking quickly and emphasising her words with tugs on his sleeve. Spiro cries.

Aaman looks around to find Juliet shaking. He supports her to a wall and holds her steady. He is not surprised by her reaction. He is calm.

"You must breathe," Aaman says. "Take one breath and then let it out. Good, take another. You are all right. There is no need to fear. It has happen, it has finished. The girl is all right."

The mother of the toddler comes towards them, unsure, reticent. She looks at Aaman and asks Juliet to thank him for her and then turns back to her children. Aaman understands but he is not interested; his attention is not taken from Juliet.

Juliet gently rubs her arm; Aaman lays his hand on top of hers to stop the motion and then just as gently takes his hand away. Juliet is crying, no sound, the feelings too deep. Even the tears have trouble surfacing.

"You can tell me if you like." The tears affect Aaman. He wishes he was bigger, not knowing if or how this would affect what he could do for Juliet in this moment. He is sitting, turned towards her. His knee touches hers. Juliet looks at him with soulful eyes.

"I was six years old. In my room, Dad was out. It was a bungalow. No stairs," she adds to help Aaman understand. "Mum is watching TV and I am meant to be sleeping. In a room at the back, past the bathroom. But something feels wrong so I call her. 'Mummy?' She doesn't answer. She often doesn't answer me. But I know something is wrong so I call again. 'Mummy.' When I call her 'Mummy,' if she answers, she would say, 'Yes, by some major error in my life!' Always 'By some major error in my life.' She is not the kindest of mothers. She is not a bad mother, she just didn't seem to have any interest in me. I think she found children boring back then and it grew into a habit. That, and some weird jealousy about me and Dad. But I had grown used to her by the age of six." Juliet explains that she had actually thought she could be no other way until she saw her talking to one of the girls in her class at school. She was kind and gentle with her and even gave her a bit of a half hug. Which had hurt her.

"But, anyway, I was calling her and this time she didn't answer at all. I could hear her laughing, watching TV. I called really loud. She answered 'Yes, by some major error ...' but she was laughing at the TV and never finished her sentence. I watched the light coming from the TV across the hall floor. I could make out the shapes of people moving. I wished Dad was home. He was great. But only Mum was there and Mum didn't come. So I went back to bed. I said to myself that if she was laughing, then everything must be fine. I curled up with my little teddy.

"The next thing I knew, Dad was picking me up but not kindly. I screeched and reached for little Emily Bear, but Dad ignored me." Juliet relates the struggle to be released, but her dad's hand pressure pushing against her head had only increased. "He ran from the bedroom. I was frightened because Dad had always been kind and loving and now he had suddenly turned into being like Mum. He was holding me too tight. My nose was against his chest but with one eye, as he opened the door, I could see the corridor was on fire." Juliet breathes fast. Aaman strokes her back and makes soothing noises.

"I realised that if I left Emily she would burn so I reached out again and tried to scream, but Dad pressed my face harder into his chest and ran. When we got outside he put me down. I felt very hot and funny. He looked even funnier as he had only half a head of hair. I couldn't say anything because something hurt. He started stripping my pyjamas off me. But they were nylon and they had melted onto my skin. I was screaming then. I thought I was screaming for Emily Bear, but now I wonder if I was screaming in pain. He sat me on his knee and hugged me tight, all except my arm, until the ambulance came."

"Your mother?"

"Ah yes, her. She had got out when my dad came home. I don't remember her being with me after Dad got me out. The fire was started by my mum's candles in the bathroom. She liked to have candles when she bathed. It was a combination of candles, tissues, and towels."

Juliet looks over to the church, now all but deserted. The doors are still open and the occasional smell of incense in the air mixes with the evening's warmth, sickly sweet.

"I was in hospital for a while. I remember Dad visiting me every day. My dad's dead now. Mum may have visited, but I don't remember. I hated her then. I thought if she had listened to me, Emily Bear would not have been burnt along with the house.

"There was a nurse who was so kind to me. I can remember wishing that she was my mum. She bought me a small bear and said the bear had a new body but inside it was all Emily, all I had to do was give her enough love and I would see for myself." Juliet exhales and looks at Aaman. He senses she is nervous with this disclosure.

Aaman sits quietly, gathering words in English. He begins by stroking her scarred arm. But the words do not come. Juliet waits. They stand in unison and begin a slow walk, kicking small pieces of gravel. They pass a pomegranate tree and Aaman picks a flower and hands it to Juliet. She twirls it between her fingers. They reach a bench, Aaman sits down and Juliet follows, putting the flower on the bench next to her.

"I know fire too, but not like you. When I was eight, I was given a chance to see if I was any good to get a job at the factory where my brother worked." Aaman says, the picture still vivid in his mind's eye.

"You give me four days' work and we'll see if you are cut out for working here." The man said, "If you are, I'll hire you and pay you. If you're not, best go home and work in the fields."

"You will see. You will hire me." Aaman stood as tall as he could for his eight years of age. His parents would be so proud of him when he came home with a job at the factory where his brother worked.

Four days, he worked at the back of the factory where paper and cotton were stored - rolls and rolls of them. His brother usually worked in the printing room but for these trial days he worked in the storage rooms with Aaman. On the fifth day, excitement ran through Aaman. This was the day he felt sure he would have a position with the factory, a proper job.

His brother was called to take some cotton pieces up to the laminating room. He pulled Aaman to one side. "You take the cotton pieces up, it will look good for you."

The cotton was heavy and it took a long time. He walked slowly on his return journey, savouring his free run of the factory. It made him feel important. He smiled at the people he met, proud to work there. When he got back to the storage yard, he ambled up to the door of the storage room and everything looked normal. But as he neared the door, something felt amiss. He put his hand out to open the door, and a wave of adrenaline pumped through him. He swung the door open. At first it didn't make sense.

There were orange tufts on the rolls on the top of the stacks. His brother was pulling these rolls off the stack and hitting them with his jacket. It was fire. Aaman's body flexed rigid. His feet anchored to the spot. His jaw hung slackly. The smoke was filling the room. Aaman stared. His brother left the rolls, the orange tufts flicking towards the ceiling. He disappeared into the smoke. Aaman wanted to follow him but nothing would move. He stopped breathing. A shape came out of the smoke. His brother all but carried one of the old workers. A fleeting thought of how big and strong his brother was drew in a breath to expand his chest. Giaan carried the old man past Aaman and put him on the ground outside.

"Stay outside," he barked as he passed Aaman. He went back in, and Aaman followed. He felt scared; he wanted to be by his brother. But no sooner had they entered the building than Giaan ran. He ran between the burning rolls, coughing and shouting to the men to get out. He came back with another old man whom he put outside. As he passed Aaman, he shouted "Get help!"

The blaze had really taken hold now, and the room grew dark and hot. Aaman hesitated before beginning to pivot on his heels when a stack of cotton rolls tumbled. They were very heavy. Clouds of dust mingled with smoke. A draft of singeing hot air hit Aaman in the face. He tried to clear the air with his hand. The rolls landed where his brother had stood. As the dust settled, he could see his brother under the rolls trying to push them off. Aaman took a step towards him but the second step never came as he knew he was too small to lift the rolls. He stood there in horror. Giaan was waving at him, but Aaman's ears would not open. He shouted again. "Get help! Run!" But Aaman's legs would not move. All he could see was his brother's eyes and his strength not helping him.

Then he was released and he ran screaming for aid. The old men were still coughing outside, and he ran manically calling everyone to come, to help. People began to stream out of their work units. First in curiosity and then in urgency. Aaman ran. Aaman shouted. The whole factory swarmed to the out buildings, the bigger men pushing to the front. Aaman ran and ran to every part of the factory he knew screaming for aid until finally there was nowhere else to run.

His legs could not move him fast enough to get back to his brother. His lungs cut like knives in their bid for oxygen. As he neared the store room, his legs began to wobble. He forced them forward, his feet twisting over onto his ankle. The door to the storeroom was open. Everything inside was fire. There was no life.

Juliet has stopped crying and finds that she is stroking Aaman's arm. Aaman looks up from his lap where he has been staring in the telling of his tale. His eyes shine with tears, and the candle flutters between them. They sit in silence. Understood and understanding.

Juliet is the first to move, shifting her weight. They stand in unison, slowly. The village streets have hushed. Noise and laughter and light come in streaks from the shuttered houses. Aaman and Juliet walk in silence, snatches of conversation coming with each house they pass.

When they reach the lane, Aaman steps away. They stand opposite each other. The mutual understanding belied by the social distancing, the rigidity of conformity. There is a need for something to be said. But neither can find the words. The minutes of struggle themselves become the words that wished to be spoken, the understanding made explicit in the time taken trying to search for them. The tension releases. They both give a little, quiet laugh. Juliet turns to go.

"Goodnight, Juliet."

"Monday?" she asks.

Chapter 8

The sound awakes him. Some sounds have no call of alarm, some do. It is a deep, guttural, wet cough coming in spasms. Aaman opens his eyes. A clean shaft of light streams through the doorless opening onto the mud floor. The bunks topped with inactive dark lumps, Sunday, a day of no pay. A black shape on the floor pulses to the coughing rhythm. Aaman shifts his position, turning away, onto his back. The underside of the bunk above provides a canvas for the passing of endless seas of unused lives. Carved, burnt and scribed dates, names, loves, obscenities, anything to make an indelible mark, an anchor to existence.

Aaman turns another quarter turn to face the wall. Carefully, with little movement, he pulls out a loose piece of mud brick. With finger and thumb, he pinches the paper that peeps from behind. His rolled savings emerge. He replaces the piece of mud brick and, spitting on his fingers smoothes the surface, his night safe hidden. His money pocketed.

The coughing subsides. Aaman rolls from the bunk and stretches. Mahmout is still asleep. There are new men on the top bunks, lying on their stomachs, talking quietly, nervously, their smoke curling up in the stillness, around and under the tiles, finding many easy exits. The air is stale and hot by day on the top bunk and cold and, if it rains, wet by night. It is never a bunk of choice for someone who has spent even one night here.

But the new men are always tricked. The farmer sells the top bunks for five cents more than the others. That gives the illusion of value. It makes him over five euros extra a week. He runs his *regina*, a cross between a motorbike and a truck, on it. Better privacy, he tells them, more head room, no one climbs over you, lets everyone else know you are a man of standing. The new men think it over and, with hope on a high, part with money that would be better spent on food. They never spend more than one night on the top if a lower bunk is free. Aaman never even spent the first night there. He did not con himself that he is here for comfort.

Through the doorway, in the brightness of the sun, the Nigerians are loading up for the day. One balances a carved elephant on one finger, another tries to retrieve it without a breakage. They laugh, the burden not so heavy for them, they have no wives, it is an adventure. They are tall, they are young, they are strong, and they help each other. Their trade is to make banter with the tourists and run fast from the police. Street sellers have no days off and no guarantee of pay.

Aaman steps past the bearded man curled on the floor whose sole-less shoes provide a pillow. The sunshine warms Aaman's sleep-stiffened muscles.

The Nigerians ignore him. There is a hierarchy even here. Aaman understands and walks past them into the orange grove to water a tree.

Oranges from the surrounding trees, his breakfast staple, are pocketed for the walk. The mud-brick barn drags all ambition from Aaman on a Sunday. The men talk of home, families they are not supporting, jobs they haven't got. He can understand their talk even if the language is not his own. No, time passes too slowly on Sundays at the barn. He sets out for the village.

No hope of work to rush for, no cold to keep at bay, the pace slow, steady, he throws his peel into the lush weeds and flowers by the roadside. Unseen tiny beasts make the high grass quiver as he makes his way by the edge of the road. A dog runs past, looking back, fearing reprimand, anxious for company. Aaman clicks his fingers, and the dog circles to approach from behind, tail wagging and haunches lowered, he sniffs at Aaman's sticky fingers. He licks his submission. They walk together, both happier for the company.

Juliet sprawls in her cotton-sheeted double bed. Sunday! A national habit of a lifetime frees her worries on this day. She stretches and yawns as noisily as she can before bounding out of bed. The cat resents the disturbance of the duvet, but stands to stretch. He greets Juliet by allowing her to stroke him before finding the warmest indentation in the bed she has left and, owning it, tucks all his extremities out of sight and closes his eyes.

The clean kitchen cupboard, which needs a coat of paint, Juliet muses, holds fresh, local organic eggs for breakfast, local olive oil bread, and a fantastic marmalade Juliet found online and paid through the nose to have delivered to Greece. But it was worth it. She flicks the kettle on and readies the coffee pot. There is just enough water from one kettle to boil the eggs and make coffee.

It is only when she lays the patio table that she realises she has no milk. She would like to be someone who could drink their coffee black, but, for Juliet, giving up milk in her coffee feels harder than giving up smoking did. She achieved the one but not the other. She half enjoys her boiled eggs, but decides to go for milk before relishing toast and marmalade with her caffeine fix.

After covering the coffee pot with a tea towel and two cushions to keep it warm, Juliet slips into flip-flops. The door opens to the brilliance of the day. The village is alive with sound, the smell of roasting lamb coming from all corners. Music blares across the valley like a duel, whining, discordant, unfamiliar clarinet solos competing with hysterical bouzouki riffs. The music mixes with children laughing, dads shouting jovially, a background of clattering plates and women chattering excitedly.

The neighbours down the lane wave Juliet to join them. She motions "Later." Greetings come from every doorstep and Juliet smiles from ear to ear. Her life is becoming complete, her dream realising.

Marina has left the shop open; she is in the back garden which spans the distance to her house behind. Between the two is an open fire pit with a lamb on a spit. Her family and friends spill from every corner and cover every chair, crowding in the kitchen beyond and creating a spellbinding cacophony of happiness.

"Come, join us!" Marina has rubber gloves on, holding a dyed red egg in each hand.

"Later. I need milk for now."

"Take it, pay another time!" A child pulls Marina by her skirt into the kitchen. She's gone.

Juliet walks back through the untended shop. Someone has been in and bought something, leaving the money on the counter. Juliet does the same.

Leaving, Juliet smiles at the sun, closes her eyes and focuses on the sounds of Greek Easter. The clarinets are still howling, the *bouzoukia* still manic. Someone has burnt something and the smell is acrid but drifts away. The milk feels freezing to her fingers. She thinks of her jug of coffee going cold and heads for home.

There is no one in the square. Everyone is with loved ones, everyone happy without a care in the world today. Juliet is happy for their joy. Content in herself, she turns onto the road. There is a man in the distance. She estimates they will cross at her lane end. She rehearses Easter day greetings and suitable

106

responses in her head. She swaps hands with the milk. It is too cold. She walks and looks up.

"Aaman!"

"Hello."

"Are you working somewhere today?"

"No, just walking."

"Are you going somewhere?"

"No."

Juliet feels prized like a winkle out of her Greek Easter fantasy. His loved ones are far away. No-one will invite him to eat with them, he does not own a house, and he does not contribute to village life. He takes and sends what he gets to his own village, his own life. He does not belong here. She knows that is how they see him.

"Do you ..." Juliet looks at the milk, starts to read one side of the carton, shifts her weight and gently shakes the milk before looking up. "Do you want to come to the house? I'm not roasting a lamb, but I was going to have toast and marmalade for now."

"Marmalade?"

"Oranges in a sugar syrup."

"Thank you, I have had oranges today. There are many oranges on all the trees and I have had so many. Every day I have many." His expression tells her that he is sick of oranges.

"Toast and coffee then?"

"OK."

They amble up the lane. Aaman silently offers to carry the milk. Juliet indicates this is not necessary. Juliet's neighbours are all so busy they don't see her

107

pass. The noise of the chatter and laughter and music ebbs and flows as they make their way.

Juliet opens the door to find the cat is on the kitchen table again. Aaman lifts it off and looks at Juliet to see if his action is acceptable. She laughs gently and offers him a seat.

Aaman sits puzzling over the tent of cushions and the tea towel on the table whilst Juliet cuts and toasts the bread. The butter from the fridge is hard and Juliet contemplates buying a microwave, just for these little jobs, she tells herself. She puts the butter on a plate and slips it under the grill tray to warm.

She joins Aaman and gives him toast. Aaman is still gazing at the centrepiece. Juliet laughs and throws the cushions back onto the sofa. Pulling the tea towel away, she says, "Tarah!"

Aaman smiles. The joke crosses cultures. They are both relieved.

"Are you OK from last night?" he asks.

"Yes, thanks. Are you? You were very brave last night," she pauses, "and when you were a boy ..."

"No, I was not brave, I was terrified. I did not jump into action. Your baba was very brave to be in the fire for you."

"I think for an eight-year-old boy you were very brave. My dad was a grown man." Juliet pours the coffee and puts marmalade on her bread. Aaman picks up the jar and examines the contents.

"You say he is dead? You miss him?" He sniffs at the marmalade.

"So much. But I missed him more before he was dead." She realises that to Aaman this will not make sense. "It's a long story. Milk?"

Aaman nods before tipping his head on an angle like an attentive bird and then sits back, coffee mug in hand, as if he has all the time in the world to listen to her.

"My dad was the best." Juliet laughs at the love of the memory. "He played with me all the time when he was at home. When I was very little, my mum worked and my dad stayed at home until I started school. Then they both worked. Mum came home before Dad but she …"

Juliet's tone deepens and her face becomes firm.

"I don't know, she always seemed cross and in a hurry, whatever we did. When Dad came home," Juliet sighs and smiles, "it was as if all the hurry and all the crossness disappeared and we'd chase round the kitchen table and play hide and seek around the house. Mum would get snappy because the airing cupboard would get messed up, or her bed would be unmade by my dad pretending to hide under the covers. But he was great."

"You were very younger when he died?"

"No. And that's why it hurts. Their arguing slowly increased. It got to a point that they had no sense of timing. They would fight openly in front of me. I was at an age when I wanted to be with my friends all the time so I tried to go to other people's houses after school. It felt good at their houses, normal.

"Then I would go back and Mum would be shouting at Dad. He'd see me and go quiet. She would carry on. Then he would leave the room and she would still be shouting. He would put his hand over my mouth and get me in an arm lock pretending to kidnap me and we would sneak out and eat fish and chips at the corner shop and not go back until bedtime." Juliet sucks on her lips to hold back the tears.

"Here I go again." She smiles, but the corners of her mouth turn down.

Aaman rocks forward, puts down his coffee cup and rests his forearms crossed on the table, looks Juliet in the eye and waits.

"OK. Well, basically he left. I was thirteen. I became friends with Michelle that year. She really helped, we would stay out from school until late, be out all weekend. Mum didn't care. She never asked where I had been. I would come home, full of our adventures and call her to see where she was. 'Mum,' I would call. 'Yes, by some major error in my life!' and my heart would sink. Even today, when I talk to Michelle, it always hurts. It brings back those times." Juliet straightens her back and looks up at the ceiling. The cat rubs against her legs and she picks him up and absently puts him on her knee.

"I don't think I am very nice to her. I mean I haven't seen her for ..." She stops, closes her eyes, fingers counting. "Twenty-two years. That's a long time, and I'm sorry to say I never call her. She just keeps on calling me." Juliet looks at Aaman, fearing his judgement. None comes.

"Anyway, she was my rock that year when he left, and for many years after. I thought he had left without a word. I didn't see him leave. He never phoned, he didn't write—or so I thought." Juliet exhales roughly through her nose, elbows on the table, her head sinking into her hands. The cat adjusts to avoid being squashed. Her voice becomes quiet and muffled into her palms. Aaman leans toward her to hear.

"When I was moving out of the house, I was eighteen and my escape route was college. They even paid us to go in those days, grants and so on." Juliet unburies her face and leans her chin on clasped hands. She cannot meet Aaman's gaze, so she stares at, but doesn't see the painted wall.

"I wanted to take everything that was mine so I would never have to go back. I was looking for something, I forget what, it might have been a shoe and I had searched for everywhere. I went to look in the bottom of Mum's wardrobe because that's where she kept her shoes, so yes, I suppose it was a shoe. Well, you can guess what I found there! They dated back to the day he left."

She strokes the cat, his fur slicking with the slight sweat of her palms. He has a quiet purr. Juliet takes a deep breath.

"The first one had no address or stamp on it so I presume he left it at the house on the day he left. It explained his position and how he regretted what was happening and how he loved me and that I could not have done anything to help. He said he'd come for me as soon as he found somewhere for us but meanwhile I could ring him at the pub he used to go to. He couldn't call me because of Mum. The next one had a stamp, two days later. He asked how I was and why I hadn't called, was I cross, if I was then he understood but he needed to talk to me and a time and a place to meet after school.

"The next letter said he had been to the house but I had been out and Mum had been angry and would I please call him. We moved sometime around then to a tiny flat and I had to move schools. I felt like I was going mad, losing my dad and all my friends at the same time. The flat wasn't far so I still saw Michelle in the evenings and at weekends, but the letters dated after that were to a post-office box. That's a box for letters you can have at the post office so no one really knows where you live."

Aaman nods his understanding and accepts more coffee.

"He said he had called round. He said he had gone to my old school. He said he had even gone into Mum's work. He said she had said I didn't want to see him and that I would contact him when I did. Was it true, he asked? You get the picture.

"There were fewer and fewer letters dated over the next three years to that P.O. Box. There were three birthday cards and three Christmas cards. He hoped I would like the gifts. I have always wondered what the gifts might have been."

Juliet stops stroking the cat and picks up her mug, tipping it slightly to look, but not to drink. She sets it back down.

"In one envelope was a Decree Nisei. That's a divorce paper saying it is final. In the last dated letter, just before my sixteenth birthday was a newspaper clipping. A one-inch report of a pedestrian killed in a car accident and my dad's name. That's how I found out my dad was dead." Juliet feels the weight of her words. She is still, and in that stillness is a crack, followed by a splintering and then the crashing of protective walls, the explosion of repressed emotions.

Aaman's eyes are upon her. She feels vulnerable as she speaks of her father's death and wonders if she can now act tough. But as she utters the words "my dad was dead," the cat stands up on her lap and rubs its nose against her chin. It is the touch of kindness that undoes the last binding. She makes no noise but rocks backwards and forwards, her shoulders raising and lowering in an impulse action to her silent sobs as she slowly curls into a ball on her chair squeezing the cat onto the floor.

Aaman puts a hand toward her. Saabira cried in his arms for so long, cried until she was asleep and awoke to cry some more. He felt responsible for her pain. He had promised to make her happy, but by creating within her a lifeless child, he had created her greatest pain. Aaman feels tears in his eyes and puts his arm across Juliet's back, smoothing and stroking.

He leans in until his hair touches hers and he makes a gentle sucking, tutting noise, as a mother to a child.

Juliet rocks and noiselessly cries, arms across her raised knees, oblivious of Aaman or his stroking hand, but falling into the rhythm of his calming sounds. The cat jumps onto the back of the seat where Aaman is sitting. He reaches his paws up Aaman's back and stretches. Receiving no attention, he curls up behind him to sleep. All three of them take all the time they need.

Juliet feels herself calming. She has avoided talking for as many years as lay between her and her loss. She has mentioned it in heartless one-line statements to Michelle here and there, almost as if Michelle were the problem, but she has not visited the emotions. She is surprised that she is still alive in this moment, that she has survived meeting with these feelings, that she has not been engulfed and eaten alive by the enormity of the pain. She half straightens and feels a weight has been removed. She is surprised and straightens some more.

Aaman takes his hand away and sits back, disturbing the cat who feels he has had enough abuse and jumps off to go and sit on the sofa.

"Are you OK?" His voice a whisper that offers the option not to reply.

"Yes, I think so. That was scary." She stands slowly and makes her way to the bathroom for tissues.

She splashes her face with water. When she returns, there is no colour in her cheeks, but her eyes are alert. Juliet feels she has gained some strength from the morning. She feels brave but fragile.

"Are you OK?" she asks Aaman, who has tears in his eyes.

"Yes, yes. It is sad. Loss. The things we do and don't do. Life makes so many choices for us."

Chapter 9

A tear balances on the rim of one of his eyes, his brown irises shimmering under a wash of saline. Juliet is not sure if it is for her or for himself. Or maybe it is for someone else. He gazes across the sitting room and out the front door. Juliet feels the need for some air.

"Shall we sit outside?" She picks up her coffee and the coffee pot and moves towards the light, the promise of warm rays on her face. Aaman follows. The village is still alive with sound. The clarinet music has stopped, the bouzouki has won, but there are many other sources of music scattered around the houses of the village, blending with calls and cheers and shouts. Someone is firing a gun to celebrate. No dogs are barking. No doubt they have all been fed scraps from the roast and lie full length under tables or in olive tree shade.

Juliet puts down the china and briefly re-enters to emerge with two awkwardly large folding chairs. When one hits the door frame, Aaman turns and hurries to help.

"They are a bit more comfortable, I think." They each unfold a chair and sit. Aaman's eyes are dry but there is a childlike limpness to his muscles. Juliet holds her head high. Her head feels clear. There is lightness to her movements.

"So we both lost someone at a young age." Juliet offers him the opening.

Aaman tenses at the invitation. He looks over the wall at the hill beyond the village rooftops. He takes himself far away. Juliet sits for a moment, but feels uncomfortable in this silence. She opens her mouth to speak but changes her mind. She looks for the cat. He is not there. She pours more coffee into her mug and holds it between both hands, sipping it as if it were a cold day.

"Giaan."

Juliet starts and a drop of coffee drips onto her jeans. She rubs it away before turning to give Aaman her attention.

"That was his name. Giaan." He leans forward and traces the letters with his finger on the table top in English, slowly, with unpractised movements.

"It means having knowledge of God or heaven. I am not sure how to say in English. It was the first thing I learnt to write in English." He picks at the edge of the table.

"Then I learnt to spell my name A-A-M-A-N. With two 'A's like Giaan." He writes this with his finger on the table top. The movement becomes more familiar with each stroke.

"Not A-M-A-N, which is the proper way." He licks his finger and writes again, turning his head this way and that to make the shapes, faint traces of his letters remain on the varnished wood. He returns to running his nail on the table edge.

"How much older than you was he?"

"He was fourteen years old when he died."

Juliet puts her hand to her mouth. She had imagined him to be older.

"When we were little, he would take me to the pipe at the end of the village and he would bang on the pipe with a stick and the rats would come running out. Then he would try to hit the rats with the stick. The first rats out always got away, but the smaller rats, the weak rats, were last out and too slow."

Juliet puts her coffee down to give her full attention.

"I watched my big brother chase rats and load wood and help with the land and even stand up to my father. I felt like one of the little rats, not beaten but always running behind, never quite fast enough."

Juliet wants to say something but the words won't come.

"My mother she praised Giaan. My father spoke to him like he was an adult. My grandparents would hug me when my parents gave Giaan this attention, like I was still a child. They did not understand what it meant to be small.

"So I tried to be like Giaan, but when he died that day, I could no longer pretend to be something I wasn't. I had done nothing to save him. I ran too slowly. I felt like I was one of the little rats running

118

out of the pipe, only, I suppose, in this case, you could say, the wrong rat died."

Juliet shook her head, her throat tightened. She is overwhelmed with the need to help Aaman forgive himself.

Juliet recalls a conversation she once had with her tutor at college one rainy afternoon on campus in the student cafe. They were practising past tenses. Juliet, for some reason, used her father's letters as the subject and, whilst struggling with the language, she said that she felt she let her dad down by not contacting him all the years he sent the letters. Her tutor replied in a very difficult sentence structure that Juliet asked him to repeat several times to understand. She cannot remember the sentence structure in Greek now, but she remembers it basically said that she could only do what she had the knowledge and power to do at the time. It was only a Greek conversation practice, but the sentence has haunted her and over time relieved, to some degree, her feelings of guilt – or maybe not.

"Aaman, I wouldn't wish it, but if this event happened again today, would you do the same thing?"

"I am sorry." Aaman pulls himself from a faraway place. He wasn't been listening.

"Suppose, just pretend, it happened today, the fire happened today, I wouldn't want it to but just supposing it did with the same room and the same factory and everything. What would you do this time?"

119

"You think I haven't thought this over and over, the different route I could have run to get to the big men faster, stopped him going in a second time, gone in with him and then maybe it would have been me not him. I have played this game many times in my life to bring him to safety, but he is still dead."

"I can imagine," Juliet's voice grows soft. "What I was trying to say was, well, when you were little, you would have thought in one way and as you get older things change. What I was mean is, has what you would do changed over time?"

Aaman leans forward.

"Obviously I realised as I got bigger, I could have done different things. When I learnt, once, about using something very long as a lever to lift a thing to make it light, this would be my dream to return and do this. This would work, even for a small boy. But if I could go back, I would do everything I could, everything." Tears are on the edge of spilling, one escapes and runs down his face and drips from his chin.

"Exactly, Aaman, you would do everything you could do and you were the same person then, so you would have done everything you could have done then. But we do everything we do with the knowledge we have. I guess that is my point, and this is something my Greek teacher once said to me. We can only do everything we could do with the knowledge we have at the time."

Aaman considers this.

"What more can anybody do than that?" Juliet continues.

Aaman looks at her.

"After he died, I got a job in a carpet factory. I felt I had to make the money that Giaan was no longer making. It was very long hours for little pay, so I would work seven days a week. It took a long time to walk there and back."

"And you were how old?"

"I was nine years old when I got the job. I wanted to be a computer programmer. That was my dream. That is every Punjabi boy's dream. But life makes the decisions. I stayed working there until I was eighteen and then I got a job in a shoe factory. It was official so I got much better pay." Aaman's mood seems to lighten a little at the thought.

"It was OK. I forgot my dream of being a programmer. I realised that you cannot escape what will happen. I was twenty one when my mother arranged marriage for me."

"Did you have a girlfriend? Were you in love with someone else at the time?"

"Oh no, no, no! But to be a husband is a big responsibility. Very serious. She was a distant cousin of my mother's, and everyone was agreed that it was a good match, not least because she was smaller than me." Aaman adds a dry laugh.

"She was so scared on our wedding night. So instead of undressing, I sat on the bed and asked her to talk. I tried to be kind and considerate in what I said, and she tried to be brave. We talked until the

121

morning. I have seen married women who are unhappy and afraid. I wanted Saabira to be happy like my mother.

"We talked for many months and held hands and kissed a little. Nothing was changing, and I felt like I was a small rat again and I needed to be a big rat. So one day I got cross and I shouted at her and she came to me to say sorry and she kissed me and there was much passion and the passion stayed. So for a long while I felt good. I had achieved a happy wife and then she became pregnant and all my family were overjoyed. For a while I was not the boy who left his brother in the fire. I was Aaman, with Saabira his wife.

"She was so happy to be with child. She would hold her sari under her belly and say, 'Do I look more beautiful if you can see the bump more?' And then she would giggle and fall on me and we would be close. Towards the end, she looked pale, but she was so happy, nothing could make her lie down. I would beg her for the sake of the child to take rest, but she said there would be no rest when the baby came so she would take no rest now.

"I was feeding the bullocks when she cried out. It was one of those noises that you know needs action, like the cry of my brother. I dropped the pail and ran so fast. She had collapsed on the floor and there was water everywhere. I put her on the bed as my grandmother came. She told me to tell my mother and that she would stay with Saabira.

"My mother came and the ladies who helped for birthing. They closed the door on me. Saabira was screaming and I felt that I had done this to her. Without me, she would not be screaming. She screamed on and off for hours. My father and grandfather went to the farthest fields to work but I could not leave the closed door.

"It was my mother who opened the door, looking away and leading me to Saabira. She was so pale and her hair all plastered to her face and she saw me and smiled.

"Who is it, Aaman? Who is our child?" I turned to the women and their faces were long. Ma handed me this bundle, but all I could do was stare at Ma. She looked so beautiful, but her face was wet with tears and eyes so sad. She shook her head from side to side and looked at Saabira, who now realised something was wrong.

"Shouldn't he cry? Why does he not cry? Aaman, why does he not cry?" She tried to get up so I hastened to her side and stroked her face with one hand. In my other arm, wrapped in a cloth, I had our lifeless baby. She pushed my hand away and moved the cloth from the baby's face and then went quiet and I saw a part of her die. It squeezed all the air from my lungs. She lay down to sleep and stayed not moving and not eating for several days."

Little sobbing squeaks come from Aaman's throat as he suppresses his anguish. His elbows rest on the table. He holds his own fist, tightly pressing it against his mouth to silence any sound, every muscle tight.

Juliet's chair scrapes against the patio as she pulls it nearer Aaman. She encircles his shoulders with one arm, stroking his hair with the other. She is happy to hold him. After a while, he twitches his shoulders, and Juliet retreats, allowing him his dignity. Aaman pulls himself up, leans away in his chair and wraps his arms around his body.

A child shrieks in play in the next yard. The cat jumps back over the wall and onto Aaman's knee. He unlocks his barrier and strokes him.

"Not only had I lost a child, but I had seen a part of my wife die. I was the little rat again, but this time it was my son who died and my wife who must mourn."

Aaman clears his throat and passes the cat to Juliet to draw his chair nearer the table and test the weight of the coffee pot. It is empty.

"So when she came up with the idea of a harvester machine for the village and we were short of the money to buy it, it was the least I could do to come to the West to make what was needed."

Aaman clearly feels safer talking about the practical necessity of his life. His voice is stronger, clearer.

"Ahh, so that's why you are here. How long do you think it will take you?" Aaman is obviously in much pain, so Juliet supports his change of tack.

"Saabira thought it would take two years but I am here now and I know that it will take much longer." He shakes his head.

Juliet has no idea what a harvester would cost, but they are big machines so she guesses in the thousands. She sees Aaman is on a futile mission.

"Something I have come to realise ..."

Juliet perks up at the sound of hope in Aaman's voice.

"Since I began this journey, I have had much silence. Silence from the necessity to be quiet or discovered, silence from lack of anyone to talk to, silence for lack of anything good to say, and in my silence I have thought a lot. It is like all my thoughts are coming together today. I thought my uneasiness of being here and my behaviour to my wife was about the sad things that have happened. But I am beginning to think something different. I must thank you, Juliet, because my thoughts began to become something different when you told me your sad life and through seeing you, if I might be so bold, I saw me."

Juliet is slightly shocked, a little weary and feels ever so slightly smug.

"Tell me."

But he does not talk of Juliet's life.

"The birth is a time that neither I nor Saabira wish to remember. She cried for so many days and I held her and tried to feed her until she eventually began to curl up with me tighter as if I could take it all away. But I knew I was the bringer of the sorrow. I had brought her the baby and so curling up next to me would not take away the pain. I knew in time we would become closer and closer and then what if another baby came? I would bring her more sorrow.

"I was so proud to have Saabira as my wife and so proud of making her happy I had forgotten everything. I was happy. But I knew if I allowed her to keep curling up to me I would want to show her that love I feel for her and by indulging my love for her I could cause her the greatest pain she has ever known all over again. So I began to make a distance between me and Saabira. It was very hard, harder than carrying jugs of water, harder than racing my brother to load wood, harder than trying to make Saabira happy when we were first married."

Juliet puts her hand on top of Aaman's hand that rests on the table.

"I was hurting too and to curl into Saabira would not have taken the pain away, but Saabira is my joy and being together could have made the pain less and the joy more ... over time.

"Today I realised that my decision to not be close, in order to protect Saabira, had made us more like brother and sister, which in itself hurt, so agreeing to this journey was a way for me to be away from the pain of the past, the pain of the present and the pain I could cause in the future if I continued to love Saabira. I realised I have run away."

Knowing his conclusion has come about by hearing the turmoil of her own life, Juliet breaks eye contact and retracts her hand. She turns her head to

126

the side and scowls. Her instincts tell her to get up and leave, but she is struck by the irony in this choice of possible action. An irresistible urge forces her to laugh out loud.

Aaman looks offended.

"No, Aaman, I am not laughing at you. I understand what you said. I am laughing at myself. At my instinct to run away."

"Running away is not to be laughed at. It is to stop the hurt when we feel we have run out of choices."

"Yes, I suppose it is. So now you have realised you have run away, what difference will it make?"

"I must stop fearing."

There is a celebratory gunshot over the hill. The cat's friend jumps over the wall and wanders into the open house and eats from the bowl of cat food, crunching noisily, staying alert, cautious and protective.

"Yeah, right, easy to say." Juliet looks at the cat inside but takes no action.

"Easy to do because what I have now is worse than what I fear. Now I have no Saabira, no children, no family, no home, and no future if I stay here. If I take the risks, maybe I can win Saabira back, maybe we can have children, my family will be very happy to see me and, it is small, but we do have a home. It is better."

Juliet feels uncomfortable by this statement. She has nowhere to go back. No family home, no village, no partner. She ran away from a wide open space of nothingness. She could not return as the welcomed hero. She slumps in her chair.

"I'm hungry again. You?"

"Always," Aaman says.

"Come on, let's see what we can find."

Rummaging in the cupboards, Juliet finds some bits and pieces from the previous week. There is also a slice of spinach pie from the bakery, with a bite taken out of it, a piece of Brie, and an open tin of baked beans in the fridge. She is not a great housekeeper. There are some tubs of spices that have been left through the house sale that are not all past their sell-by date. Juliet finds the tubs that are three years old or more amusing, but Aaman cannot see why throwing these tubs away makes her giggle, nor can she explain it.

Juliet is in charge, but it is quickly apparent that cooking is not one of her skills and so Aaman takes over. He selects what he can from the vegetable rack. Juliet offers to wash and chop. Aaman begins with oil and spices in a large pan, and the house fills with incredible smells. He washes his pots and pans as he cooks, using the same ones again, even though Juliet points out she has more than one of most things.

By the time he is clapping and rotating chapattis, Juliet sits watching with fascination.

"May I ask something?"

"Sure," Juliet says.

"Do you make money now you have no husband or does he still support you?"

"I make my own, always have, ever since the boys started school."

"How can you when you are so far from your home country?"

He stacks another chapatti.

"On the Internet. I translate documents from Greek to English. In fact, I have just been offered some more work by the British Council in Athens, so I'm going to be really busy soon."

Aaman is silent.

"What was that you said about your boyhood dream to be a programmer?"

"I think it is every boyhood dream in Pakistan. Everyone thinks it will be easy money with no labour. For me, I think I would really like that it is logical. Also, I like languages."

"Yes, your English has improved unbelievably. I thought you only had a few words of English when we first met, but you are nearly fluent."

"I have been listening to you and learning. Saabira has a degree in English and she was very patient with me. I never had the chance of college but I think I am a quick learner."

Juliet reels at her presumption. The thought of Saabira having a degree doesn't fit with the image she has created in her head. She imagined an unreal person from a developing country. Not a person like her, like her boys, with a degree.

"You went to school though?"

"I finished school when my brother died. We had the idea that he was going to help our family make the money so I could go to school to become a programmer. But really I don't think there was enough money."

"Oh. Does anybody manage to become a programmer in Pakistan?"

"Yes. They would have to come from a family who could afford education."

"Ah."

Aaman brings food to the table. Juliet gets knives and forks, and Aaman puts them to one side. Juliet follows Aaman's lead and eats using the chapatti. She is amazed at the quality of the food given her bare cupboards. They eat with no talking and, for Juliet, no thinking.

Aaman dwells on what the Western world has to offer, jobs through the computer, enough money to buy houses in countries you are not born in, translating languages to make a living. The world is so big. He so wants, he wants ... he wants to stop thinking like Mahmout. Wanting brings him misery.

After the meal he wanders to the pomegranate trees and feels the fruit. Although they have grown they are still nowhere near ripe yet.

Chapter 10

They sit for a long time over their late lunch. The Easter celebration noises in the village show no signs of abating, the music continues at a loud volume, and the children gain their second wind. The sky begins to darken; there are one or two single fireworks. The still air is pierced with a series of festive gunfire shots. Someone over the hill puts on a firework display, and the whizzing and cracking is heard over the sound of the bouzouki.

Aaman and Juliet move onto the patio. The cat sits on Aaman's knee. The cat's friend circles Juliet's chair. She *pshhhes* at it, but it flops onto its side and licks its paws to clean over its ears.

Aaman's face is blank, and Juliet assumes he is now the one who is not thinking. He settles onto the hard-backed chair as if it is made of duck down, his limbs slack, his legs crossed, the upper dangling parallel to the lower indicating his leanness, his lack of size. Juliet's mind is rolling through the events of the day, the things that have been said, the thoughts she has had.

"You know you said earlier that my life had shown you that you were running away? What did

131

you mean? I mean, what in my life were you talking about? Exactly?"

In the interlude before Aaman answers, she raises a postponing finger and slips inside to reappear with a bottle of wine and two glasses. She clamps the bottle between her knees and pulls, producing a satisfactory pop. She pours; it can breathe while they drink.

"There you go." She clinks her glass against the one on the table.

"No, thank you." Aaman looks at her, trying to express something without words. Juliet's realisation comes suddenly and makes her feel foolish.

"Oh, of course. Would you rather I didn't?"

Aaman grins at her and wags a finger. She grins back and drinks.

"So come on, what did you mean?"

"Tell me more of your life, after you left home."

Juliet is happy to allow Aaman's direction.

"I moved out and went to college and promptly started an affair with my tutor, who was old enough to be my father." Juliet lets out a short, humourless laugh. "Which lasted until he decided my flat mate was more attractive than me, and I dropped out of college, became a loner, pulling pints in the Irish club until I met another lost soul, Mick. But there you go again! He was Irish, my dad was Irish. Mick was older than me, had no job, no home, he was wandering. Michelle tried to warn me, but after what my friend at college had done to me, I no longer believed in friendship. So I married Mick thinking we could, the two of us, escape the world in our bubble. Which we did until the reality of Thomas and Terrance happened. My beautiful boys."

Juliet gets up and reaches through the front door to the table just inside. She returns to her seat with a picture of her boys. The boys are in school uniform, about eight years old. Smiling and proud, she looks at Aaman to see his reaction. He appears clearly distressed.

"You have left them. Why?" There is an edge to his voice.

"Oh, no! They are not this age now. No, they are grown up. One is doing an MA and will follow that with a Ph.D., and the other's got his degree and has immediately landed a job at a bank. He's even been promoted already. They do a lot of in-house training so he's happy. He has a girlfriend and I think they may get married, but they haven't said anything yet."

"They are lucky to have so much education."

"Yes, it's harder now, there are fees. But Terrance, that's this one," she points, "has two small jobs and both me and his dad are helping him through."

The phone rings.

"Excuse me." Juliet takes the photograph in with her as she goes.

"Hello?"

"Hi Juliet, how's it going? Did your house boy show up?"

"Hi Michelle. I am a bit busy at the moment."

"Oh, OK."

133

Juliet clicks the phone off.

"Sorry about that, Aaman."

"Why did you do that?"

"What?" Juliet looks around her for what it is she is meant to have done.

"Not talk to your friend Michelle who helped you all those years?"

"Well, I, em, I didn't really want to." Juliet's cheeks have warmed and she rubs her arm through her long-sleeved t-shirt.

"Why?" Aaman asks slowly.

"There is no why. I just didn't want to." She cannot meet his gaze.

"You asked me earlier what I saw in your life."

"Yes, and?"

"And I ask you why you do not want to talk to Michelle."

"Would you like coffee or tea, seeing as you're not drinking?" Her tone is breezy and impersonal.

"No, Juliet, I do not want tea or coffee, or wine or anything else."

Juliet stands and then sits again.

"I want to run," she says.

"Yes, I can see that."

"OK, I don't want to talk to Michelle because she asks 'what am I doing' all the time. She wants to know what is going on in my life."

"Isn't that what friends do?"

"Yes, but that is my point. I didn't ask her to be my friend."

"Have you asked her to stop being your friend?"

"What? No, of course not, you don't ask people to stop being friends!"

"What would it be like if she no longer was your friend?"

"Oh my goodness, the thought of Michelle not being around is unthinkable." Juliet widens her eyes and raises her brow. "I mean, I don't phone her and most of the time I don't want to talk to her, but the thought of her never ringing again, I would feel so, so ... oh my God, I would feel so alone." Her body slumps boneless. "I am such a bitch." Juliet cannot find a pleasant place to rest her eyes as they look inward. "She has stood by me all these years and persisted with a one-way friendship, which, as I have just found out, I would feel alone without. So why, oh why do I not want to talk to her? Unless I am a class A bitch!"

"Or?"

"Or? Well, she does remind me of all the horrors of my past. But we did have fun staying out all weekend, going into pubs when we were only fourteen. We did get bored on weeknights a bit, but generally she was great. I loved her."

"Yes?"

"What do you mean, yes? As in yes I loved her? Well it's true, I did."

"And now?"

"I am not a kid any more. Things change."

"Do things like that change? Have you stopped loving your dad?"

"No, never, but Michelle is not my dad."

"She was with you when you went through a lot of pain."

"Yes, she wasn't around much when I went through the pain of college and I could have done with a friend then. You know I really thought I loved John. Dr John Brooks, that was his name. I thought it sounded so educated, above the sordidness of life. I saw him as my salvation. How wrong was I? I saw our relationship as a sign that I was an adult away from all the hurt of my childhood. I thought it was a new chapter in my life. But guess what? It was just more pain.

"Actually the pain was almost worse from losing my best friend of the time to losing him. Jenny." Juliet pauses to drink some wine.

"We met in fresher's week. That's the first week of term when you are new. We got on so well. We went everywhere together, discovered life away from families together, explored our freedom together. I guess I loved her too really, until ..." She finds no reason to finish her sentence and stops to swig down the rest of her glass and pours some more.

"It just seems that everyone I love goes and bloody well hurts me."

"And what have you found is the best way of getting away from that hurt?"

Juliet's eyes dart left to right and then she nods her head and smiles sadly.

"I couldn't get away from the pain of losing my dad. But I left home to get away from Mum. I left college to get away from both John and Jenny. And

Mick? Let's not forget Mick who has been hurting me for the last twenty-five years. I left him and, well I came to Greece. I have matured from a short-distance sprinter into a long-distance runner."

"And Michelle?"

"Michelle? I have never run from Michelle." Juliet can almost feel Aaman's next question and begins to answer, leaving it unasked. "Why? Because she has never really hurt me. She could have. She could have been like Mick or Jenny or my mum, or dishonourable Dr John Brooks, but she isn't and she hasn't hurt me because ..." Juliet stops. It has hit her. She turns to Aaman, shifts her position and takes his hands. He smiles. "I have pushed her away. I have not allowed her close to avoid the pain just like you and Saabira."

She lets go of his hands and throws her arms in the air, letting them fall onto her lap.

"I am such a bitch! Poor Michelle, year after year trying to be my friend and all the time I am pushing her away, not allowing her close. Twenty-something years we haven't seen each other all because I was scared of the possible pain, not even the actual pain. That is so sad, and stupid." She looks Aaman in the eye.

"I need to be like you, Aaman. I need to overcome the fear."

There is a knock on the gate. It is a neighbour.

"*Ella edo!*" The neighbour clearly does not intend to step over the boundary and calls Juliet to her. Juliet jumps up and walks towards her, inviting her in. She returns holding a large plate brimming with meat and vegetables.

"She asked why I haven't been to share their Easter food with them. Presuming I was busy, she brought the food to me. How kind is that?" She goes inside and returns with two forks. She pulls off the plastic wrap that covers the plate, puts it in on the table and pulls her chair close.

"It's goat." Juliet beckons him to join her and feels slightly smug for having remembered that he probably wouldn't eat pork.

"So come on, Aaman, seeing as we are fighting fire tonight, what do we need to do next?"

"You are doing it."

"What?"

"You are being brave, fighting your fear."

"What? By coming to Greece, you mean?"

"No, by letting me in."

"What? To do the garden?"

"No, not the garden, Juliet." He laughs at her, and Juliet is aware that she doesn't want to run. In fact, she wants to stay.

"What about you, Aaman? Will you return to be close to Saabira?" Juliet does not like the thought of him going.

"I do not know how I can. I have no money to return with and no money to buy the harvester. I would return in shame and I would have to try to get a job back at the shoe factory, if they have work."

"Hang on. I think I have a plan." Juliet scrambles to her feet, reverberating with excitement and nearly

138

jumping on the spot. There are fireworks across the sky, but she doesn't see them.

Aaman is not easily given hope and his countenance does not change.

"Listen." Juliet cannot stand still. "I still need the gardening doing and ..." She turns to him so she can see his face.

Aaman's face goes slack, as this will not provide the money he needs.

"No, listen. I need the gardening doing, and this work will be paid whoever does it so it might as well be you, but better than that I have a computer and you are an extraordinarily fast learner. I am sure there will be programming courses online. You can learn by yourself and when you return, I will write you a reference saying you have been here, writing programmes for me. Ha, you will have the pick of jobs. Brilliant!"

"That is not honest."

"Then I am formally asking you to write me a website for my translation business and I will pay you for it. Then it will be honest and you will have a large sum towards your harvester."

She has gained Aaman's attention; he is sitting bolt upright. He begins to smile and it breaks onto a grin as big as Mahmout's.

"I do not need all the money for the harvester, only my portion." He calculates on his fingers and holds up his hands to show her how much.

"Then I don't think you will have any problem at all. You can return with the money as a programmer. How fantastic is that?" Juliet grabs her wine glass.

"To you, Aaman. No, sod that. To us! May we both overcome our fears and create a better future for ourselves."

"And our loved ones."

Juliet drinks it down in one.

"Right, come on." She marches indoors.

Aaman is comfortable where he is and has no idea why Juliet has gone inside. He feels reluctant to move. He is comfortable. It takes a few seconds to lift his back from the chair. The village is quieting now, the noises are less harsh, some shutters have been closed. He stretches and goes inside.

Juliet is sitting on the sofa with her laptop on her knees. She pats the seat next to her without taking her eyes from the screen.

"Here, what about this? Teach yourself C++ in twenty-one days. Is that any good?"

Aaman is mesmerised. He reads the screen and then scans the keyboard. There seems so much to learn and it thrills him.

"What do you think?"

Aaman is momentarily lost.

"I would have to work on the garden for free to pay for the use of your computer."

"Oh no, I wouldn't dream of it."

"No, it is right, it is business."

140

"OK, here's the deal, you work in the garden and get paid, and you use the laptop as a friend, because that's what friends do. If you want me to stop being your friend then you have to ask me to stop." Juliet laughs and the cat that had been sitting on the arm of the sofa takes the opportunity to try to walk across the keyboard. Aaman picks him off and puts him down. The second cat comes in and licks the first cat.

Aaman is grinning now, his hand eager to take the laptop and start. Juliet hands it over and shows him the basics of using Google and then stands up. Aaman doesn't notice. He is searching and reading.

"Call if you need me." She doesn't expect an answer, nor does she get one. She strokes both cats and wanders into the garden through the back door.

It is spooky by night, the pole with the vine sticking up in the middle of the garden. There are two smaller poles now, both with vines hooked to them. The olive tree in the far corner rustles, a dense black against the deep, dark blue of the sky. It is beginning to get cool. Juliet wraps her arms around herself and wanders onto the waste site. There is no more mess; The Mess has gone. There is nothing to trip over, no buried bits poking out. It is all weeds and roughly turned soil. She considers turning it into lawn. It would need watering. But if she planted trees, the lawn could grow in their shade. Fruit trees.

She walks the length of the house and round the end. The space at the end of the house would be good for vegetables. Next door's disused barn would provide a small amount of shade at either end of the day and she could set up a watering system from the house.

The front of the house is mostly gravel, which needs weeding. But down the edge against the wall where the three orange trees are, she could have a herb garden. Basil, oregano, rosemary, thyme. Oh, and lavender. It will be nice to have the smell of lavender as she comes in from the lane.

The patio looks bright compared to the garden in the moonlight. The folding chairs give it an air of comfort. The table and chairs make it look very Greek. Perhaps she could hang a hammock somewhere for when the boys come over. They will come over, surely.

Juliet suddenly feels far from home. It may be a while before Thomas can afford the time to come over. Terrance will not be able to afford the money even if he had the time. Her Greek neighbours are lovely, but she needs more than a passing chat. Michelle is right, as usual. It takes more than the language to merge cultures.

Michelle. Poor Michelle. How mean she has been over the years. Never calling, never giving her the time of day. She has become her punch-bag. What was due to everyone else, she gave to Michelle, who just kept coming back for more. A true friend. And she, Juliet, has been a true bitch. Something needs to be done about that, but she isn't sure what. She will call her soon. No big drama, she will just start treating her with respect, as Aaman would treat a friend. She is sure he would be calm, thoughtful, and attentive. He was towards her and it made her feel calm, important, cared for. She will do the same for Michelle.

Juliet stays on the patio and listens to the last of the sounds of Easter diminishing in the village. The dogs have started barking again, their midnight telegraph conversation. They are keen for the early morning, for their owners dressed in khaki, for the rabbits to be retrieved. The moon disappears behind a wispy cloud and the village submerges under a dark blanket. She turns to go back inside, the glow from the window in the door encouraging her entry.

Aaman is engrossed and does not hear her enter. She picks up the book she has been trying to read and settles in the battered leather armchair. She is grateful that the house has come with some contents. The previous owners saw no value in their inheritance and the furniture that remained was left piled in one room. To Juliet it is treasure. She tucks her feet under her and settles to read. She is asleep within twenty minutes.

Aaman moves once to find a blanket and lays it over Juliet. After that, he becomes motionless, engrossed in a programming course he has found on the Internet. He falls asleep just before dawn and awakes only a couple of hours later, feeling an urgency. Opening his eyes, he sees the computer, remembers the urgency and begins his studies again.

When Juliet surfaces, it is as if he has studied straight through the night. She smiles and stretches.

Chapter 11

Aaman insists that he start work on the garden at eight and continues until four before resuming his studies on the laptop. Juliet relishes this sense of order, limiting the hours in which she can do her translation work. She knows she will be more productive within these confines.

Aaman seems to devour everything he finds online. He sits motionless for hours and then frantically taps away until the next period of reading. Juliet looks over his shoulder once or twice, but it means nothing to her, and she spends her time in the evenings painting the kitchen cupboard doors.

At eight o'clock, Juliet asks if he is hungry. Aaman immediately leaves the laptop and offers to search through the kitchen for things he can use. Juliet yields and produces a pen and paper, suggesting that Aaman give her a list of things she should buy for the week, and he begins the cooking whilst he dictates a list of everyday ingredients. The air becomes infused with heated spices and Juliet's stomach is clawing.

Juliet looks forward to sitting with Aaman and lays the table on the patio in the warmth of the evening. Aaman brings the dishes out and sits. Once the table is laid, he slows his whole pace down, looks over the food, offers to serve Juliet, selects choice pieces for her and then himself and eats slowly. Juliet enjoys the reverence of the process. She asks how his learning is going and if he is finding suitable courses online. He says he is and asks what will be next for the garden. They discuss the best layout. Aaman likes the idea of making the garden a fruit orchard and agrees that vegetables at the end of the house will be a good place. The conversation meanders.

"What's Pakistan like, your village?" She picks up a cherry tomato with her fingers.

"Pakistan is beautiful, but the most beautiful is the Punjab. I live in the Punjab."

"I went to India, before I had the boys, before I met Mick, when I was at college. Anyway, I went to India. It was beautiful. Bombay was amazing, so full of people, life, noise, and bustle. I loved the cows everywhere, just wandering the streets."

Aaman picks up the jug and fills Juliet's water glass and then his own.

"I met a little girl who happily showed me her hand where there was a spot the size of a coin, leprosy. She seemed to be so pleased with this spot. It gave her the power to beg. All I could see was how she would be in a few years, still with a beautiful face but with only one useful arm. I looked it up when I got home, her fingers would shorten and deform as the body absorbs the cartilage.

"Anyway, in the bit of Bombay I was in, Colaba, the tourist area, I suppose, there was a hospital just

146

down the road where they could treat leprosy and I knew the admission fee was a very small amount so I gave her the money and pointed to the building."

Juliet pauses to drink.

"She obviously understood me because she laughed when I gave her the money, but I saw her ten minutes later with her friends and they all had ice creams. They obviously had a different view of life to me. Even though they had leprosy and no money, they seemed happy. They had each other, they were laughing and pushing each other, totally lost in the moment."

She puts the glass down.

"I also went to the Taj Mahal. Have you been?"

Aaman shakes his head.

"The people were lovely on the train. Families all sitting together and strangers making friends and sharing their food. Everyone seemed really happy to be there and to be with each other even though they initially didn't know each other. I bought a ticket for a berth, but it was filled with people sitting on it. Eventually an old lady lay down on it and I had to sit up all night. She had her family and they all cuddled up around her, her grandchildren, I think, from their ages. She had her family and I had my berth ticket. She was a poor old Indian granny and I was a wealthy, lucky Western woman."

Juliet finds that she can't stop talking. Her life seems to need to escape from her, many images of the past need telling. High points need sharing, low points explaining. She is spilling over with the need to talk, her tongue needing flight.

"But I didn't say anything to the old lady. It's just a matter of where you are born as to what your luck is. I mean, if I had had different parents that could have been me, that little old lady, with no money and lots of family love. It's just luck, there is no fairness."

Aaman is finishing his meal.

"Can you understand when I talk quickly?"

"I know many of the words. Fairness I know."

"Yes, and unfairness."

They sit for a while. Juliet listens to the sounds of the evening, the village becoming quiet, shutters closing. Children called inside. Goat bells as the animals are brought in for the night. Aaman's foot jiggles. Time has slipped by and he is clearly eager to return to his studies. Nevertheless, this is Juliet's dream, this is the essence of what she has wanted. Being with someone else has allowed her to sit longer, enjoy it more.

Aaman's foot twitches rhythmically. Every moment on the computer is precious, a chance, an opportunity he must take and use to his advantage. There are no such possibilities back at home and time is passing. Each minute could be a minute learning something. But Juliet? Juliet, she is making all this happen for him. If she wishes to sit, then he will sit. He calms himself until Juliet stands to go inside.

Juliet continues with the kitchen cupboards, which becomes a bigger task as one of the cats rubs against one of the newly painted doors, leaving a trail of fur on the door and giving itself a very pleasant, muted sage green patch, which it objects to having washed off.

It is late. Juliet feels tired and wonders how far Aaman has to walk to get home.

"Do you need a lift home?"

Aaman is startled and tries to tear himself from inside the computer. His shoulders face her before his head, his eyes coming last.

"Oh, ah, no. I am sorry I am keeping you up. It is just such an opportunity." He carefully puts the laptop on the sofa and stands to put his coat on.

"Is it far?"

"No." He is ready to leave. Unsure of how to depart, he sticks his hand out. Juliet takes his hand and he shakes it. "Thank you, Juliet. Thank you for being my friend."

She watches him get smaller and smaller down the lane.

The next day he arrives at eight o'clock, works through till four, studies till eight, cooks, eats, washes and dries the dishes, and studies again through till eleven in the evening. This becomes their routine for the days to come. Juliet declares Sunday is a day of rest. Aaman says that he thinks it is good if they rest from the garden, but would it be too much to ask if Sunday could be his main study day?

She spends the next few Sundays going through the treasures left in what will be the guest room. She discovers five hats stacked one on top of the other and several pruning saws with the price tags still on them in drachmas. There are various goat bells, an ox's yoke for ploughing. The brass bed seems to be complete, but with no mattress, and there are two wooden pails.

Her greatest find, hidden behind a loose board lining a cupboard built into the thick walls, which she is cleaning out, is a very old-looking rusty revolver. The handle inset has gone, just leaving a metal outline, and the trigger has been purposely bent beyond usage but the barrel still revolves. It reminds her that Greece has been a very uncertain place until relatively recently. She wonders what family lived here in such insecure times that they had need to hide a gun. She chats to Aaman.

Aaman does not hear her talk as she clears the room. His mind is fully occupied, leaving no room for any digression.

Over these days, the garden makes progress. The trees are selected and planted and the grass seed is scattered handful by handful. Juliet has no idea how thickly to sow grass seeds.

"One handful for the ants, one for the garden to have grass, and one for the gods," Aaman declares for each step of their steady march, as they fling seeds in an arch. The vegetable plot is planted and tended, and Juliet cultivates her herb garden that Aaman visits for his cooking.

They rig up an irrigation system for the vegetable plot. Juliet buys coils of plastic pipes and bags of connectors. Aaman trails the main pipe along the edge of the plot and takes off spurs to each furrow they have planted.

The hoses have holes in them at regular intervals, and Aaman folds the ends back, fastening them with cable ties. Juliet, to make her life simple, orders an electronic timer that they can connect to the hose at the tap so it comes on at regular intervals, but Aaman likes the thrill of turning the system on and off manually, and it is a while before he connects the timer.

After just under two weeks, Aaman looks up from the computer one evening.

"I have done it, come and look."

Juliet, who is now painting the walls in the guest room, puts down her brush and wipes her hands on an old tea towel. She is still wiping them as she stands behind Aaman, who works at the kitchen table. The screen is filled with code until Aaman switches to another window and there is a page dedicated to her. There is her name, a description of her services, her specialties, and a form to fill out to contact her to use her translation services.

"Wow! That's amazing. You have learnt to do that in these few days?"

"It is HTML, it is not difficult. Next I will learn PHP so I can write active pages that can do processing and call a database."

Juliet smiles encouragingly but hasn't a clue what he is talking about.

Juliet jumps at the shrill sound of the phone and picks it up quickly so it doesn't disturb Aaman.

"Are you busy now?"

"Hi, Michelle. No, I'm not busy now."

Aaman looks up from his work and smiles at her.

"So tell me about the house boy!"

Juliet turns from Aaman, who is already lost in his own world again, and goes through to her bedroom. It's cooler in here, the walls are two and three feet thick in what is the oldest part of the building. Juliet slouches onto the bed and pulls the covers over her legs. The cat appears and settles down on her warmth.

"He is not a house boy." Juliet giggles.

"So what is he?"

"He is a pretty nice person, actually."

"So tell me again, he's doing your garden and he is illegal, right?"

Juliet brings Michelle up to date.

"That's an interesting turn of events. Is he staying with you?"

"No, he goes home each night."

"Oh, and where is his home?"

"I don't know. I haven't really asked."

"I don't suppose it will be much from what you have said. What he expects to get paid is less the price of a hotel room. How do you get in touch with him if you need to cancel?"

"The thought hadn't occurred. Anyway, how are you?"

"Are you feeling all right? Or do you want something? You never ask me how I am!" It is Michelle's turn to giggle.

"Well, I am now so how are you?"

"The social reply is I am fine. The real reply, if you want it, is I am pretty fed up actually. I didn't tell you that I caught Richard out, did I? It was about a year ago, with his secretary for pity's sake. How clichéd is that? Well, I confronted him and, to cut a long story short, I filed for divorce and it came through last week." Michelle draws a breath.

"Oh my God, Michelle, why didn't you tell me?"

"We've been so out of touch these last couple of years. Besides, you had your problems. I just need to get on with mine." There is a touch of humour in her tone and Juliet realises she has been remiss and her lack of effort has caused hurt.

"So where are you? Are you at home? What happened to the house and everything?"

Michelle laughs.

"I was made into partner two years ago. I could have taken him to the cleaners. Anyway, he pretty much just wanted to walk away so that made it easy. It's just the evenings when it's quiet, or at night when I wake up and I have forgotten and I find I'm alone. But you've been there, Juliet." Her voice drops and becomes quieter as she speaks.

"Yes, I've been there, and it is tough no matter how much of a sod they've been. But it is just an adjustment, nothing bad is happening. Soon you will be like me and loving the freedom."

"Actually I already love that part. No one to answer to. After work last night, I took the train into the centre of London and saw a show. I couldn't be bothered with the hassle of public transport to go home afterwards, so I booked into a hotel. That kind of freedom is priceless. I can't imagine what Richard would have said if I'd done that when I was still with him."

"Good for you. But I guess it wouldn't harm if I called you more often in the evenings then, just to remind you that you are not completely alone!"

"If this is what Greece does to you, then maybe you made the right move."

Juliet can hear genuine pleasure in her voice. She opens the door a crack so she can see Aaman. He is still intent on his work but he is smiling.

The sun grows hotter as spring merges into the beginning of summer. The garden needs less and less work as the days pass. Aaman is rebuilding a stone wall at the front of the house that has collapsed over time. He and Juliet have made several runs to a nearby riverbed, which is dry in the summer, for boulders and stones to finish the wall. Juliet sits drinking a well-deserved coffee as Aaman thoughtfully reconstructs the wall.

"Do you think we should paint it when it is finished to match the white wall behind the pomegranate trees?"

"I think that is up to you." He continues at his own steady pace. Juliet looks over her cottage with a sense of accomplishment.

"What's it like where you stay, Aaman?"

"It is in an orange grove."

"That sounds nice."

"No, it is not very nice. It is a barn that the farmer has made for illegals to sleep."

Juliet creates a picture of a wooden-beamed, stone-walled barn with single beds dotted around the walls, a huddle of armchairs at one end, and a flagged stone floor.

"It doesn't sound too bad."

"No, I am grateful."

"I'm going to the village shop. Is there anything extra that we need? No? OK, see you in a bit."

As Juliet walks down the lane, she notices that all the weeds have gone. It looks oddly bare. The edge of the road where it meets the wall is entirely clear of nettles and grasses. Juliet misses the dots of colour the wildflowers brought, but is glad the spiky, variegated leaved plants are no more to be seen, or felt. The vines that creep over the fence of the disused barn next door have been trimmed, and the lemons harvested from the untended tree next to the barn. The house next to that, which, as yet, has shown no sign of inhabitance to Juliet despite the well-tended front yard, is clear of the weeds and leaves around the gate. There are signs of Aaman's care and attention everywhere.

Two dogs hurry after each other in the road, and a lady leading a ram says good morning. The square has tables taken from the *kafenios*, and clusters of farmers at each drink small cups of Greek coffee and the occasional ouzo shot. The warmth is bringing the life outside.

Juliet stops to look at some of the headlines on the newspapers that have been pegged on a line outside the shop. She can hear Marina chatting inside.

"Yes, she has met a boy. He is nice boy. His father? He has the land with the mandarins down by the old river. Yes, that's right, you were at school with him. Well, his boy has been in America for work all these years. Yes, twenty eight and never married! Yes, I know, the same age as my eldest. No, she is still single. One such a baby and married and already divorced and meeting this nice boy and the other such a woman and no thoughts of marriage at all! What can you do? So I arranged for his family to come to me at Easter. It was a very good time, we ate, we drank, we sang, When the evening was finishing I see them sitting quite close and talking quietly. I do not say anything. You know me, I will not interfere. It is best. Ah, here is Tzuliet, Goodbye, Mrs Eleni. Tzuliet, how are you? There is much talk in the village about you." Marina still struggles with Juliet's name.

"Really, Marina? What on earth about?"

"They say you are making the old farmhouse into a palace. The postman says the garden is bountiful with food you are growing and you are planting trees and making everything beautiful."

"It is a palace and the garden is looking amazing, but your garden is the same." Juliet loves this banter.

"Ah, the same, it is the same, but maybe I did not do it so quickly."

"I have help."

"Of course you have. Why wouldn't you? What can I do for you today?"

Juliet reels off her list, and between them they gather the goods.

Walking back home, the sun directly in her face, Juliet muses on how nice people are and what a nice spot it is in which she lives. The village feels idyllic, just like the dream she searched for when she moved out here, the situation only improved by someone to share it with. It feels perfect, she feels lucky.

Chapter 12

That night, Aaman wakes to an unfamiliar sound. He listens. He can sense that some of the other men have woken too. There is a stillness, the snapping of a twig. A bird flaps. A leaf rustles.

A sound of many feet. A shout. Flashlights outside. A burst through the doorway. Light beams on startled eyes. Many shouts. Power wielded. Ugly laughter. Fluent Greek. Guns at the ready.

The men are pulled from their bunks. Aaman scrabbles to check his savings are well hidden. He misses his chance. Pulled away, patted down, handcuffs slapped on, linking them in a chain, pushed through the door to waiting hands. The black shape on the floor is kicked. A small groan but it doesn't move. It is kicked again. There is no groan. The bunks are cleared. The men lined up outside. Full moon. Sharp contrast.

There is a discussion about the black shape. They turn him over. A shiny black beetle runs out of his beard.

"*Nekros!*" The policeman shrugs.

"*Afiste.*" The man in charge pats the air as if telling a dog to drop a bone.

The illegals, blinking in the moonlight, are chained one to another. The cold metal blinks in the starlight. Cuffed hands wipe sleepy eyes, reshape sleep-torn hair. The police foot-scrape the mud floor corners of the barn to see if anything has been left, secreted in the shadows. There is nothing. They march the men to the edge of the orange grove to a waiting van.

Aaman turns to see his last glimpse of the barn, his paper hoard. The orange trees cup the mud building in a quiet embrace. The moonlight slices the tops of the trees, reaching down through the door, spotlighting the floor where the bearded man lies, unmoving, face in the dirt.

And there, behind a tree, a face, a grinning smile. Teeth. Mahmout.

Aaman is in the back of an army truck with all the familiar, and some unfamiliar, faces from the barn. The Nigerians still heavy with sleep, mumbling, limp-boned hands make decisions about what to do with rolled euro notes missed in the pat-down, notes they had down their trousers whilst sleeping. There are three new Indian faces. They look scared. The two tall Russians are there, which surprises Aaman as he thought they had never been in the barn. They must have fallen on hard times. The rest are the usual Albanians, Romanians, Croatians, and Bulgarians.

Three of the policemen throw armfuls of shoes and sandals that have been collected from around the barn into the van with them. The chain of illegals pulls against each other in the scramble to reclaim footwear. The men snap and curse each other as the bracelets cut and pinch.

The truck is green, inside and out, mesh at the windows, and smells of stale smoke. No police ride in the back with them. One of the Russians lights up two cigarettes from a pack and a lighter he has hidden under his hat. He passes one to his friend. An Albanian asks for one but is ignored. The Russian says something to his friend, and they both laugh heartily as if they are at a party. The Albanians speak in hushed tones, planning, plotting damage control. The Romanians and Croatians lean back as if this is the thousandth time they have been in this situation and they are thoroughly bored with it. One has a torn jacket which he inspects. It must have happened in the raid. Several are already back on the edge of sleep, heads rolled back, mouths gaping.

Aaman watches through the mesh. The orange grove gives way to a road. They are heading for the nearby town. They pass the nursery where he and Juliet chose the fruit trees, her hair glowing gold in the sun. She had a white, floaty blouse that day and the strap on her sandal broke. She leant against him as she hopped back to the car.

The Russian burps. The truck slows as they approach a large, square, modern building set back from the road on the edge of the town. Aaman reads phonetically, out loud to himself, the sign on the building. One of the Albanians hears him, translates into English, the common language: Police.

They are unloaded into the car park and taken inside in a line, one handcuffed to the next, through the large, glass front door to the reception beyond. It is bright, marble, shiny with a very high ceiling, a useless space. Aaman thinks of all the rooms that could be contained within this room. The jobs it would create to convert it, the men it could house, the income the rooms could earn, the wealth it would generate to employ more men to build more rooms. Aaman concludes that the West has its head on backwards.

The policeman at the desk in the main hall is drinking a coffee and eating a slice of cheese pie. He listens intently to the officer leading the men and then waves a dismissive gesture and resumes reading his newspaper. The officer who has brought them in insists on something from the man at the desk and pokes a finger at the man's newspaper to accentuate his point. The policeman eating his pie, drinking his coffee and reading his newspaper is highly affronted. There commences an argument, and Aaman can see bits of pastry spat into the air. One large piece falls out of the policeman's mouth onto his jacket, and he picks it off and eats it before continuing to push his point.

Aaman thinks of Juliet drinking her morning coffee. He looks around to find out the time. He is near enough to the arguing policemen to see that the one nearest has a watch on. Aaman waits until he gesticulates, his sleeve rising. It is nearly six a.m. She will not be awake yet. It is only a matter of the

161

minutes ticking past. His time is over, they intend to make him leave the country, he feels sure of that. But to which country will he be sent? No country to the West wants illegal immigrants. They will forbid it. If they take the immigrants to a more Eastern country, they know they will just return to Greece as it is the route to the West. They won't know where to send him. They may put him in a detention centre. He has heard of people held there for years.

They stand in the lobby for over an hour, the two officers arguing, leaving occasionally to find some paperwork or another officer who comes and joins in the heated discussion. At one very angry point of the discussion, one takes out a cigarette and is about to light it when he reaches for the packet again and offers one to the man with whom he is arguing. He accepts. They stop to light up using one lighter, the one accepting mutters something, and they both laugh before resuming their positions and continue shouting their differences.

Aaman shifts his weight, limbs responding as if in treacle. His eyes blink slowly. Even the barn's wooden bunk feels attractive. There is a yank on his cuffed wrist as the line tension changes. The Albanians try to sit on the floor but the Russians shout at them as they pull on their handcuffed wrists, the metal digging into soft skin. One of the Indian men is crying silently, talking to himself. Aaman understands the dialect. His wife is in a village twenty miles from here, and he is expected back. He has been an illegal for twenty years, his children go to school here, his wife cleans floors in a government building, he was just staying overnight as it was too long a walk from his village to the town and back in one day.

Aaman turns away. He looks down a corridor with rooms off to the side. At the end of the corridor is a green wooden door. There is a moth at a window above the door. The window is dirty, streak marks from where a damp cloth has been wiped over it form arches of sunlight. The moth starts at the bottom of the arch, banging itself against the glass, hoping for an exit, a passage to freedom, and each time it buffets against the window, it gains a little height. The dance takes it to the top of the arch and down the other side until it takes a rest, its little feet on the wooden frame. It crawls for a while and then begins the process again, sometimes at the other end of the arch, sometimes at the same end, seeking the elusive light, the freedom of unimpeded flight.

The officers have stopped shouting. A man in civilian clothing has entered the lobby holding high a copper ring hung from which, on a tripod of metal ropes, is a copper tray. On the tray are two small Greek coffee cups. The arguing policemen have stopped to order coffee from the delivery boy. The Russians sigh and pull the Albanians to the floor as they themselves now give up and sit, leaning against the wall. The whole line follows suit as each is pulled down by the last. Aaman is the little one on the end.

Once seated, Aaman sleeps, one eye open. Some part of him hears the police eventually make their peace and the one behind the desk makes a phone call. He is not surprised when the arresting officer pulls them to their feet and takes them back into the yard and into the truck. The Russians complain loudly, they mime the need to pee and Aaman's mind takes in the Russian words. The Russians' complaints are ignored as though they are whining dogs. The policeman leaves the door open and goes to drink his coffee, sitting in the sunshine with his new found friend, the reception officer.

More time passes. One of the Russians pulls the line about so he can pee off the edge of the truck. The sitting policemen jump up and hurry over, drawing their batons and calling him a dog. The Eurasian aims at the police so they cannot get near. He finishes, the police call him more names and then dismiss him as a concern as they return to their ashtray of smouldering cigarettes and steaming coffees.

The men sort out their line, settle down, and fall asleep. Aaman imagines that Juliet will now be awake and wondering where he is, and this thought hurts him. She has been so kind, so caring, so generous, she will think he has not taken what she offered with any value. His solar plexus knots. She will think he took it for granted. She will think he has given up on his studies and does not value the work. She will think he was just using her for his evening meal. But the worst pain of all is that she might think he did not value her friendship. She will wonder where he is and then she will grow angry. She might even feel disappointed that she was so kind to someone who was not worth it. And it is absolutely a possibility, although not very likely, that she may feel a little bit alone by the end of the day.

His chest aches at his yearning to be at her cottage. His eyes fill at the pain of how she might see him. His lost opportunity to learn more on the computer and give himself such a good future makes him nauseous. Altogether, he feels dizzy and that he may pass out. He opens his drooping eyelids and gasps for air. The doors bang shut.

Juliet has come to love waking in her bed with its cool cotton sheets, looking up at the roof beams with the sun pecking in stripes through the slats of the shutters. Now the sun is strong, the strips of sunlight make the dust dance, specks of fairy dust, now you see it, now you don't. She eases herself up. A cat paw claws under the gap at the bottom of the door.

It feels different somehow. The sun too strong. Too warm. The cat awake. No cockerels crowing.

"Oh my God, I've overslept." Juliet pulls on her jeans and sweatshirt and wonders how long Aaman must have been waiting.

After a brief journey, Aaman is unloaded again. He watches the Albanians climb out and laugh when they realise where they are. One of the Russians, as he ducks his head to climb down, asks in very bad Greek why they laugh. They say this place is called

Little Albania. The Russian groans. "You mean the detention centre?" No-one bothers to answer him.

Aaman is shackled to the Indian man who is still crying and talking about his wife and wondering who will take the children to school. Aaman does not respond. He imagines Juliet on the porch drinking her coffee and stroking the cat. She will be scorning him, thinking him unworthy, that he has betrayed all her kindness. A new thought comes to him. What if this becomes to her another experience of someone letting her down, going away with no notice? He hopes he isn't that important to her. Just a gardener, he tells himself. I am just a gardener.

The first in the line has his handcuff removed and is ushered through the wire mesh gates. Each in turn is yanked in after him, uncuffed and pushed forward. There is a window next to the main door, where they are each asked to turn out their pockets. Cigarettes and matches are allowed, lighters and money and everything else is confiscated. Two lighters, twenty-five cents, nine mobile phones, and a spoon is their total. They are then ushered into another room where they are told to strip, bundled through a cold shower and given back their clothes once the guards have felt through them. Tired and hungry, they are shown to a block with more men than beds that backs onto a yard full of men coming and going out of many other blocks. The dominant language is Albanian. He learns two words in the first few minutes he is there, the first being Hello and the second obviously a derogatory obscenity that can

166

be used as a negative or for camaraderie. It makes Aaman smile, but he is not sure why.

As they are now unshackled, the Albanian men soon disappear into the sea of their brethren. The Russians look around for other Russians and soon find their corner. The Romanians and Croatians don't seem interested in finding their own kind, but after an hour or two, their own find them. The atmosphere has something of the holiday camp about it, but with a grim undertone.

The Indians sit on the floor, not knowing which are their bunks. They hail Aaman over, but he is not there for his own comfort or to be social.

The room with the bunks and the mattresses stinks. He walks past one of the bunk beds anchored in the corners, which is four levels high, and then on past the two-level bunk beds pinned against the walls, picking his way down the narrow uncovered area of floor between them and the central floor which is laid with abutting mattresses. Aaman is distracted by the clothes and bedding that are everywhere, hanging off beds, scrunched into corners, strewn across mattresses. He wanders outside into a cauldron of people. He knows the advantage of being a little rat is that big rats are seldom interested in little rats. Big rats fight other big rats. Aaman feels glad he is not a big rat in this place.

He estimates that the yard is big enough for about two hundred men to move with ease. He guesses there is double that. Some of them are old enough to be retired and some of them so young they should be at school. There is every race east of Greece represented, all trying for a better life in the West. Most of them are clearly harmless people. Very few have the aura of criminality. The Albanians stand out in the crowd, with a hardness about them, even at a distance. Aaman sees it in the way they stand, walk and look at each other. There is an aura of threat from them, a sense of being ungoverned. Aaman finds a corner of ground by the inner wire fence and sits on the floor, his back against the fence support. Above the plethora of people, there are two guards in a raised tower. One reads a magazine, sitting in a chair rocked onto its back legs, his feet up on the safety rail. The other looks out over the sea of people as if he were a tourist in a new city, momentarily interested but not alert.

Aaman searches out beyond the double fence where dry scrub land hills meet deep blue sky. Life has not been kind. He does not seem to be given a chance. When chances are offered, he takes them, but then the good things are taken away again. He tuts at his own negativity. That sort of thinking is ungrateful. Life owes him nothing. He is very indebted to be alive at all. He has his health and there is always hope. He will not start thinking like Mahmout.

Mahmout!

Like a dream remembered, he recalls the face of Mahmout behind the tree next to the barn. Grinning. He was grinning. Aaman does not wish to think badly of anyone. Maybe there was a reason why he had been there. He could have gone out to relieve himself and just got lucky. He could have been going for an early job, or a job very far away that required a long walk. He could have met friends and stayed out very late. But for Aaman none of this rings true. He was grinning. Why would he grin when all the men were in chains and the bearded man dead on the floor?

The day turns into evening and the men make their way inside to the bunks. Aaman presumes that the bunks around the wall will be favoured. The big rats will sleep there. The central mattresses differ in thickness; there will be a pecking order for them. He finds a really thick, unoccupied one and waits. It is suggested by a fairly big Albanian that he move on. Aaman tries to assess the size of the man to the depth of the mattress. He finds a second unoccupied mattress that is not as thick as the first but still would stop the warmth of his body being sucked out by the cold of the concrete floor. This time, a smaller Albanian tells him to move on. Aaman decides not to stand but instead exercises his newly learnt Albanian vocabulary. The Albanian goes away. Aaman is not pleased with his enjoyment of his power.

As the sun sets, Aaman wishes Juliet good things in life and wishes also that she will not think too badly of him. There are no lights in the blocks. As the men quieten, there is the occasional shout from one block to the next. A piece of banter, a string of comradely expletives, proof that their souls cannot be tamed. All becomes silent as the sun disappears, just

169

coughs and whispers, prayers and sniffled tears. The guards high up in their tower are laughing. The sound of a television gives a clue to cause of their mirth. They get paid to watch television because their mothers are Greek and he, Aaman, gets deported because his mother is Punjabi. Through the birth of their mothers, their destinies are carved. The mothers feed and love their sons. They both want the best for them, but even in the wider sphere of life, there are big rats and little rats and everyone is somewhere.

As Juliet hurries out of the house, there is no Aaman at the gate, and she wonders if he has come and gone. She has let him down. She curses herself. He is sure to return in a while, when he thinks she is up and about.

As usual the morning coffee tastes good, and the toast and marmalade make a perfect breakfast. She makes a mental note to buy some more of the marmalade online. Maybe she should order a box. Expensive, but so worth it. It does seem that Aaman is leaving it very late. Juliet looks down the lane, hopeful.

Returning indoors, she decides to complete her first translation assignment at the desk in the bedroom. She does not wish to distract herself by continually looking down the lane. She opens the window so she will hear him if he taps on the metal gate. It is natural to presume that Aaman has taken the fact that she was not up to open the gates as a sign that she does not want him to work that day. It is logical, reasonable. The rest of what she is feeling is out of perspective. It is a surprise to her how much she misses his company. She chastises herself once more and hopes he will not have taken offence at her laziness. Through her bedroom window, the garden seems incomplete without him squatting, tending to plants or appearing into view from round a corner busy with something.

After a late lunch, alone, in the kitchen, looking at the cupboard doors that still need a second coat of paint, the cats begging for morsels, Juliet becomes fidgety. Aaman will arrive soon having finished his day's work elsewhere. What should she say? Should she say anything? Should she be cross? After all, it was she who didn't have a gardener all day. Should she apologise for not getting up on time? But then again, if he has found work elsewhere, then he has lost nothing if they have paid him and fed him. She is abashed when she realises her discontent is that she is just missing him. He, on the other hand, is just fine.

Four o'clock and Aaman is not there. Juliet feels sure he will arrive in time for his studies. Neatening her papers on her bedroom desk, she takes the laptop into the kitchen where he will use it to study. The cat rubs her leg, and she picks him up to find his friend also rubbing her legs. Juliet picks up the second one and holds them together, pushing her face between two warm, fluffy bundles. There is no Aaman.

The cats jump down and they all go onto the patio at the front. Juliet looks down the lane but there is no-one. It doesn't feel right. He would not miss his studies. She grabs her keys and heads for the village, leaving the gate unlocked, just in case.

Chapter 13

"I am so glad that she is seeing this boy. Yes, the one whose father has the mandarins by the old river. They are so right for each other. Last night they went to the bouzouki bars and she was not home until very late. Did you want eggs? I heard them from my bedroom window, they were saying goodnight and they took so long to say goodbye. You have two packets of rice here. Did you want two? But he was being shy and she was being shy. No, we have only bread for toast, the village bread is finished. I wanted to shout out 'for goodness sake, kiss her,' but I am not one to interfere. But they did agree to meet late in the week. Is that everything? Yes, OK, goodbye. Ah, Tzuliet."

"Hi, Marina."

"Why so worried?"

"The man who does my garden didn't come today. Have you seen him? He is small about my height, he has—"

"Oh no, they would not come in here. They go to the kiosk. He will be asleep somewhere, or someone will have offered him more money. Don't you worry, Tzuliet, you take another help, there are many men for your garden."

Across the road the kiosk's lights are just flicking on. Vasso puts some beers and soft drinks in the fridge before returning inside the booth.

"Vasso, did you see the small Pakistani man today? Not the one that grins."

"I saw the one that grins. He was here this morning, but he was the only man to be here looking for work today. Maybe they have done a raid."

"A raid? How do you mean?"

Vasso comes out from inside the kiosk to straighten the shelves. She slides her feet to keep her slippers on.

"Oh, every once in a while, the police try to clean up the area, if they find where they are sleeping, for example. They don't tend to pick them up during the day because they all just run. I have seen that a few times. Like rats they are, scattering in every direction, so the police get no-one. But if they find where they are sleeping then they raid and catch them all."

"Do you know where they were sleeping round here?" Juliet looks at the choice of chewing gum to try to appear casual. She can hear the sound of her heartbeat in her ears and her mouth has gone dry.

"I think Old Costas had them on his land for a bit, up on the road past the hill. Did your man not show up for work today? Why don't you just wait? It won't be long before there are new illegals here."

Vasso shuffles back into the kiosk and sits down. She tips coins from a bag and starts to count them.

"Can I just have this please?" Juliet buys a small bottle of water.

As she passes the lane end, she glances up to her house, but the gate stands as she left it. She swallows a lump. The road splits, and Juliet takes the way to the right up past the hill. She does not know Costas' land. Her head turns right and left, scouring the orange groves for a sign of a building. A car passes, forcing her onto the long grassed verge. Some of the orange groves are fenced, gates lying open; some are open to the road. After a mile or two, the way narrows and little stones are heaped down the centre, grass breaking through here and there. On the left is a building several rows of trees back from the road. Juliet feels an expansion of hope and wades through the grass, bowing her head and pushing branches to the side.

The breeze-block hut has a metal door, which is chained. The window has bars but no glass. Standing on tiptoe, Juliet can see the hut is full of pipes and machinery. There is a hissing sound from a forceful leak, and water sprays the inside wall. She sighs.

Returning to the road, Juliet hurries her steps. The road divides. Juliet's stomach turns. Her situation feels cruel. She looks down one road then down the other, hoping to spot a clue, a sign. She looks back along the way she has come. There is nothing, no markers, no way to make a choice between the two roads. How to decide? How long are the roads? Nothing comes to her. Her mind searches for answers, but none come. She waits for inspiration, but nothing arrives. She stuffs her hands in her front pockets and lets out a heavy exhalation of air, tears

175

on the precipice of falling; she looks down at her feet and twists her toe in the gravel at the road edge. A dried cigarette butt emerges from its hiding place beneath the layer of chippings. Juliet turns to walk back home, head down, shoulders slack. She trails her feet along the verge where grass meets tarmac. Another cigarette butt and a match. Who would stand in such an out of the way place and light a cigarette?

Juliet's head jerks up. With purposeful movement, she turns on the spot and returns to the road's divide, her eyes searching the gravel boundary. She walks several yards down the first road, scuffing the verge, pace quickening. Frantic movement, heart beating. No cigarette butts. No matches. She runs back to the divide. Second road. Scanning the verge. One yard. Two. A match. Three. A cigarette butt. Juliet lifts her head. She is sure. She looks left. She looks right. She stoops to see under the trees as she walks. One hundred meters. Two. The road runs out. A dry, dusty track continues. The trees thicken.

There! To the left. A track through the trees. Juliet runs three steps and then slows. She sees a building the colour of the soil. A dark red, buried deep in the trees. What if someone is there?

She stands still, listening. A bird sings. Something tiny runs in the grass. A tractor coughs far away. Each step considered. Ears alert. The track widens. Signs of life. Two large stones, big enough to sit on, small enough to move, talking distance apart, shiny on top, cigarette butts and burnt matches between.

The barn close, no windows, no door visible. She rounds the end, under the trees, ready to hide, ready to run. The front of the barn. A clearing. Logs for seats. A pan with no handle. Empty water bottles. A rag. Quiet.

The opening has no door. The inside is black. She ventures.

"Hello?" Juliet's best defence.

No answer comes. There are drag marks at the entrance. Juliet steps on them into the dark. Blinks. It is too dark. She closes her eyes for a second. She opens them and sees. A dirt-floored, empty room. There is nothing.

There are no little beds, no comfy chairs at one end. Instead there are dried mud brick walls and a mud floor and what look like deep shelves bolted to the walls. This cannot be the place. She turns and steps on something. She looks down. A shoe. She pushes it with her toe. It turns over. It has no sole. Juliet turns to look in the barn again. There is a heaviness in her chest. She steps up to the shelves and puts a hand on the edge of one. It is smooth, smooth with wear. Her eyes are fully adjusted now and she can see carvings in the wood. Dates. Names. Juliet's silent tears fall. She looks at the shelf above. She can see the marks inscribed on the under surface of the top shelf. Hearts and names. Four lines with a strike through. Many times over. Many, many times over.

Juliet sits on the bottom shelf, hunches her shoulders and weeps. Tears splash in the dried dirt, creating tiny smooth craters. Her world expands. Beamed ceilings and cosy corners exchanged for soleless shoes and blanketless boards. She could not imagine. She had to experience. She turns to lie on the bunk. Her mind fights reality. The board has no give. Dust falls from the wall. It smells dank. The board above only a foot from her nose. Messages and words gouged in pointless effort. Tears run in her ears. She rubs her nose on her sleeve. Focus sharpens. There above her head the name Saabira and under that in capitals JULIET. She ruptures into a thunderous sob, unexpected sound, her body spasms against the board, finger-tracing her name. She lies until the tears subside.

Dark is falling by the time Juliet gets home. The gate still unmoved, the house dark, and the cats meowing at the door unfed and unloved. Juliet scrapes the remains of an open tin from the fridge into their bowls and throws the fork in the sink. It misses. She leaves it. Shuffling to her bedroom, she wishes for all thought and emotions to shut down. Flopping on the bed, sleep engulfs her heaviness.

There is no bounce in her step as she climbs in the car the next morning. The grey, square, concrete building looks incongruous with its shiny, full-glass doors. There is a chubby man in uniform behind a high desk, eating something between sips of coffee.

"Good morning. I believe you have taken my house boy." Juliet purposefully does not try to hide her English accent. She knows the positive reaction her accent ignites, memories of allegiance during the war, of British support in their war of independence and more recently a refusal to side with the Turks over the Cyprus conflict. Teaching and memories that create ripple effects in her life today. When it comes to bureaucracy, she has learnt to lay it on thick.

"Madam?" The chubby man puts down his coffee, brushes the front of his jacket with his hand and stands.

"You have my house boy and I want him back." It seems best to underplay their relationship, easier for others to understand an English woman wanting a servant. Even in this day and age, it gives her authority.

"Sorry, who is your house boy?"

"A Pakistani, from the village, small."

"Ahh, the raid. They've gone."

"Gone where?"

"Little Albania."

"Where?" Juliet takes out a notebook and pen. The policeman looks over the top of the notebook to see what she is writing.

"Little Albania, it is a detention centre that way." He points in the general direction north.

Everyone she asks on the way knows the way to Little Albania, but each tells her that she does not want to go there. The smooth roads give way to potholes. The orange trees to forestry land, scrub-covered or barren.

She arrives at the place, but thinks she must have taken a wrong turn. It looks abandoned. Large lumps of cement are cracking away from many of the walls, areas of rising damp discolouring the corners. The only indication of maintenance is the relatively new corkscrew of barbed wire atop the inner of the two layers of wire mesh fence. The gatehouse stands sentry to other large block buildings, creating an inner circle. There are narrow gaps between the blocks hinting at signs of inhabitation, glimpses of movement, the impression of many people in a yard beyond.

Juliet stops the car and pulls on the hand brake, feels the car move on the slight hill, pulls it on one more notch and puts it in gear for extra safety. She puts anything on the dash of any value to her in the glove compartment. Her focus stays on the building. There is a forgotten aura about the place. As she steps out, she can hear the distant hum of many people. She locks the old car. The surrounding land is arid. The sun is hot. The air is dry. Juliet's mouth is dry. As she marches towards the gates, a man in black uniform with a rifle steps from a side door in the gatehouse. Rifle across his bulletproof chest, gadgets of restraint around his hips, he saunters towards the gate as if on a catwalk, big boots on thin ankles.

"You have my house boy." Juliet speaks in English.

The man clearly has not understood her. He looks a little flustered. This was Juliet's intention.

180

"I want my houseboy." She continues to use English.

The guard turns to a man who is looking out of the window at them from the gatehouse. The man in the window raises his hand and twists it from the wrist, fingers loosely apart, palm up, his eyebrows raised. The Greek gesticulation of "what?"

"*Ti*?" he shouts.

The guard with the gun shrugs.

"English," he shouts, pronounces it very badly and then laughs.

The man behind the reception window beckons Juliet with all four fingers. The outer gate is unlocked, and Juliet marches through, ignores the thin man with the gun and heads straight for the man in the window. The dust kicks up around her feet. The buzz of a large number of men from behind the blocks grows. The disintegration of the building becomes more apparent.

"Hello. May I help you?" His English is fair, and he enjoys his opportunity to show off to the guard.

"Yes, I understand you have my house boy and I would like him back!"

"We have many house boys. Which one you want?" He shows no sign of being serious, apparently delighted by this break in his tedious day. He looks at his colleague before recalling he cannot share his joke in the foreign tongue. Juliet remains stern.

"I have been given to understand that he was brought here yesterday."

"We had thirteen men brought in yesterday. None of them had papers on them, so we presume all of them are illegal. Here is where illegal people are put, so he is in the right place." He finishes his speech with a grin.

"I will make him legal."

The man thinks this is highly amusing, but tries to keep a straight face and turns to repeat Juliet's sentence to the guard in his native tongue. He too is amused.

"It does not work like that." He turns back to Juliet and barely manages not to laugh out loud.

"It can if you want it to. Just hand him over, I will take all responsibility." Juliet's ground is turning to quicksand. She forces her facial muscles not to quiver. She puts her car keys in her pocket to stop herself fiddling with them.

"I cannot do this."

Juliet considers bribing him, but is not sure how to do it. If she is obvious and he takes offence, she could be arrested. It is out of her sphere of experience.

"Can I talk to him?"

The man sighs and strokes his moustache, long and curling at the ends. It is not so amusing now he has to do something. He searches on a shelf under his desk, which is at right angles to the window, and pulls up a large, dark blue ledger. He drops it onto the top of the desk, causing a breeze of papers to escape from under it at either end. One paper floats off across the room. The man watches it and sighs again. The man with the gun makes no effort to retrieve it even though it lands near his feet. Moustache returns to the book, which he opens at yesterday's page. A long ribbon attached to the spine marks the place. The ribbon is pink and Juliet finds this incongruent.

"What is his name?"

"Aaman."

"Aman what?"

"I don't know, but Aaman is spelt A-A-M-A-N, if that helps."

The man sighs again. The effort is exhausting him. He runs his finger down a list in the ledger.

"Yes, Aaman, no surname, no, you may not talk to him." He seems relieved.

"Why not?"

"He has gone." He is smiling now. Sitting back in his chair, relaxed. The guard behind him picks up the paper by his feet and returns it to the desk.

"Gone where?" She tries to hide her tone of desperation.

"He was taken to Athens or maybe Fylakio this morning." He runs his finger along the line, puzzling over the destination. "He will be sent back to his country. Did he steal from you?"

"God no! So was he taken to Athens or Fylakio?"

"Who knows? If he didn't steal from you then consider yourself lucky and find another house boy. There are many." He shakes his head, blowing through his nose at the size of his endless task. He wishes her good day and closes the window. The armed guard strolls out from the side door and walks with her to the outer gate, his eyes assessing her figure. Juliet wants to run. He unlocks the outer gate and holds it open just enough for her to squeeze through. Juliet forcefully pushes it open wider and the edge of the gate nearly hits the man in the face. He jerks his head back in response and the lecherous smile drops from his face.

Juliet remains rigid. She marches back to her car, drives a mile, stops and deflates.

There are hundreds of Pakistanis clustered outside the embassy in Athens. The building stands back from the road. Solid bars divide the pavement from its courtyard; a thick, barred gate set in pillars of stone offers the only entrance. Some men hold the bars high above their heads, resting their weight. Some stand unaided, some sit, one relieves himself against a much-stained wall. Some are in their traditional dress, some in Western shirts. Most hold papers. They fill the pavement, lean against parked cars, talk in groups in the middle of the road, moving slowly in response to horns and shouts. Juliet weaves up to the gate. Some of the Pakistani boys sense that something may happen and they gather round, hoping it will benefit them.

Juliet presses the bell push at the top of the pillar by the gate. Nothing happens. She presses again and waits. One of the Pakistani boys tells her it has been disconnected. His English is good. Juliet asks how she can get in. The boys shrug. She draws out her mobile and calls directory enquiries, and is transferred. The Pakistani Embassy has an automated service to select between Urdu, Greek, and English. She selects English and waits for an operator. And waits. One boy asks what she is doing. She explains, and they all start talking at once. She will never speak to anyone that way, they have all tried it, no-one ever answers. One says the only way in is by helicopter. Another says by parachute. They grow excited by the possible ways to gain entrance. Arms start flying with ideas, the chatter becomes loud. Juliet puts her hands to her ears. They are so excited they talk over her, forgetting she is there. She is buffeted. Within a minute, a guard comes to the gate. All the men who were sitting stand when they see him and thrust their papers through the railings at him. He ignores them, opens the gate and lets Juliet in. She is escorted into a room with three reception windows, each with a chair for the enquirer. No-one is in the room, no-one queueing at the windows, no-one serving. The guard opens the door at the far end, and lino gives way to carpet. She is shown into a room with a desk.

"Hello, Mrs?"

"Please call me Juliet. I am here about my house boy."

"Your house boy?"

"No, actually my friend. He was taken by the police to a detention centre. I want to help him. I thought that you might be told where they are taking him. His name is Aaman, two A's at the beginning."

"Oh dear, oh dear, you have lost your friend. A great shame, a great shame. He will be lost now in the Greek system. If only you had come sooner."

"I didn't need to come sooner if he wasn't detained!"

"No, but if you are his friend, as you say you are, then coming sooner we could have got him papers maybe. If you were willing to employ him full time, we could have got him a blue card, a work permit. And maybe, depending on how much of a friend he was, for a little money, a passport." He licks his lips until they glisten and smiles. "Such a shame. Such a shame. Would you like some tea?"

Chapter 14

The lane is flooded. The water seeps from under the gravel of Juliet's drive and runs down the lane toward the village. Juliet unlocks the gate in haste to find one of the watering connections for the garden has popped apart, the timed water no longer reaching its intended destination.

The beans look all but dead. Juliet lifts a sad leaf and lets it flop. She crouches among the seedlings. They have shrivelled to nothing, and some of the plants have slug holes in their leaves, flowers gone. The lettuces have melted. Juliet drops her bag by the seedlings and scrabbles in the dry soil for the water connector and pushes it home. She stands and stretches her back. The vegetables need weeding. The grass needs cutting. The edges by the wall need trimming. The vines need a pergola. There are no tools poised for action. No trowel waiting in a flowerbed. No lawn mower momentarily left halfway to the lawn. The garden looks back at her blankly.

A glass of wine and a cold tin of beans. She forks the beans straight from the tin and balances her wine on the back windowsill. Her stomach fills, the wine relaxes her but does nothing to relieve her emptiness.

Just in the time she has been away the weeds have sprung up and the trees have budded, the late April rain and damp giving the wilder side of nature an adrenaline shot. But her tender vegetable plot has suffered from the lack of care and regular watering.

To Juliet, the garden looks bare. Her body is glad her travels are over. She sits slouched, bottom on an upturned paint bucket, legs stretched out before her.

Too tired to move, she drops the can of half-finished beans on the floor beside her. They land on a stone and balance. She pulls her high ponytail free and rests her head back against the wall. The bean can tips over and the juice puddles on the floor. She wonders where the cats are. But she has been gone a day longer than she planned.

Greek bureaucracy and red tape! Officials who found her funny, officials who didn't have the time, computer systems that failed, logs that hadn't been filled. Men who didn't know their jobs passed her from department to department, from people who didn't care to other people who didn't care. Juliet is glad to be home even though home has a piece missing.

Aaman is gone. Juliet doesn't know if the Greek system is as bad as it has appeared or whether each and every one of the people she came into contact with blocked her progress to save themselves work, to stop further hassle, use of their energy. The laid-back ease that attracted her to Greece is now the very thing that frustrates her.

The paint bucket begins to feel small and hard. The temperature has dropped a fraction as evening takes hold. She looks at her glass of wine, which, since she sat, has been just out of reach on the windowsill. A slight movement in the grass at the edge of the lawn calls her attention. A snail peeks out between the blades and begins its slimy trail to the upturned beans. Its ommatophores extended, waving muscles make slow progress. Juliet pushes a tiny twig in its path with her foot. The snail glides smoothly over, unimpeded. She determinedly stretches for her wine, the bucket creases on one side under her redirected weight and she slithers onto her hip on the floor. Slowly standing, she brushes her jean leg, gathers her wine and fork, and carefully steps over the feasting snail to return indoors.

The laptop sits open on the expanse of kitchen table. The screen unblinking, black, useless, no-one giving it purpose. Juliet pours a second glass of wine. She will have to mow the lawn herself. But, by the power of wine, she will ensure herself a good rest tonight.

Aaman turns on his mattress. His legs itch. Knees to chest, he looks and scratches his ankle where there are many pinprick bites. The man on the mattress to his right is restless, glottal sounds on the in-breath, wheezing on the out-breath, a minor part in the symphony of sleep that fills the room. The dawn sun hits the farthest walls, wakefulness following its spread across the room.

He lies on his back, in his head the rich, thick smell of coffee with buffalo milk, the quiet of sitting at Juliet's kitchen table, the cool of the computer under his hands, the aromas of Saabira's cooking promising lunch, a perfect existence. A boy of no more than eight pads his path across Aaman's mattress to the sole toilet, shared by eighty men and boys.

He doubts he will see either Saabira or Juliet again. His savings tucked in a hole in a mud barn miles away. There are whispers of people remaining in these detention centres for years. The man next to him wriggles in sleep to face him and exhales loudly. Aaman turns from the fetid smell of his breath. The boy pads back from the toilet; an old man stands from his mattress and shuffles to replace him. Someone passes wind loudly.

There is no sound of the outside world. No dogs barking, no cars on the road, a strangled, hushed silence of hundreds of men sleeping, grunting, snoring, scratching.

The old man returns, another takes his place. Aaman realises that soon all will be waking and the one toilet will become awash. He stands and picks his way to the cubicle, across the uneven mattresses, avoiding limbs under spread blankets. The toilet stands surrounded by thin, half-height metal walls in the corner. The smell is obnoxious. In his hesitation, an Albanian pushes past him, his bare feet slipping in the wet as he stands rigid, unconcerned if he hits his mark.

Aaman wonders if there is a corner outside where he can relieve himself. There is no door to the yard. There are no doors and no windows anywhere, only gaping square cavities in the cancer-ridden cement. The only cavity with a door is the one that brought him in. Aaman wanders into the yard.

There are several men on their knees silently bowing and praying, facing Mecca. Two men stand talking in hushed tones by the fence between two of the blocks. There are no guards visible in the tower but faint sounds of the television betray their presence. Aaman steps towards a corner between block and fence. As he nears, the stains of a thousand before him are noticeable before the lingering stench invades his nostrils. The consensus of a thousand like minds before him. Aaman looks, as he stands, between the blocks, out through the double fence to the scrub land, barren.

He finishes and turns to find another man walking towards him, his hurried steps announcing the need for the corner.

No alarms sound, no bells or klaxons. The men wake when they like, rubbing eyes, stretching, scratching. They seem to gravitate towards one of the blocks. Aaman treads carefully, manoeuvres to observe, waits. Men leave the block with cups and bread. He joins the growing queue. The man in front smells acrid. Aaman folds his arm across his face. Inside the block there is an internal window with a hatch. They shuffle by, each receiving a cup, and a grubby hand offers something that looks like crumbly bread. The man in front snatches his piece and eats quickly and it is gone before he takes his cup. Aaman is hungry and eats slowly. He steps to one side, out of view. Watching the big men return for seconds and, after a while, the window is boarded before the line is all served. Those not served do not complain.

The day settles into the expectation of nothing. They are weary before they begin, bored before sleep has left them. Men in twos and threes but mostly in groups of five or more squat on haunches, knees in armpits, waiting for the heat of the day to build and the inevitable overcrowding in the shade of the blocks as the temperature soars and the sun burns. Aaman keeps to himself, watching and learning about his surroundings. No-one approaches him.

The day progresses slowly. One of the guards in the tower comes out and stretches. His arms clasped above his head, his mouth wide, he leans backwards, showing all the signs of being equally as bored as the prisoners. There is the sound of a vehicle on the road, and the guard unclasps his hands and points to it and turns to talk to another guard who also comes out stretching, crucified, in the sun. Lungs filled, limbs limbered, they stand, side by side, arms across bulletproof chests, discussing the vehicle, which changes down gear and grinds to a stop.

A scuffle. In the yard corner, like rats skirmishing. A Russian is pushing an Albanian. The Albanians gather, back their man. The Russian puffs out his chest. Towers, to show his size, but backs off. Boredom returns.

Some areas of the yard still have shade. These areas are taken by the big rats. The big rats stand. Out in the sun squat the Indians and the Pakistanis. They are used to temperatures of over thirty-eight degrees. Aaman does not notice the heat of the sun. The temperature often reached fifty when he worked on the land with his father. He nods if the Pakistanis look towards him, but he does not join them. A single man can sit where he likes.

The two guards on the tower nonchalantly take out their guns and stand ready. Aaman looks around to find the cause of their caution. There is a stirring by the huts nearest the gatehouse. A whisper runs through the yard. One of the Albanians pulls one of the Indians up by his arm. The Indian looks surprised but does not protest. It is the man who was worried about his wife awaiting his return in the next village. He is pushed by the Albanian towards the gatehouse block. The other Indians stand to ask why they are taking him. The Albanian's answer is heard by those nearest him. The remaining Indians are pushed towards the block that leads to the gatehouse. Aaman stays quiet.

The Albanian who has taken the lead role returns to the yard and looks around. He organises the rounding up of a group of Pakistanis. The compound then turns on his neighbour, each looking for an Asian, a moment of power. The man next to Aaman

193

nudges him and Aaman walks to the block, shrugging off his escorts.

Huddled by the door that leads to the reception building are the Indians and Pakistanis, Afghans, and one Uzbeki. There are several armed guards at the door. They do not enter the compound. They wave the group through with their guns. Aaman keeps to the middle of the group. The door shuts behind them. The men left behind cheer and jeer and bang on the closed door.

None of the guards speaks to them. They re-house their guns in low-slung holsters, momentarily standing like cowboys, enjoying the perk. They chat for a while with the gatekeeper and the gate guard. Aaman understands the words 'Indians, easy, simple, good.' His Greek has not improved since taking the job with Juliet. He wishes he had learnt more, but he cannot dwell on his lacking; the tension within the group has ignited his fear.

"Please to tell us what is happening?" he asks a guard without becoming visible from the group.

"English!" The guard laughs and turns back to his conversation, ignoring the question. They say their goodbyes, a slap on the shoulder here, a handshake there, and four of the guards herd Aaman and his group to a waiting van. Grilles at the windows, smelling of piss and cigarette smoke. Aaman wonders if he smells; the man in front does.

The van rattles as it starts, the clutch shrieking its reluctant consent. The journey winds along narrow roads, and the truck sways. The other men try to predict the outcome of the journey. The consensus is Fylakio, a large detention centre near the Turkish border. Those who have not heard of it grow fearful. Those who know are resigned. The road straightens. The truck falls into a rhythm. Aaman sleeps.

He wakes with a start to someone banging once, very hard on the side of the van. He orientates to a cacophony, horns blaring, people shouting, the drone of heavy traffic, motorbikes buzzing, and the van no longer moving.

He thinks to ask the other people how long they have been stationary, but he cannot see the point. He waits. They all wait. One says he needs to pass water; the others shrug. It is hot. Another says he is thirsty; the others do not bother to shrug. They wait. Aaman drifts in and out of sleep. There is a smell of urine.

The van door opens and a guard beckons them out. They are at the back of some building. Aaman blinks, adjusting to the light, and a force in his back propels him towards the open door. They totter down the corridor into a stairwell. Several other police have appeared. The police laugh as if the day is a joke. They beckon one of the group, one apiece. Aaman is chosen by a tall man who has his black uniform bomber jacket and white shirt open to his waist. His hair is lank and his fingers yellow from smoking.

Aaman is pushed into a room by the tall guy's baton. The room is pale green. There is a metal table and two plastic chairs. The tall policeman sits heavily and indicates for Aaman to sit. He has a form and a pen. He takes out a cigarette but does not offer one to Aaman. He lights it, picks tobacco from his tongue and begins.

"Name?"

"Aaman."

"Surname?"

"Aaman." Aaman's face is rigid.

"Aaman Aaman?"

"Yes."

"*Ox Aman!*" A Turkish phrase of exasperation. The guard rolls his eyes. "OK. Are you here legally?"

"No."

"Have you any papers?"

"No.

"By coming to Greece without papers you have committed an illegal act. You have twenty-four hours to either get papers or leave the country." The tall man stands, opens the doors and indicates that Aaman should leave.

"I don't understand."

"You have twenty-four hours to leave the country or get papers."

"I can go?"

"Yes."

"Can I ask something?"

"Yes."

"Where are we?" Aaman is standing but has not made a move to leave the room.

"Athens."

"Thank you. Can I ask another thing?"

"What?" The tall man is shifting his weight from one foot to another, ready to close the door after them.

"How am I supposed to leave the country with no money and no papers?" Aaman walks out of the room.

"That, my friend, is not my problem." He closes the door and walks off down the corridor, leaving Aaman alone. Another policeman who passes him points to the exit sign. Aaman walks out onto the streets of Athens. He has been in custody for two days.

He stands still for several moments.

The man from Uzbekistan comes out of the same exit. "So what now?"

"I have no idea," Aaman replies. "We are no more or less illegal than when they picked us up. We are just further from what we know."

"I suppose that they have cleared the area where we were to only increase the number of illegals where we are now. There is no money or time to ship us back. We just get passed on, someone else's problem. Well, God be with you." He pats Aaman on the shoulders and walks off down the street.

"Hello." It is the Indian who was worried about his wife. Aaman doesn't reply. "I have heard it told but I never believed it."

Aaman concedes to the man's insistence. "What?"

"That the police let the Indians go easily because they don't make paperwork. They don't pretend to be legal so there is nothing to check on, no false trails.

We are easy so they deal with us first." He smiles as he speaks. "I could be home in a month, God willing. It will take that long to earn the money to buy the ticket home. So long."

Aaman starts walking. The names of the streets are meaningless, the buildings tall and impersonal. He has no sense of direction and nowhere to be. The cars travel four deep on the roads, motorbikes nipping between them like impatient small dogs. Horns sound, people shout. Men driving, one elbow on the windowsill, cigarette dangling, sunglasses on. Another motorbike, no helmet, white shirt being pulled from his back by the wind he creates. Women clacking along in high heels, lots of makeup. Men in suit trousers, bellies pushing shirts over trousers on hips, ties loosened. People sitting outside their shops on stools, smoking, chatting to the next person sitting outside his shop on a stool, smoking, chatting. Taxis, yellow, stopping, starting. People in. People out. Aaman feels dizzy. He leans against a shop.

An Indian man passes carrying a tray of bread rings.

"Excuse me?" Aaman uses his native tongue. It feels strange.

"Yes, hello. You look like you are having a hard time, my fellow."

"Where is the best place to go to find work? I need to earn enough to get back to the lady I work for."

"Nowhere and everywhere. Good work is hard to find. If you want any work, go to Omonia Square and ask around. Best place to start as any." He hands Aaman a bread ring and continues his trail.

"Thank you. Which way?" The man points. Aaman walks.

Chapter 15

Juliet pretends she is still asleep, not really lying there listening for the metallic tapping sound on her gate at a ridiculously early time in the morning.

Cockerels are crowing, light creeps in between the shutters and warmth seeps under the door, indicating the night is over.

Juliet gives up diving for dreams and sits up. She is still pleased by the sight of her beamed ceiling, the white walls, her own little nest. She reaches for the clock and knocks over the wine glass, one of the several from the night before. The glass pieces shatter as far as they can in every direction, the red wine stains at the point of impact, a bullet wound on the white floor. She recalls why she drunk so much.

She curses and tiptoes across to her flip-flops, which for some forgotten reason she hung, one on the window handle and one from an old nail in the wall, the previous wine-filled night.

She pulls on her jeans and t-shirt, leaves the crime scene and heads for coffee in the kitchen. The back door has been open all night, and the cat has returned and is asleep on the table. She lifts it off and dumps it on the sofa, where it yawns and stretches before orientating itself enough to recognise Juliet is in the kitchen area and runs over meowing its excited anticipation. Later in the day, the second cat reappears, looking slightly fatter than she remembers.

After a week of steady watering, the bean plant, twisting around a tripod of canes, regains some strength. Some leaves drop, some recover. The beans themselves do not plump out. They remain skinny and dry, hidden amongst the leaves. Juliet's thin fingers caring and tending.

The grass needs cutting every few days, the garden vibrant with growth and energy before the onset of the real heat of the summer. Juliet struggles with the electric lawnmower, fearful of cutting through its umbilical cord. Weeds grow overnight. Tucked behind the gate post, a large, spiky succulent manages to reach a foot tall before Juliet notices.

It creeps on Juliet like bindweed; he is not coming back. As the days pass, the bindweed coats her limbs and she feels heavy. She cannot find a reason to care for the garden, her translation falls behind.

She wanders aimlessly around the house and garden.

The tools lie neatly organised and ready for use at the back of the house. Crafted from boards, stiff wooden vegetable boxes, old wooden broom handles, and uprights of wood Aaman must have found in the original mess of the garden are shelves that house the tools. The shelves bring tears to Juliet's eyes.

"Bye, Tzuliet. Ah, Mrs Sophia. Yes! She is still seeing the boy. She has been seeing him most weekends. Yes, you are right. They are well suited. I thought when they met it would have been instant, but they are taking their time, which I am pleased about. I am not one to interfere, but I think I will invite his family over again, just to be sure."

Juliet waves as she leaves, armed with postcards and stamps. Now filling her days with volumes of translation, Juliet is blinkered by her solitude. It is safe, it is painless. But after some time, thoughts of the boys push themselves behind her stockade. Time seems to have stretched out and Juliet is not sure how long it has been since she talked to them. She'll surprise them with cards.

The grass is dry and soft, and she lies on her stomach, sunglasses on, hair in a high ponytail, bikini bottoms, and a long-sleeved t-shirt. She takes out a postcard and looks at the picture of an old man bent under the weight of the bundle of sticks he carries. It is in sepia tones to make it look old. To Juliet, it is a daily view of her village life. The second card is of a sepia-toned man with a herd of goats, shepherd's crook in hand, and a handlebar moustache. Juliet looks closely. He is wearing Nike trainers. She laughs.

Dear Thomas, Old-fashioned snail mail!

She puts the pen end in her mouth. She has no idea what to write.

The garden is looking lovely. Unfortunately the man who was helping me has been called away, so I guess it will be up to me. I have more and more translation work all the time. The British council have me on their books, and I seem to be getting a regular supply of work from them, almost too much, both by email and by post.

I hope you and Cheri can find the time to come and visit. I know that both time and finances are short so no pressure

Much Love,

Mum

The cat comes to investigate what Juliet is doing lying on the lawn. He climbs onto Juliet's legs and walks up to settle in a ball in the small of her back. Juliet tries to bend her arm around to stroke him. The cat digs its claws in to stop from sliding off as Juliet's contortion unsettles his bed. She rolls over on the grass as the claw tips make contact with nerve endings and the cat leaps to safety. Juliet calls him back but he heads for the edge of the lawn, disappearing under a dense plant with purple flowers. The sun lulls Juliet into a brief snooze. She wakes gently and resumes her postcard writing.

Dear Terrance,

I hope your studies are going well and your landlord is happy! I love Greece although a friend of mine left recently and I miss him. He has been gone two weeks already! I am sure I will make more friends although some people are just special. Talking of which, have you seen any more of the girl who was helping you with your thesis? It would be lovely to see you over here but I do understand. No more room. Love M xxx

Juliet rolls onto her back and feels the sun on her face. The cat jumps on her chest and she strokes it. It is time to get back to her translation.

After some days of intense translation, Juliet feels she is on top of the recent glut of work she has received. With no structure to the day, she often finds herself working into the night and getting up too late to enjoy the next day. When Aaman was around, the day had structure, work got done earlier, which meant she had time to make progress on the inside of the house. Work on the house has ground to a standstill.

The paint tin is stiff to open, and Juliet looks around for a piece of paper to stand it on to catch accidental spillage as she prizes open the lid. All the paper that she uses for translation work is in the bedroom on the desk. There was a slightly scrunched piece next to the telephone. Juliet puts down the paint tin and the screwdriver and crosses the room to the telephone. The paper has Michelle's name written at the top and her number written below in bold handwriting with the words RING HER in capital letters at the bottom. It is Juliet's handwriting.

She recalls the way Aaman smiled when she was last on the phone to Michelle. She wipes her hands on her painting shirt, just in case, and picks up the receiver.

"Michelle? It's the evening!"

"Yes, it is. How nice of you to call."

"Is it a lonely evening or one in which you are busy and I am interrupting you?"

"It is not a lonely evening. It's amazing how quickly that seems to be wearing off since I spoke to you. However, you're only interrupting me from painting the office, so I'm glad you have called."

"I was just about to paint the door to the guest room. White. How about you?"

"Shocking pink! He had that room dowdy colours for so long I decided to openly overcompensate. How's your house boy?"

Juliet's tongue dries, her heart beats a little faster.

"Are you still there or have I said something to make you slam the phone down? Juliet?" Michelle is giggling.

"He got arrested." Juliet rubs her eyes with the finger and thumb of her free hand.

"What? What did he do? Are you all right? Did he steal from you or hurt you? Oh my God, are you all right?"

"Stop, stop. I'm fine." Juliet sighs. "He was taken because he was illegal. I tried to find where they have taken him to try and help, I don't know, help him get his papers or something, vouch for him, something. But they couldn't find him. They have shipped him from one detention centre to another but the paper trail got mixed up and no one knows where he is." Juliet can no longer hide her tears, and she sniffs loudly.

"Juliet, are you crying? Are you OK?"

"Yes, I'm OK, I'm all right, I'm fine." There is a pause, Juliet looks around, sniffs again and reaches for tissues from the table.

"So this house boy ... come on, I can't keep calling him that. What's his name?"

"Aaman." The word brings peace to Juliet and her crying stops.

"Aaman got taken for being illegal, you've tried to find him but haven't had any luck, and you're crying because you haven't found him. That's what it sounds like. Is that what's going on?"

"Yes."

"Are you crying over Aaman because he was a great gardener or did something happen between you guys?"

"No, yes, no, not really. We just talked. He is, or rather was teaching himself to programme through the Internet in the evening on my laptop. He works all day in the garden. He built shelves at the back for the garden tools. He put the vines on poles ready to build a pergola."

"Juliet, have you fallen for this guy?"

"No! He's married. He loves Saabira. He plans to go back to Pakistan as a programmer. He's going to buy a harvester with the rest of the village. He wants to have children with her."

"That's a lot of personal talking you guys have been doing if he's just a gardener. Can you hear yourself?"

Juliet sobs and blows her nose.

"Yes, I can hear myself. I can hear how it sounds. He's my friend, Michelle. He was in a fire when he was eight, he lost his brother. I care about him."

"Ahh, that sounds heavy. Have you no idea where they took him?"

"I spent days trying to trace him. I went to the Pakistani Embassy. I even went to the British Embassy to see if anything could be done from there or if they could tell me what to do. I've been to the police station where they first took him and then every police station from here to the northern suburbs of Athens. I've even rung Fylakio. That's a jail up near the border of Greece and Turkey."

"Can he write, I mean does he know how, in English?"

"Yes, but if he is in a detention centre, are they allowed?"

"I don't know. How long has he been gone?"

"It's a month now."

"That's not so long, Juliet. Do you know what the usual routine is? I presume they'll want to deport him. How do they do that? Do they fly them home, or just hand them over at the nearest border to their home countries? If they have sent him home, it may take time. He's bound to write when he gets home if he feels the same way as you."

"I have no idea how he feels. He is kind and considerate and cautious and thoughtful. But he could just be doing it for the job, I don't know."

"People don't talk about trying for children with their wives to keep a job, Juliet. That goes way beyond."

"I think he thinks I am a good friend who is lending her computer. I shared some of my life with him, and he shared some of his life with me."

"You shared about the fire?"

"Yes, and my dad. Which, by the way, reminds me, due to him, I owe you an apology."

"Apologise to me? This is too confusing. Because of Aaman?"

"He made it 'visible,' I suppose that is the word, that I have not been, well, very nice to you over the years. When my dad went and my mum being the way she is and then finding Dad had died and, well just the whole everything, I realised I was scared of you so I pushed you away."

"Scared of me? Why would you be scared of me?"

"Not scared of you exactly, scared that you might ... like Dad did, or become a bitch like my mum or that girl at college who went off with John. It just felt, well, safer, I suppose, not to be friendly, and I'm sorry. I am really sorry. You've stayed by me through all of this and even through my Huge Mistake with Mick." Juliet hiccups out a laugh at the thought of the Huge Mistake with Mick. Michelle mirrors the laugh back.

"Juliet, this guy has really shaken you up a lot, hasn't he?"

"I miss him so much. I thought he was a gardener, then I thought he was a friend, then, well, then he was gone and my reaction has left me not understanding myself. I was just so comfortable with him, I loved him being around. Oh, and I went to see where he used to stay. He said it was a barn, and I thought of an old English barn with little beds and comfy chairs at one end like a hostel and, oh my God, Michelle, it was awful. It was made of mud brick, it had a mud floor. A tiled roof that you could see the daylight through and no doubt let the rain flood in. No comfy chairs, no chairs at all. And the beds! They weren't beds, they were shelves in the wall. Just enough room to lie on. They were all worn smooth on the edges and there was so much graffiti carved and written. Names and dates and days counted off like a prison cell. And he lived there! And each night, I spread out in my double bed with clean sheets and a duvet and my cats."

"Cats? More than one now?"

"Two. By accident, I found the bunk he must have used. He had carved the name Saabira, his wife's name, and then under that, in capitals, he had carved JULIET and now he is gone." Juliet breaks into tears anew.

"Hey, listen. Juliet?"

"Yeah, yes, I'm OK." She blows her nose.

"Listen, you've had a hell of a ride. You divorced the Marvellous Mick, and not before time, but before you had a chance to adjust to single life, you moved to Greece. Now I'm not saying there's anything wrong with that, but you were very displaced when you met Aaman. New to the country, new to the village, new to being single, and with no immediate support. If he was kind to you, he's bound to have become a bigger person in your life than, say, if you had met him back here with your boys just a car ride away, when you still went to your yoga group twice a week and coffee with half of them on the other days, and when you still had weekly meetings with the ex-Greek teacher and so on. You get the picture?"

"Yes, I get it. But he has experienced fire and loss, he understands. I haven't met anyone else who seems to understand the way he does. He allows me to feel. He gives me time and space and the safety to feel what I have never dared face."

"I can hear you and I love him for it. But if he's gone then he's gone, and there's nothing you can do about that."

"Just like my dad."

"Sorry?"

"Gone just like my dad and then I found out years later he loved me, but it was too late because he was dead." Juliet begins to cry again, but half of her watches and is amazed at being a forty-eight-year-old woman crying for a dad who died twenty-seven years ago.

"Your dad didn't want to lose you, and it sounds as if Aaman had no choice either. Neither of them wanted to abandon you. Aaman going is about Aaman, not about you."

Juliet stops crying and wipes her nose. Her brow unknotted, she makes an effort to inhale and exhale steadily. Michelle's words filter through her.

"You know what? You're right. He didn't want to leave. It wasn't his choice. I've been thinking about my loss all this time, but what about Aaman? He had so much more to lose."

At Omonia Square, Aaman's first job is to sell wind-up rabbits that hop half-heartedly with flashing red eyes. The owner of the mechanical rabbits has assured Aaman it is a good job and kindly subbed his food for the first day, "Whilst you get going," he says. There are three other people selling the same wind-up rabbits on the corner he is stationed on. The toys are cheaply made and they are meant to ask five euros, "Accept four if you have to", out of which they can keep one euro for themselves for the first two they sell in a day, two euros from the rest. He must work whilst the sun is up. He sleeps in the square, under a tree, with a stray dog he names Lucky.

After a week, Aaman sees that the odds are stacked against him. He spends all he makes on the cheapest food he can find. Some days he doesn't sell a rabbit and he goes hungry. He also still owes the rabbits' owner the sub for his food on the first day. He sees the trap that it is, ensuring his return day after day or the alternative consequences of owing such a person money. He works two more days, without food, to get free of his debt, the last day spent not so much trying to sell as observing his surroundings.

Omonia Square is a congested roundabout with openings to the underground strategically placed, the central island large and open with trees and benches. The area is busy, predominantly with foreigners, illegals. At the hub of the island are mostly Georgians, Turks, and Armenians. They stand in knots, looking casual in stance and alert in their eyes. Occasionally one will break away and take long, bouncing, running strides to the Pakistanis or Indians who stand at the traffic lights, at the entrances to the roundabout, offering to wash windscreens, sponge in hand, buckets at their feet, hopeful for tips. The Armenians collect up these tips from the pockets of the Indians, tip a bottle of water in their bucket, tell them to work harder, then return to their group in the square's centre jangling their pockets like returning warriors.

Someone kicks one of Aaman's rabbits. Thin white trainers, one with no laces, the woman stands there, her body contorted in impossible angles to stay vertical. Involuntarily bending from the waist, her knees begin to give. Her face vacant, eyes rolling. She looks like she will fall at any moment, but each time a force within her returns her to vertical and the collapse begins again. Her head just keeps nodding and, somehow, her balance remains. Aaman rescues his rabbit and shifts down the street a couple of yards, avoiding other vendors and areas of sick and dog dirt.

Another man breaks rank from the centre and goes to another windscreen cleaner. He pockets the money and returns to his colleagues. The nodding lady sees him, her eyes gain some focus, her impossible gait propelling her towards him on the central isle, cars stopping, horns blaring, windows being rolled down, shouts, hand gestures. She reaches the man in the centre and scrabbles in her pockets. The man watches her struggle until finally she brings out some money. She passes the money over and he hands her something small from a bag around his waist, under his shirt. He grins as she leaves, a car narrowly missing her as she staggers back from the island and all but falls down the steps into the underground.

Aaman stays squatting by his rabbits until they are collected from him, his day done, the last repayment made, money left for him. The windscreen washers have their buckets and sponges taken away by the men in the middle. Aaman crosses the road to surreptitiously join them. It is a large area with sculptures and different levels and trees. Aaman finds a nook behind a tree not far from the group of men and waits.

The night has fallen and the men still talk and only break to hand small somethings from their waist bags to people who don't stay near them for longer than is necessary. Two of the men with waist bags also have buckets and sponges lying idle by their feet, ready for out of work Indians the next day. One has a basket of rabbits with mad red eyes.

The girl is halfway across the road when Aaman sees her again. She staggers and falls against a car that screeches to a stop. She gives the driver an obscene hand signal and continues to her destination, a motorbike narrowly missing her. She lumbers toward the group, madly feeling through her pockets, digging deep, toppling but never falling. Aaman sees potential trouble and readies himself. He moves closer behind another tree.

The girl asks for something, and the man holds his hand out for money. She begins her own body search again, each ploughing of her pockets sending her off balance, she sidesteps to regain. She has on a long cotton coat with large pockets, stained in many places and with a rip across the back. Her eyes are rolling and her mouth stays open. Her hair is plastered to her head down one side, on the other it is frizzy. Last pocket, she is frantic, she bends low to reach the bottom, her balance goes, she stumbles into the men. They stagger in turn and shout. Aaman, like a small rat, runs between them and makes away with a bucket and sponge; they don't even notice.

He runs for a few blocks and then finds a corner, at the back of a building, between some pipes and a wall, behind a bin where he sits on his haunches. Bucket in hand, sponge under his t-shirt, he lets himself drift in and out of sleep till morning, grateful that it isn't cold.

The next morning, Aaman picks a corner with no Armenians in sight and touts for work for a few hours. He cleans two windscreens but only one driver pays. Twenty cents. He buys a bread ring and moves on.

He is stopped at the next corner he tries by a Russian who wants to know the name of his boss. Aaman says he has no boss and the Russian laughs as he brings an elbow up under Aaman's jaw. Tongue bitten, eyes roll. Balance lost. Elbows take the weight of his fall. He sees feet move. Weight rebalanced. A swinging foot. A sharp pain, he curls up for protection.

"Now you have a boss." The Russian grabs him by an arm and drags him away from the road under a flyover. Aaman remains curled. The Russian sits down on a rock. Aaman can smell cigarette smoke. He waits. He falls asleep. Awakes to residual pain. Opens his eyes and uncurls. The Russian is still there, now with a friend. Aaman slowly sits up. His tongue is throbbing.

"Ah, my worker awakes!" The Russian and his friend laugh. The friend gets up and walks away across the road, saying something in his mother tongue.

Aaman glances at the Russian. He sees his chance being lost by the actions of this man. He feels an unfamiliar emotion, identifies it as anger. He puts his hands on the floor to stand, his fingers curling around a rock.

"And where do you think you are going?" The Russian finds his role amusing. "Sit down!"

But Aaman does not sit and the Russian stands to take action, feeling his own anger at Aaman's defiance. He lunges at Aaman to push him back down. Aaman ducks and sidesteps. He swings his arm towards the Russian's head, his fingers clenched around the rock. It makes a grating thud as it makes contact. The Russian's eyes open wide and an expletive passes his lips. He stands tall and turns on Aaman.

Aaman is terrified. The Russian is much taller than him. He knows he is going to swing for him. His legs are straddled for a sure base and his eyes are menacing. Aaman doesn't have time to think. His foot has come up between the straddled legs and the man folds, a sweet acid expulsion of air passes his lips as his head lowers to his knees. Aaman brings the rock down on his head with a solid crunch and the man falls to the floor.

Aaman grabs his bucket and runs. He heads off the main road and finds a street with high-fenced houses. He is gasping for air but dare not stop running. He eventually staggers to a halt by an old house. The bushes outside the fence on the pavement are dense and covered with flowers. Aaman pushes his way past the canopy of foliage to disturb a cat curled by the trunk of the bush. He takes its place and stays hidden in the bush until nightfall. His tongue throbs slightly less and the pain from the kick to his stomach has decreased, but his heart is still beating fast.

By the light of the moon he takes his bucket and runs through the suburban street until he can run no more. Dawn is breaking. He wonders if the grapevine on the street will have every Russian in Athens looking for him. He steals a yellow t-shirt from a washing line, swipes a baseball cap from a garage. He finds a corner to work on and stays twice as vigilant.

Aaman keeps moving to avoid the Russians, Georgians, Turks, even Greeks. Traffic lights here, street corners there, moving constantly, each step closer to her computer, her garden, her house, Juliet. Street by street, mile by mile, day by day, cents turn into euros. The euros are eaten away with the need for food. Water fifty cents a bottle. A Sisyphean task. Some days he takes no food to save money, some days there is no pay. He is nearly at the end of Athens. He takes his money and buys a ticket for as far as it will take him. He will walk the rest.

Chapter 16

The village outskirts feel so familiar. The woman sits in the shade by her aging petrol pumps. Girl and woman, she has sat there, now neatly dressed in black, knitting. A dog runs to him, black with a wide collar, reacquainting. Aaman pats its head, it runs on, free of its work with the sheep for a few hours. The bakery closed, it is late, the pharmacy dark. The kiosk lit like a fun fair, full of promises and temptations. Aaman sits under the palm tree, stretches his legs and rubs his feet.

With his remaining cents he buys a box of matches. The road out behind the hill, the familiarity only brought by the repetition of walking. The fork in the road, nothing new, the road becomes a track, the trees thickening and there, the track on the right. Aaman slows his pace, listening. Is there life? An owl. The track so familiar. The moon bright, cloudless. The clearing and the barn. Hope builds. He steps on something. A roof tile snaps under his weight. It is handmade, lichen-covered. He looks round. There are more. No roof means no business. Rounding the corner to the front, he half expects to see the dead man and Mahmout grinning behind a tree.

There is the pan. A fork stuck into the mud door frame. All is abandoned. Roof tiles littered, a deliberate act. The moon shines down through the beams, some tiles holding fast, polka dotting the floor. The shelves pulled from the walls, some on the ground, some falling away, some half out, a methodical destruction to render useless the illegal camp.

Aaman has no interest in the broken history. The bunk that was his is gone. Where it was pulled from the wall there is a hole, the mud bricks have crumbled, brown dust and straw. Aaman's fingers feel the wall, around the hole, scanning to recognise what has gone and what remains, his mental map shifted by the missing pieces. He feels in his pocket, lights a match to see.

He finds a brick with carving on it that he recognises. He lights another match. He traces the route, back four, down three. Yes! There! Spit-smoothed mud. Aaman looks around for a twig, a stone; he runs and grabs the fork. Scraping and twisting the fork into the dried earth, it crumbles with ease. The tip of something paper. He lights another match. He nips it with finger and thumb and pulls. The notes uncurl as they slide out. The first few leave some behind. Nipping and pulling, Aaman retrieves all his savings. A smile spreads across his face and he laughs out loud, muted and buffered by the dense grove of orange leaves. He lies back on the plank that was once his shelf, looks up to the star-filled sky and, with a smile on his lips, falls asleep.

Up at seven and all translation work finished by tea time, Juliet finds she is much more productive and happy. This morning, she has a new piece to work on, but there is no urgent deadline. But it is important to answer an email about the book someone wants translated. That is a big job, lucrative.

She turns over and stretches, the silkiness of quality, tight-woven cotton against her skin. The sheets twist round her smooth-shaved legs and the cat meows for his escape. Juliet sits up to untangle the cat. Its face comes out first, relaxed and unhurried. Eyes open wide, ears tense and turning, he can hear something. Juliet smooths his fur with a lingering hand.

"There, there, puss with no name. What's wrong?"

The cat relaxes to only tense again. Juliet listens. A tapping, a metallic tapping? Juliet stops breathing to listen more intently. There it is again. Not the postman's blast on his moped horn. A tapping. Juliet flings her legs off the bed into her jeans, pulls on a top as she runs for the keys, flings the front door open. Stops still. Aaman!

Does she run, does she hug him? How did he get back, why is he back, does he feel the same, is he staying?

"Aaman!" Juliet has no choice, her legs are running.

She stops a foot from the gate. He puts out his hand. Juliet is not sure if she is to take it or shake it.

She reaches for it, their fingers touch as if to slide into a handshake, movements slow and slur, his fingers reach her palm, hers his. The touch light, thrilling. Juliet makes a tiny almost unnoticeable stroke with the middle finger, his thumb curls around index finger, his little finger curling around hers, they slide their hands slowly apart only to rejoin, her ring finger and little finger interlocking with the soft flesh between his, her thumb stroking his wrist. He intakes a breath, their eyes locked. His fingers reach her wrist, feeling her pulse, sliding down across her palm, fingertips touching, exploring, uniting, intertwining, his circling her palm. She takes a breath, eyes still locked, he takes her hand, encompassing her thumb, helpless.

"Hello, Juliet."

"Hello, Aaman."

The hands have not separated. Fingers interlock, squeezing, releasing, holding, caressing, brushing, clutching, the tender, thin skin between fingers exploded, the edge of the nail smoothed, the speeding pulse felt, the life line exposed, the mound of the thumb kneaded. Neither noticing their actions, both absorbed, gazing in silence until the cat jumps on the gate between them and nuzzles for attention.

"Oh, sorry." Juliet releases his hand, as the cat's head butts her arm, to fumble with the gate key. She steps back to let him in. He enters over the threshold, puts his hand on Juliet's shoulder, softly, tenderly. He couldn't escape her eyes, transfixed, his hand trails the length of her scarred arm, smoothing, feeling, absorbing all the way down until he remains supporting the tips of her fingers.

Juliet, paralysed, her desire to hold him, melting at his touch, stands unmoving, smiling, mesmerised. He releases her fingers and breaks the spell, replaced by a calm that folds over them.

"Please come in, Aaman." Her words are languid. She puts her hand on his shoulder and leads him to the house.

"Are you hungry?" His jumper feels dirty. She removes her hand to make a quick scan of his condition. His clothes are visibly dirty, and now she has noticed them, she becomes aware that he smells. They go into the kitchen. Juliet pulls out a wooden chair for him to sit on and begins to make him a sandwich.

"Actually, I wonder if you would like a bath? The water is hot and I think I can find something that might fit you." She smiles at the memory of that last time she offered him clothes.

"No, no, Juliet I am fine. I came to explain."

"There is nothing to explain. I heard they had taken you. I tried to find you, I went to the Pakistani Embassy and several police stations but they seemed to have lost you. I presumed they had deported you. I can't believe you are here. What happened?" Juliet was expecting the excitement to fuddle her words, her thought, but instead there is profound tranquility about her, as if she has the rest of her life to find out Aaman's tale.

"You went to the embassy to find me?" His mouth is open, he processes the information. She is still looking at him, enquiring. "They let me go. I had twenty-four hours to become legal or leave the country."

"Or what?"

"Or I will be an illegal immigrant all over again!" He is smiling as broadly as Juliet has ever seen. She laughs, the final tension relaxing.

"It is so good to have you back." And before she can think, she hugs Aaman, they hold on a little longer, he breathes in, his nose in her hair, she feels the tension in his muscles. She pulls away, embarrassed by her feelings, unsure of their reciprocation.

"I insist you have a bath. If you have been in a detention centre you will definitely need one. I will be happy to wash your clothes. I can find you something to wear." She opens a trunk by the bathroom and brings out a thick, fluffy, cream towel, which she hands to Aaman. He hesitates to take it, it is so clean. Juliet pushes it into his hands as she passes him to run the bath.

She returns to find Aaman has taken his jacket and his t-shirt off. His chest is hairless. Juliet averts her gaze and leaves the room to look for some spare clothes in her bedroom. Once in her own room, she sits on the bed and reminds herself that she is a grown woman as she waits for her pulse to subside.

She finds the pair of unisex jeans she offered him before and, taking a needle and thread from her

223

desk, sits and stitches the hole. Away from his company, her thoughts launch a deluge on her tranquility. Why has he returned? Is he here to stay? Will she be in trouble for harbouring an illegal immigrant if she knows he is illegal? Could she legalise him? Halfway through the sewing, she can no longer ignore her unease. She puts down the sewing and returns to the sitting room for the telephone. She can hear Aaman splashing in the bath.

Having dialled, Juliet tucks the telephone under her ear against her shoulder and returns to her bedroom, closes the door and picks up the sewing.

"Michelle?"

"Why are you whispering?"

"Aaman's back."

"Fantastic! How?"

"They just let him go, but listen, I feel out of my depth. I'm not sure why I have rung, it's just that ..." Juliet snaps off the cotton and puts the trousers to one side on top of a t-shirt she has found.

"What, Juliet? It's just that ... what? And why did you say we are whispering?"

"No, I'm being ridiculous. Sorry to bother you. Better go, bye, call you soon." Juliet clicks the phone off and takes the trousers to the bathroom door.

"Aaman? I have left some clothes outside the door. I am going in the garden." Juliet steps out the back door into the sunshine. The sky is clear, the air is thick, the warmth exaggerated by cicadas rasping. Beyond the orange groves, at the back of the house, the tinkle of goat bells signals the herd's return.

Towards the village, a car door slams, and up by the hill the grumble of a tractor fades away. But there is another sound. Juliet focuses. It is small but insistent. She tries to hone in on it. It stops. There it is again. She treads toward the wall.

"Juliet, thank you." Aaman is rubbing his head with the towel. He looks revived, relaxed. The jeans fit but the t-shirt is baggy, his feet are bare.

"We'd better get you some shoes. Listen!" Juliet hears the noise again and pauses. Aaman hears it too, moves nearer the wall. Juliet hears it quite distinctly now. She lifts the ground-covering plant where the cats love to sit in the shade, and there is the cat's friend with four blind kittens.

"Ahh, how cute." Juliet reaches out to touch the small balls of fur. Aaman's hand encloses on hers.

"No, don't touch them. The mother may reject them if you do." His hand releases its pressure but he does not let go. He looks from the cats to Juliet, arms abutting, her breath on his shoulder. Juliet thinks of Aaman's dead child and Saabira.

"I wouldn't want that." She withdraws her hand and puts it in her pocket. "Come on," Juliet breaks the bubble, "let's go and get you some shoes."

Aaman has not sat in Juliet's car since the first day she employed him. It feels unsettling. In one world, he was handcuffed and in the back of a van, in another world he is in the front seat of a private car being taken to have the gift of shoes bestowed upon him. Grateful for the shoes, but impatient with his lack of power over his own life, Aaman sits with his knees neatly together and his hands loosely folded in his lap.

Juliet chats gaily as they pull out of the lane onto the road that leads to the village and on to the town. She talks about the replanting of the vegetable garden, and wonders if it is too late for this year. The sound of her voice to Aaman is like honey, it speaks of freedom and wealth, choice and power. It speaks of kindness and consideration, tenderness and love.

Aaman turns his gaze to look out of the window. There are two illegals in the square. Aaman can spot them immediately. They are new faces.

Past the kiosk, Aaman looks down the little side street where an old man sometimes tried to sell the illegals cups of coffee first thing in the morning. "Extra income for me, everyone's happy!" he said. The road flashes by, but he sees, without a doubt, Mahmout sitting on the stool by the old man's door. He opens the window for the breeze, wipes the sweat from his palms onto the jeans Juliet has given him, all stitched and ironed.

"So we will find some shoes, see if we come across a t-shirt that fits and pass by the nursery, OK?"

"You are very kind. But I must repay you."

"When is your birthday?"

Aaman has to think when it is, where they are now.

"It has gone."

"I'm sorry I missed it. I would like to buy you a belated present of a pair of shoes."

"I would be very happy with some slip on sandals, in plastic if I can choose because they are better in water and mud."

Back in the village, their shopping trip complete, Juliet pulls up outside the corner shop. "Just going to pop in for cat food for our new mother. Anything you want?" Aaman shakes his head.

"Ah Tzuliet, isn't it fantastic?"

Juliet feels thrown. It is fantastic to her that Aaman is back, but she is unable to see the connection with the shopkeeper.

"He has asked her and she has said yes! They are engaged. Isn't it wonderful?"

"Who? Oh! Yes, your daughter. I'm so pleased for you and her."

"She is divorced like you, so you see there is someone waiting for you right now, somewhere. Just the cat food? Eighty cents. Bye."

Aaman is waiting, sitting silently and still, his hands wedged between his knees. He is looking at his feet, his new shoes. Juliet thinks he looks like a small boy and realises how unhappy that would make him. She becomes aware of how little he is but also aware of how life treats him as if he is so small he is unable to decide for himself.

"Would you like to start back on your programming today?"

"I am so grateful for your kindness. I did not come back to be bought shoes and offered such generosity. I came back to tell you that I had not left from my

227

own free will. That I did not take your kindness for granted. That I valued your kindness to me."

"I am grateful to you too." Juliet cannot add any more on to the statement. She does feel gratitude towards Aaman, but can't explain, even to herself, why exactly. She wants to hold him. She feels safe. She pats his arm, lingering.

Aaman gets back into his studying that day. Juliet looks at his form sitting at the table. His straight fringe hangs from his forehead as he bends over the keys. His small hands move quickly over the keyboard. His back curves just enough to soften his silhouette. His shape pleases her. She wishes she could draw as she would like to study him hour upon hour. She makes him a coffee and places it by his work, resting a hand on his back as she sets it down. Aaman turns his face towards her, eyes on her mouth. He murmurs, "Thank you" before a thought that passes behind his eyes causes him to turn back to the computer and frantically type.

Aaman finds he has not forgotten where he was with his studies. It flows and feels natural. He hadn't realised he had made such progress.

The day slips by. Juliet visits the kittens every few hours, just for a peek. Aaman doesn't move from his position. The evening draws in, and Juliet thinks about opening a bottle of wine but then decides perhaps she would be better having something to eat.

"Do you fancy going out to eat, Aaman?"

"Out? You mean a taverna? No, thank you, but if it is time for me to go then I will go."

Juliet steadies herself with the kitchen table.

"No! You mustn't leave. I mean, I'm not suggesting you leave, just that I am getting hungry ..."

Aaman cooks and they eat on the patio. The salt is passed with fingers that dwell. Aaman tells of his journey, his slice of police shortcuts. Juliet tells her tale of the chase, her slice of people's shortcuts. Aaman speaks of his physical discomfort as if it was an experiment, it mattered little to him. Juliet speaks of the mental frustration, as if it was a personal vendetta. They both listen more than they speak.

After dinner, Juliet tells her story of visiting his barn, but does not mention seeing the carving of her name.

"Aaman, you cannot go back there."

"It is safe now, they think it is gone."

"What do you mean?"

"I went back before I came here. It has been destroyed. They think it is no longer habitable, so it is safe."

"It is not habitable. The boards are hard, there is nowhere to sit. You cannot go back there. You must stay here."

"That I cannot do."

"You must."

"I cannot."

"Why?"

Aaman gives her a long stare. Juliet crosses her legs and leans away from him. She cannot return his stare.

"Look, have you anywhere to stay?"

"Yes, the barn."

"Apart from the barn. I mean, if I was in the police I would go back there after a month. It's an obvious place to go. Everyone thinks it's safe so they go back, so it is an obvious easy raid. So, no, no barn. Anywhere else?"

"No."

"So, to keep you safe you need to be somewhere legal. Can you afford anywhere legal?"

"Yes."

"And then how much would you save?"

"Nothing."

"So here is my thinking. If you are going to go back with enough money for your harvester, then you need to stay somewhere cheap or free. I have a spare room. You work here all day, you study at night. It will save time and effort if you stay."

"How is this possible?"

"OK, you once said to me that you wanted the job of working inside my house as well as outside. You used the term house boy. This will also make it possible for you to get a blue card, a work permit, maybe even a passport. It could make you legal."

Juliet explains the details she found out at the Pakistani Embassy. Aaman sits attentive. He leans forward in his chair, resting on the table, his crossed hands a finger length from hers, his little finger extended. It could be a reflex. Juliet extends her finger in response, the tips of their fingers touch. Aaman looks into Juliet's face, his eyebrows raised in the middle.

"Thank you, Juliet. I can see it is logical. I would like to accept. Please tell me my duties."

"You are talking to me like I am a stranger."

"It is better if we are clear." His eyebrows still arched, he turns his hands palm upwards on the table.

"Well, still do the garden. I would love it if you would prepare the meals, and if you could just help a little round the house, keeping it tidy and a bit cleaner perhaps. A bit of painting occasionally? But you are my friend, Aaman, and no amount of duties or rules will alter that." She puts her hand on top of his. His lies limp, he does not respond. Juliet retracts hers. He smiles softly at her and draws his hand to his lap. Juliet smiles in return and withdraws her own hands.

"The guest room is yours." Juliet stands and goes inside and returns and places a key on the table in front of Aaman.

Chapter 17

Aaman dreams he is on a soft plank in the barn. The shelf bends in the middle and gives way to his weight as he turns. Surfacing slowly, eyes still held shut by involuntary muscles, he waits for harsh reality to return. He turns onto his back, the illusion of softness still there; he slides his hands to stretch above his head. Surprised, he stretches upwards only to be hindered by a puffy softness under his head. Consciousness comes rapidly. Aaman opens his eyes. The ceiling is beamed but in rich, honey-coloured pine timbers, not gnarled, dark-stained walnut with missing tiles.

A smile sparkles in his eyes and his hands slide over the pillow to complete his stretch. Feeling every inch of his body against the smooth cotton sheets, he twists and contorts, awakening the muscles in his back. His feet feel heavy, and he looks down to see the male cat sitting on his ankles. His smile turns into a chuckle. He lies back, hands under his head, and stares at the ceiling, planning a future. Eventually he is called to the bathroom; he slips his feet to the floor and pulls on the jeans. He feels the need to get underwear now he is staying in the house, but this is something he will not discuss with Juliet.

The door opens with a squeak. Aaman looks at the hinge and makes a mental note to find some oil. He has a full-time job now and he must look out for all the things that need attention. He pads to the bathroom and taps gently. The door opens on his tap; it is empty. Aaman makes sure the toilet is clean and the lid is down and washes his hands thoroughly. He hesitates to wipe his hands on the towel on the rail as it will be Juliet's. He shakes his hands and leaves the bathroom wiping them on his jeans. He looks up to see, across the sitting room, Juliet in the kitchen. She looks over to him, with a spoonful of coffee paused over the jug. Aaman becomes aware of his shirtless torso and scuttles to his bedroom. He comes out again wishing her a good morning as he pulls on his oversized t-shirt. The neck wide enough to expose one shoulder, he hitches it up.

"How are you feeling?"

"Very excellent indeed! I thought I was waking in the barn, but then I felt the softness of the bed. It is truly wonderful this kindness you show to me."

"I am sure if I was in your country in the same situation, you would do the same for me."

"Of course, I would love to be able to repay you one day. I hope you will come to our village." Aaman stutters over the last few words as he thinks of the basic facilities he has. How little he could offer Juliet, whilst she offers luxury. "We don't have much, but you would be welcome to all we have."

Juliet can picture the degree of kindness and consideration she would be offered by Aaman and his family. She blushes at the memory of how she treated him when she first had him work for her. She feels sure that Aaman's family would not have to wait to get to know her to offer kindness or to be asked for water on a hot day. Juliet turns away with these thoughts then turns back and looks at him directly.

"Thank you. Breakfast?"

They take their toast and marmalade, which Aaman appears to like very much despite its orange origins, out to the back garden. The trees are stretching now their roots are in soil and have lost their plastic boots. The grass is growing but the vines are still propped on the poles that Aaman put them on to protect them when he was clearing the land. The pomegranates are fattening and tinged with red. Juliet takes a big bite of toast and studies the garden.

"I think," breadcrumbs held in by skill and practice, "we should think about putting up a pergola to support the vines. They have been very patient." She swallows. "But," she adds as she feels Aaman energising himself next to her, "I think we should do that in a day or two. Let your body recover from your ordeals. Regular meals and good sleep for a while first."

"I ate twice yesterday, I am having breakfast now, and I have slept like a prince for ten hours. I am ready to build a pergola!"

Juliet hears the enthusiasm in his voice and recalls that he is probably a bit younger than she is.

"How old are you, Aaman?"

"Thirty-two, I think. Yes, thirty-two."

Juliet scans his face. He has boyish looks but with an age of experience that shows through. At a glance, he looks younger than his age, but she had presumed he was older, a good few years older. A quick sum tells her he is sixteen years younger than she is. She swallows, her throat feeling curiously tight. She looks younger than forty-eight, but the reality knocks her. She feels ashamed of her feelings. A predator.

They both look up as they see the mother cat carrying one of her babies across the lawn to the woodpile. She glances furtively around as she steals back for another one. She completes her task, all four moved and stands protective in front of the hollow in which she has placed them. Her babies. She dashes madly across the lawn, glances sideways at Juliet and Aaman as she sidles in through the back door and into the kitchen. They hear the sound of crunching cat biscuits before she dashes back to her vulnerable young.

Aaman laughs.

"More coffee?" Juliet asks. They continue their plans for the pergola. Aaman says he can use some of the old beams that lie against the wall at the back of the house that were there when Juliet bought the place. Some are rotten, but others are good. Juliet asks if he will need help. He says if he prepares everything, she could give him a hand when it comes to putting the uprights in if she wants. It is agreed. Juliet says she will work from her desk in her bedroom with the window open and he can call her when he needs her.

Aaman insists on washing and putting away the pots and breakfast things. Juliet settles at her desk. The garden lies before her through the window. A bird lands on top of one of the vines, but flies off when Aaman comes out. Juliet turns to her work.

Aaman takes his time to lay out where the uprights should stand. He places markers and then wanders around the garden and along the back of the house to see how his placements will alter or improve the view if that is their final resting place. Once happy, he digs the first holes. After a couple of shovels of dirt have been removed, he takes hold of the pickaxe.

Juliet looks up at the change in noise as the pickaxe drives into the deep compact soil. Aaman, sweating, has taken his shirt off. His skin has a sheen like gold. He is lithe to the point of thin, but his skin has a depth, a firmness that softens the edges of his muscles as they tense and release in his work. His hair falls like a mop, spiking into points. She presumes he has poured water over his head to stay cool.

He lays down the pickaxe and shovels the loose earth out of the hole he has made. Different muscles come into play. He stops and rolls his jeans up to the knee. His calf muscles flex with the movement. Juliet tries to concentrate on her work, but Aaman corrupts her interest. He shovels in another area now, digging deep, muscles taut. He strides over to the sand and cement Juliet has had delivered. He scoops a spade or two of cement and several spades of sand into the wheelbarrow and turns on the hose which snakes across his feet. He introduces it to the sand and cement and mixes, turning it over with his shovel. He is careful in his movements, avoiding splashes.

"Juliet, you want to come and help?" he shouts as he transfers the mixed cement into a waiting bucket. He turns his back on the window and Juliet breaks her gaze. Scrambling to her feet, she grabs an apron as she passes through the kitchen.

"Where do you want me?" Juliet asks.

Aaman lifts a beam, using its central point for balance. He carries it to the farthest hole and tips the beam's weight until the end sits in the hole. He walks away, holding the beam, and then when he is a good distance away, pushes the beam towards vertical, walking in as it gains height. Juliet runs to help. As the beam makes it to upright, Aaman's hands are half over Juliet's. Aaman looks her in the eye.

"Would you like to hold the beam or get the cement?" he asks.

"I'll hold. It seems balanced."

Aaman carries the cement bucket to the pole and pours it in around the base. He gathers some short pieces of timber and wedges them around the pole for support, then claps the dust and cement off his hands.

"One!" He smiles.

Juliet lets go, smiling.

They complete six uprights before Aaman thanks her for her help, and she decides to pop to the nursery for some climbing plants to train up the poles.

She returns with a selection of border plants and only one climbing plant in a wooden box. Aaman jogs up to help her unload it from the car. She seems excited and Aaman presumes it is from having the garden done. Out of curiosity, he asks why she hasn't bought climbing plants. She is completely distracted.

"Aaman, how good are you with the programming?"

"I am further on than I thought. I am learning PHP which allows queries to search a database and perform other server side processing tasks. Why?"

She shields her eyes from the sun with her hand.

"The man in the nursery says he needs a website. I said I knew someone who would do it and he said to ask how much!" She is grinning.

"I will not charge him."

"Why ever not?" Juliet drops her hand.

"It will be a good way for me to learn. It will take time and it may not be perfect."

"You will charge him and you will use it to learn and he will give you a reference which I will officially translate into English!"

"But I will be slow. I will be learning as I go."

238

"He does not know how long it takes to write a website. Besides, he said he would like it ready by next year. Nothing happens with any speed in this country." Juliet laughs.

"I must talk to him to find out what he wants exactly."

"I took the liberty of asking him, and he has written it out for you, what he wants it to do and so on, I will translate it for you and if there are any questions, I have his phone number. Isn't it great?"

Aaman seems nervous. Juliet reads the signs: he is already inside his head, thinking, working.

"I think it might be an idea if you left the cement to dry, do extra tomorrow, and go start work on the website now. What do you think?"

Aaman is already tidying the tools, pulling on his shirt.

It takes just over six weeks to write the website whilst juggling his time with finishing the pergola and keeping the garden and house perfect. He declares it is not a complicated site and that he has been slow to learn.

Juliet is amazed. She ensures that the nursery man pays before taking control of the site, and Aaman spends a few evenings showing him how it works, and practises his Greek in the process, and Juliet stands by intervening when necessary as translator.

Aaman lies on his bed. He is reading the translation of the reference from the nursery man who was delighted to enter the digital age. He gloats over the roll of money in his hands, which has grown considerably in size following his payment for the website. He is almost beginning to believe that he will be able to pay for more than his share of the harvester, help out his village, his distant, faraway, dreamlike village. He expands his chest, the returning hero. The thought slices through him. His yearning to see his mother, Saabira, his father, his grandparents, even the oxen, pulls hard. But then here and now is strong, Juliet, her garden, the house, her world, its kindness, ease, comfort yanks his senses. Juliet, who is so much older, and yet not. She understands. He almost allows himself to think 'like an equal,' but he recoils. It does not seem right. She is doing all the giving, he the taking. That is not equal. This hurts.

It is only days after the completion of the nursery's website that Juliet is approached by Stella who runs the village takeaway. Her best seller is souvlaki-meat on a stick, chips and salad wrapped in flat bread, *tatziki* dripping from the wrap. She needs to expand, she tells Juliet, to welcome tourists. Her husband is not content with the business they are doing. Juliet asks if there are a lot of tourists in the village, not having seen any. Stella replies that there are not but a website will change all that. Juliet is not convinced, but Stella insists and also neatly corners Juliet into promising English lessons once a week.

Juliet feels Aaman did not charge enough for his last job and this time quotes more. Stella seems very happy. Juliet suggests a more modest sum for the lessons; it is important to become part of the community.

Aaman completes the task in two weeks. Stella's English will take much longer. Aaman has learnt now and his skills flow. Besides, this site is easier. It needs a way for Stella to alter the prices and update the menu. She loves the design. Aaman studied many English websites for cafes and restaurants before designing his own.

His bankroll grows. He keeps it behind the boards that line the built-in cupboard where the gun was found. He reflects on this. Things change, and he must change with them. He looks down at himself. He is lying in the jeans Juliet has given him and the oversized t-shirt. He needs to change. He pulls the door to the guest room open with his toes whilst remaining lying on his bed.

"Juliet, I have a very big favour I wish to ask of you." There is no need to shout as Juliet is on the sofa in the sitting room.

"Yes is the answer."

"No, you must not say that. It might be too big a favour."

"OK, what?"

"Next time you are going into town, please may I take the time off from the garden so I can go and get some new clothes?"

241

Juliet closes her book.

"Aaman, I am going into town now. Is there anything you want? Would you like a lift?"

"No, you are being too kind. But the next time you go?"

Juliet stands up and pushes her feet into her flip-flops. She walks to the door and picks the car keys from the hook - the hook Aaman put up to stop her from losing them.

"So are you coming?" She does not wait for an answer but goes through the open door, the heat lapping from all sides. She opens the gates and returns and sits in the car.

Aaman has not moved. She starts the engine. He is standing by the front door. She turns the car around to face down the lane. He runs to the car and jumps in.

Aaman asks Juliet to leave him whilst he shops, which suits her as she has some dry cleaning to collect and a hard copy translation to send. There is always a queue at the post office so she has her book with her, which she is still struggling with.

When they meet up, Aaman astounds Juliet. She expected he would, that or he would have bought something too garish on which she would not be able to comment. He has bought a lightweight jacket, a starched white shirt and some dark trousers. He has even bought some summer shoes. Nevertheless, what impresses Juliet the most is that he has also been to the barber, his floppy fringe gone, the back, which over the time she has known him grew to shoulder length, is short. The barber has gelled it, and Juliet wonders how it will look after a day in the garden. Juliet notices that she also feels a curious sense of jealousy, as if the world can now share her view of him.

"You look amazing! Let's go to a cafe and sit in the sun and watch the world go by."

Aaman has watched people sitting at cafes and watching the world go by for, how long, a year, longer, shorter? Time seems to escape him. At the beginning he counted in days, then in weeks, for a while in months, but now? He casts the thought aside. He does not want to think in those terms, how long he has been here, how long he has not been there. Nonetheless, to be one of those people sitting watching the world go by feels like huge step.

"Is it very expensive?"

"My treat."

"I would not like that."

"Sorry, Aaman, I know I can be very insensitive. Look, this cafe shows the prices."

Aaman looks. He covers over a sharp intake of his breath with a small cough and wonders how people manage. He is grateful more than words can say to Juliet. If it cost even a whole day's pay it would be no more than if he gardened free and he would gladly do that for Juliet, every day.

"My treat!" Aaman takes Juliet by the elbow and leads her to a table.

Aaman orders coffee and Juliet the same, and just as the waiter is leaving their table Aaman orders ice cream.

"Strawberry, vanilla, chocolate?" the waiter asks.

"Juliet?"

She forms her lips to say 'no', but looks at Aaman. He is offering half a day's wage. She reshapes her lips into a 'yes', and smiles. He is delighted, they are now equal.

"Vanilla, please." She smiles. "It has been a long time since I have had ice cream."

"Two vanilla, please."

The ice creams arrive in glass dishes with wafer straws, strawberry syrup poured over them, and a sprinkle of nuts. Aaman wonders how much the extra things will cost and tries to remember how much money he brought with him and how much is left from his shopping trip. He excuses himself to the lavatory and makes a quick check. He has plenty. He returns relieved.

The afternoon glides into evening. They talk of gardens and people and perceptions, the West, the concept of work, how unfair the world is, colours they like, one topic merging into another.

A tall Nigerian man approaches their table. He opens a case showing row after row of watches. Aaman looks in the man's face. He has not met this individual man, but he feels he knows him. Aaman shrinks inside himself, mindful of the pecking order. The Nigerian addresses them.

"Nice watches, good quality, very good price to you, sir. I can see you are a man of taste and distinction, it would look very nice a watch on your wrist. Madam?"

Juliet pulls a face and turns her head from him.

"No, thank you." She sounds almost cross at the interruption.

"You, sir," he turns his back on Juliet to face Aaman, "you look like a successful man. You should have a nice watch to show your success."

Aaman's mouth opens and he readies himself to speak, but words are lost to him. He glances at Juliet for guidance. Her head is turned away, watching children at play in the square. He looks back at the man, recalibrating their relative social positions. He is aware of the uncertainty of his life, but to this man he appears successful. He feels the unease of being a fraud, and he looks down only to be reminded of his new clothes. He is wearing shop-bought clothes, head to foot, and he is sitting at his leisure in a cafe. Aaman looks around him. He wonders if all the people sitting at this cafe all struggle in some way, as he is, and if the clothes and the casual postures are as thin a veneer as his. The watch seller looks at him with expectancy. Aaman shifts his weight as he realises that he could, if he wanted, afford one of these watches. A waste of money, but to be in a position to buy one! Maybe he is who the vendor perceives him to be.

Aaman straightens his back and pushes himself farther back in the chair, growing in height. He is aware that he has nothing to draw on to know the correct verbal response in this situation. Nevertheless, his muscles relax and he begins to smile. He looks in the man's eyes and is startled to see the hunger, the fear, the loneliness. He sees the possible brutality, tempered to fight for his survival. Aaman swallows and tries to settle the stir of feeling this ignites, but his struggle takes time. The man moves on. He is at the next table now, same watches, same words, and same smile.

"Are you all right?" Juliet asks. "You look like you have seen a ghost."

"Yes. I am fine, really fine!" Aaman comes to terms with the side of the fence he is on.

Juliet smiles. He shakes his head to himself and snorts a chuckle before his attention is taken by some children jumping to catch bubbles blown by a street vendor.

They sit a little longer people-watching, enjoying the sun. Juliet puts her hand on his and gives it a squeeze before letting go. He smiles, and they get up to go home.

Chapter 18

August shrieks its presence every morning at dawn with the voice of a million cicadas and builds an oppressive wall of heat by nine a.m.

Juliet concedes defeat and joins the rest of the country that seems to have taken the month off, the only exception being those civil servants who have drawn the short straw and who sit immobile under the air conditioning units in their dingy offices, mopping pools of sweat, stunned into submission by the heat and who, if it were possible, are even less inclined to get on with any actual work than in the cooler months.

It's been a good year so far with plenty of translation work, and her bank balance is healthy. Juliet tells herself she deserves some time off.

The cafes and beaches overflow with Athenians and foreign tourists, both equally conspicuous, and Juliet begins to feel like a proper local in the presence of these intruders.

Aaman is finding August less restful. Two more people have come forward, having heard of his reasonable prices, and have asked for websites. Stella, after one of her English lessons with Juliet, asks if Aaman can do another site for her. She wants to re-open her father's candle factory and sell to Greek communities abroad. "There are more Greeks," she says, "living abroad than in Greece. Melbourne, Chicago. We will make international businesses. "But please," she adds, "not to be telling my husband."

Aaman tells Juliet, after Stella has left, that he thinks this is the beginning of the Internet boom for Greece. America is first in all things he says, followed by Britain, followed by the countries of Europe taking their turn, the farther to the east, the later to catch on. He says he is delighted that his speed and skills are growing quickly. But he also says he has explored other programming languages and begins to see the breadth of his chosen path.

Juliet points out that every new skill he masters increases his scope for employment. He says there is something new to learn every day, and each new thing he learns serves to show how much more there is to learn. It is a happy Catch-22 he says, pleased with the Western term he has picked up. He lets the words roll around his mouth as he says them.

Juliet is washing out the brushes and Aaman is bringing the furniture back into the sitting room. The kittens get under his feet.

"That's the last room!"

"Your bedroom?"

"No, I did that first before you came."

"So that's everything?"

"Pretty much. The kitchen cupboards and the built-in cupboard in your room are done. The wardrobe in my room is wooden and just needed polishing. The bathrooms are 'usable by local standards,' as they say, and the garden is absolutely perfect!"

"So I have no job now." Aaman is not sure if she is joking.

"Oh no! Now it needs maintaining. Round and round every year. Actually all the shutters will need painting, after the summer, ready for the winter, so we are not finished yet."

"You have paint in your hair," Aaman says, picking the kittens up one after the other to give them all a stroke. The mother cat is crunching noisily in the kitchen. The male cat is on the sofa.

"I'll wash it after I have done these brushes."

"I'll do the brushes."

"They're done now. I'll go do my hair."

"I'll do your hair then." Aaman laughs.

"OK." Juliet laughs and goes into the bathroom and runs the shower. When the temperature is right, she takes the showerhead off the wall and kneels over the bath. She is getting all her hair wet when his hands take the showerhead from her. She laughs.

"I was only joking!"

"I know, but I would like to do something for you."

He massages her head; his hands feel stronger than the force he is using. He puts the shower in the

249

bath to pick up the waiting bottle. The shampoo is cold against her head. His fingers work from the base of her neck up, picking out knots of tension, working slowly, deliberately up to the crown. His fingers hypnotic, making small slow circles down towards her ears, the pace steady, rhythmic, stimulating follicles, relaxing thoughts. Juliet can feel herself transported, drifting.

Juliet's hair feels silky and smooth, soft and feminine. Aaman is not sure where his gratitude ends and his masculine feelings begin. She has been so kind to him. Without her, he knows how different his life could have been. He thinks of the bearded man, alone, in the moonlight, lifeless. He had no Juliet. Aaman feels strangled with indebtedness towards her. But appreciation did not make the angle of her chin, nor did it make her stride, the whites of her eyes, her conversation, the thoughts in her head, this head under the slow caress of his fingers. The head whose thoughts create the possibility of a new life for him. Her thoughts are part of a world that he wishes to conquer, win, and return to her on a plate. But how much of these thoughts and feelings are thanks and how much is his own ego? If he removes his thanks and his ego, is there anything left that might just be the golden glimmer of something so precious for which men are willing to die? Aaman allows his fingers to dissipate these thoughts into the skull at their tips. He passes the golden glimmer, the feelings that men have died for. His breathing quickens, his heart beats faster and tears trickle down his face.

"Juliet," he murmurs.

"What? I can't hear you I have shampoo in my ears." She tries to raise her head but Aaman's hands push her head under the shower.

"Nothing." He rinses her hair soap free, reaches for the towel, wipes his eyes in passing and wraps it around her head. Juliet stands and looks at him enquiringly. She can see his eyes are rimmed red. She steps towards him, puts her hand up toward his face. Aaman swallows, anticipates. She strokes some shampoo bubbles from his hair and shows it to him. Aaman decides it is time to tell her.

"I must start to think about returning to Pakistan."

Juliet gulps some air and tears well in her eyes. She says nothing. Aaman waits. She looks into his eyes. There are gold flecks in the brown. His pupils dilate as she stares. Juliet responds by putting a hand on his arm as if he were leaving immediately. Aaman puts his hand on top of hers. She can see a tear form, rising from his left tear duct, welling, swelling, spilling and rolling down his smooth skin, hanging on the edge of his jaw. She cannot bear to see it fall.

It falls. It is too much. Her gulp turns to a gasp, which becomes a sob. Aaman pulls her to him like she is a child. Juliet reaches for him. They fall together, his arms encompassing her, her head on his shoulder. She cries, silent and deep. He strokes her hair to comfort himself. He resists touching the wet, tangled mass with his lips. His shirt is soaked, sticking to his chest. His heart pounds, Juliet's sobs fall to its rhythm, unity. They cling to it.

Aaman turns his body, still holding Juliet in the pain-filled harmony. He walks her to the sofa and sits with her. Replacing their loss for words is an agreed silence. Juliet grows still. Aaman begins to breathe more steadily. Slowly, choreographed like a ballet, a flower uncurling, they begin to pull themselves a little straighter; Juliet takes her head from his right shoulder. Aaman lets his left arm drop from around her shoulders, his hand now resting on hers on her lap. Juliet sits up fully and Aaman lets his other arm fall from her shoulders behind her, sliding it through the gap now between them onto her knee. Their hands seek to intertwine.

Juliet sits unsupported, her face wet, eyelashes clustered together. Finally, she steadies her voice. "Of course."

Aaman's tears still flow, well upon well, chasing each other down still wet paths. No noise, just tears.

"I am sorry," Aaman says. "For so many things but do not know where to start." Juliet nods her head.

"I'm not." Juliet's voice is small but sure. "To leave, you have to have been here, and I'm not sorry that you have been here." Aaman's lip quivers. He sucks in some air. He seems so young, so vulnerable. She puts her arms around him, his head on her shoulder and he weeps. Juliet kisses his hair, brown and soft. Strokes his back, his hair, his head. She makes a sucking, tutting noise to soothe him. She rocks him ever so gently.

Aaman stills. He pulls from her, slowly. They sit side by side.

"When?"

"Soon. I do not know."

Of all the things Juliet would like to say, what she actually says is the very last.

"I will help."

In a clean shirt and with his trousers ironed, Juliet accompanies Aaman to the embassy. She had the foresight to take the direct number of the man she spoke to previously, and they have arranged an appointment. Outside the gates hundreds of Pakistanis sit and stand in the road, papers held tightly, hopefully.

Juliet phones to announce her arrival and they wait. The Pakistanis around them beg from Juliet and chat to Aaman. Juliet feels the gulf between them widen a fraction. She releases her grip a little and her heart tears a fraction more.

The guard comes out of the building and walks to the gate. All the waiting Pakistanis thrust their arms through the fence and shake their papers at him. They shout the reasons why they should be considered, why they are different, how long they have waited. Aaman answers in his mother tongue. Shown through the gates, he enters into the building. Some of the waiting men look at him like he is a traitor to his race.

Juliet does the talking. She charms and flirts with the official. He responds fully, and a blue card is arranged on the spot, a permit to work. Legal. Aaman is happy. Juliet reads his body language and knows he is about to stand. She touches the outside of his legs lightly, an unnoticeable gesture by anyone watching. Aaman understands and complies, settling himself back into his seat.

"Now here is the main thing." The man listens to her intently.

"I want to visit your country, and when I get there I want to stay for a while. Learn a little about your culture, your country, so I need to rent a house, take on servants, that sort of thing." Juliet wonders if she had overdone it, but the man is still listening. "So I would like Aaman to go over first and arrange this all for me. He knows my tastes, I trust him with my petty cash, and he could have everything ready when I get there."

"How can I help you, madam, in this endeavour?"

"I would like to go next month. Well, you can see the problem. How can Aaman arrange everything by next month if he cannot leave the country legally? It will take him months and risk much hardship if he goes by the 'back door' across land."

"Ahh, you would like a passport for him to return so he can fly."

"Exactly." Juliet hears Aaman's heart beat beside her. Or is it her own?

"Madam, this would not be a problem. Passports to go back are easy. They just take a little time and a

254

little money." He smiles. The thought of money pleases him.

Aaman opens his mouth to speak but Juliet silences him with a raised finger, playing the Colonial Employer.

"Aaman, would you get me some water please? I saw a water fountain outside in the hall."

Aaman takes his leave, pulling faces behind the official's back. Juliet ignores him. He returns with a paper cup.

"So I will do that then and it will arrive by post in two weeks?" She puts an official-looking envelope in her bag.

"Exactly, Madam, precisely no trouble at all." The official beams at her.

"You have been so kind, I thank you." Juliet holds out her hand and he shakes it smartly, bowing a little as he does so. Juliet takes Aaman by the elbow, which makes her stifle a giggle, and they both leave the embassy.

The men waiting in the street all rise as they leave the building and they rush to thrust papers at the guard. He unlocks the gate, and Juliet and Aaman push through the clamour.

"Are you really coming to Pakistan?" Aaman asks.

"No." Juliet looks at him, eyebrow raised. He understands.

"What will you do for the passport to arrive by post in two weeks?"

"Have a passport picture of you sent to the embassy."

"And the money?"

"Well that bit is between me and him."

"Don't, Juliet. Give me my pride."

"How can I not do this for you? If you go by yourself, you have left me. I would always feel abandoned. However, if I make it happen, if I pave the way, then you have not left me, I have sent you, sent you home, where you belong. Besides, you want to go home, and I want for you what you want for you. If going home is your greatest happiness, please allow me to give that to you."

"Do you want this water?" Aaman is still holding the paper cup.

"No."

Aaman drinks it. Juliet takes the cup and puts it in a bin they pass.

The two final websites go well and Juliet 'officially' translates the references into English.

They are both strangely surprised when the postman parps his horn and Juliet is asked to sign for Aaman's passport. They had held off buying the plane ticket as neither of them really believed it would ever arrive.

They search online for plane tickets and agree to split the airfare between them. Aaman's need to do this is as great as Juliet's.

Juliet suggests that Aaman does not travel with his money in cash. When he arrives home, she says, he open a bank account with a little of the money and she can send the rest over by bank transfer. This thinking is new to Aaman. He comes from a cash culture. In his village, they swap and lend and barter. In the towns, they use money. The idea of money existing without it really existing is alien to him. That it can travel from one country to another without anything physical actually moving seems unreal. He researches it online before he agrees.

Aaman also researches software houses in Pakistan. He finds over three hundred and fifty in Lahore alone. Juliet suggests they send off emails to all of them in batches. Juliet scripts a letter as if she is the head of a bespoke software house where Aaman works, saying that she is sorry to lose him and could they offer him a job on his arrival in Pakistan.

"That is dishonest."

"No, it is not."

"Juliet, you know it is."

"No, it's not. A company is 'an association or collection of individual real persons.'" She traces her finger down a Wikipedia page as she reads it out. "And a bespoke software house is 'A company who specially develops software for some specific organisation or other users.' So you and I are a collection of two individuals and I have found the work for you to develop for specific organisations or other users, have I not?"

"Surely we would need to pay taxes here for that to be strictly true."

"Until a very short time ago, you were an illegal immigrant. Now you do not want to write these letters because you haven't paid your taxes?"

257

Aaman raises his hands, palms upwards, and shrugs. She types.

"Besides, they only need these letters of introduction to convince them to try you out. Once you start working for them, your work will speak for you, these emails will be forgotten."

She is shocked when she gets two hundred and ninety-eight replies. She passes them on to Aaman to deal with. They all want to ask questions and some want to meet him.

Eventually they run out of things that need doing and the storm of action leaves only the devastation of the parting date.

Aaman looks smart, and worried. Juliet is casual but fragile. Aaman takes her hand as they walk out of the main door of the house. He escorts her to the car and opens the door for her. As he crosses to the passenger side, the kittens get under his feet. He picks them up one by one along with the mother cat and says his farewells. The father has not been seen for a while. Just before Aaman gets into the car, he puts a finger up for Juliet to wait, and he runs into the back garden. The vines are doing well and grapes hang in huge clusters, purple, brushed in white. The pomegranates are enormous, and Juliet slips out of the car, plucks one, and on returning to the car, slips it into Aaman's bag as a surprise for him when he unpacks in Pakistan. Aaman has walked past the grapes; they are not what he wants. Juliet bought and Aaman planted another climbing plant because the man said it grew fast. He noticed the day before that the first flower had opened.

He climbs back in the car and presents the flower to Juliet, who gasps as she takes it. A circle of white petals laid over with a thousand purple tentacles, banded in purple and white, deeper hues towards the centre, topped with the deepest purple and ridiculously tall stigma.

"Oh, my goodness, that is so beautiful. Is it from our pergola? What is it?"

"A passion flower." Aaman blushes.

Juliet leans towards him. Aaman backs away just a little. Juliet plants a delicate kiss on his cheek, and pokes the flower behind the driver's mirror.

"Right then, we'd best be off." The quiver in her voice belies her.

So familiar. Aaman watches. The lane turns into the road which turns into the village. He is glad she is driving slowly. They pass the kiosk. There! Down the side street is Mahmout.

"Please stop the car a minute, Juliet."

Juliet draws in, presuming he wants something from the kiosk. She follows him through the driver's mirror.

Aaman walks with stiffness; a pulsing begins in his abdomen. Mahmout sits there drinking coffee with the old men.

"Mahmout!"

Mahmout sees him and stands as if to run, but sits down again grinning.

"My friend! How are you?"

"How did you think I would be?"

"I do not understand you."

"I saw you behind the tree. A man is dead because of that raid. Why, Mahmout?"

"He was nearly dead anyway."

Aaman is so shocked he loses his words. He stares for a second.

"Why, Mahmout?"

"It is a dog-eat-dog world, my friend, and I happened to see where the big Nigerian man was keeping his money." He grins smugly. "And, I believed we would get more work with everyone else gone!"

"You mean you would get more work with everyone gone. So you went to the police?"

"Oh, no. Not exactly, it was not like that at all. I overheard some police saying that they would like to clear up the streets a little, so I just walked past and suggested they check out Costas' barn."

"Exactly. You went to the police!"

"No, not exactly at all! Well, yes, but you would have done the same in my position. It is a tough life!"

The old man on whose doorstep Mahmout is sitting and whose coffee he is drinking at twenty cents a cup looks blank. Aaman tells him in pigeon Greek that Mahmout has ratted on his brothers. The man looks disgusted now. Mahmout's Greek is clearly not good enough to understand what Aaman has said as he continues to grin. Aaman turns back to Mahmout.

"Mahmout, I am not sure whether you are a big rat who has acted small or a small rat who has acted big. That is not my problem. I know that as long you are a rat someone will be chasing you with a big stick."

Mahmout stands up and looks around him, to see if Aaman has come with friends with sticks. When he sees there is no one, he grins. Aaman leaves life to take its own revenge. Mahmout shouts after him.

"You would do the same had you been smart enough to see where they kept their money." He raises his coffee cup as if to say cheers and then bends his legs to sit down, but the disgusted old man has taken his stool away and has quietly closed his door on him. As Aaman walks away, the last he sees of Mahmout, he is sitting on a nonexistent chair and falls on his back like a cockroach in the gutter, hot sweet sticky coffee over his chest and face.

"Everything OK?" Juliet asks, aware he did not go to the kiosk.

"Yes, just tying up loose ends. Questions I may ask myself later if I do not answer them now."

Juliet does not want to understand. She wants to be numb. They travel to the airport in mostly a sober mood, with occasional pushes into joviality. Juliet takes Aaman's hand on two occasions. Aaman takes hers on three. On each occasion, it is brief.

The sight of the airport's control tower signals their arrival. Juliet parks the car in the short-term car park and walks across to the departures entrance. They find his check-in counter; the queue is short.

"Aaman, I have a confession." Juliet is smiling, her sadness hidden.

Aaman is not sure he wants a confession. Juliet continues.

"I needed a new laptop anyway." Juliet smiles. Aaman frowns and then smiles. He points to his suitcase that is disappearing through a black plastic curtain. Juliet nods. Aaman hugs her. The woman behind the desk asks them to step to one side.

There is a maze of rope dividers in front of passport control.

"You go through there. They will check your passport, and then follow the signs for the gate number." Juliet points to the gate number on his ticket. "Before you are allowed into the waiting room for the gate they will ask you to take off your jacket, belt, and remove the coins from your pocket onto a tray that is X-rayed. You then go through a metal detector, you know, for guns and so on. If it bleeps, they will scan you by hand and maybe pat you down and then you redress and go through to your gate and wait. They will tell you when to board. I imagine once you are on the plane, they will speak Urdu. So, have you got everything, do you understand everything? Oh, and here are some sweets to suck because as the pressure in the plane changes, your ears feel funny, and sucking helps."

Juliet remembers the time Terrance went on a skiing holiday with the school. They were late and it was up to Juliet to usher him through the airport to meet up with his beckoning class. She had tucked some sweets in his pocket as he left.

Aaman's concentration is distracted by everything. He is in a world he thought would always be denied him. He is glad to experience it, but he is not sure it is better than oxen for ploughing and jugs for carrying water. Just different, a different struggle, money in larger quantities, more people, less personal. He draws his attention back to Juliet. There are no words big enough to express all he wants to say.

He leans towards her; she has tears in her eyes. He places his closed mouth on hers. She is still; he does not move. Lips upon lips, trying to pass over all he feels. He pulls away even more slowly than he had advanced. Juliet struggles to keep herself composed. It is time.

Chapter 19

"Hi, Michelle. It's me."

"How are you doing? How is Aaman?"

"He's gone."

"Again?"

"No. This time he flew."

"He flew? Flew where?"

"Pakistan."

"Deported?"

"No, I helped buy the ticket."

"Why? What do you mean? Has he gone for good? I can't keep up!"

Juliet tells Michelle about Aaman's quest to help buy a harvesting machine for the village. "Once he had the money to do that, he had no reason to stay."

Michelle is incredulous that a migrant worker could have managed to do this in such a short space of time, which leads the conversation onto his programming ability. She is suitably impressed.

"So are you staying in touch?"

"I don't know, he said he would write, but his old life will take over and I think he will forget me."

Juliet imagines his returns will be glorious. Arriving in Lahore where he has arranged to stay for a week before contacting his family. Together they emailed so many businesses that he will need five or six days in town to see them all. He said he would not leave Lahore and go home until he had a job. He said it would honour his brother, fulfil their dreams. He will arrive in his village employed. His family and friends will celebrate his return with a feast, and he will be swept along until she, Juliet, will be a distant memory.

"He was one lucky man to bump into you," Michelle says.

"I think he blamed himself for his brother dying in the fires. His programming fulfilling both their lives, exorcising demons. It was the only thing that would account for such intensity, as if his life depended on it. Which, potentially, it did I suppose. You know what I mean?"

"A bit like your intensity to study Greek all these years because Greece and its attitude remind you of your dad." Michelle pauses slightly between the last few words, the final word comes out almost like a whisper.

"What?" Juliet says.

"Well, the Irish are quirky and warm and humorous, and the Greeks are quirky and warm and humorous. At least they were when we were there twenty million years ago. Don't you remember, you even said at the time that everyone you met reminded you of your dad? You even said, 'It's like southern Ireland, but warm.'" Michelle laughs. "We had such a good time. Do you remember that barman who just kept giving us shots and then he ended up

265

dancing on the bar? Remember? He banged his chest and said, 'Life depends on what is in your heart.' And we cracked up laughing."

Juliet laughs. "That was such a good holiday. I never thought that it would lead to where I am now." Her tone drops and a sadness enters her voice. "His intensity will get him the job though."

"And after he gets the job?"

"I suppose he will go to the village." Juliet can imagine Saabira running to greet him, his mother kissing him all over, his father shaking his hand, and the whole village gathering around him. Some will say, "Did you get the money?" Aaman will ask, "How much is the village short?" Someone will tell him. "Not any more, I will cover it all!" he'll cry. The village will cheer. A real hero's return. Juliet laughs as she cries.

"Aw, Juliet, I don't know what you guys had together but am I getting the feeling, maybe, that it wasn't such a good idea. Do you regret it?"

"Absolutely not! He is the most spectacular thing that has happened to me since my dad rescued me from the fire. He has opened my mind, my prejudices, and my heart. It is easy to think you're OK if you don't know what you're missing. He showed me so much, Michelle. I feel a different person for meeting him. A better one."

"Sounds like love to me."

Juliet blows her nose.

"Juliet, you'll be OK. It's not as if he left you because of you. He would have stayed if he wasn't married, by the sound of it."

"Yes, it is more like he has died in a way, you know, because nothing has changed between us. There has been no falling out and no change of heart. But then again, he is not dead because we could write, or email maybe. I am hoping at some point he'll get Skype so I can see him."

"And his wife?"

"You know, that is strange, I don't feel jealous of her at all. In fact, from what he has said, I think I would like her. His was an arranged marriage and he has worked hard to make it a happy one. I was not an arrangement. I was a choice, of sorts."

"What do you mean, 'of sorts'?"

"Well, he worked for me and the relationship grew because we spent so much time together, and, as you pointed out, I had no-one else and he had no-one else. So how much was choice and how much was proximity and human nature?"

"Good idea, Juliet. Take all the romance out, dissect it until it cannot hurt you and it becomes worthless. Pick it to pieces until you have nothing to run from. Go on then, time to slam the phone down."

"No, I hear you."

Michelle clears her throat, a short contemplative sound.

"But do you see what I mean?" Juliet asks.

"No, you're talking rubbish. You're saying that with any man you invite in to do your garden, you're going to find this connection. If that were the case, they wouldn't advertise Date Line, they would advertise Garden Line. Get real, Juliet. These connections are rare. I wish I had had such a connection to someone. All I've ever had was lust, familiarity, practicality, and divorce. No, treasure it, and be thankful he was not around long enough to spoil it."

"A little bit longer would have been nice. Like ten years or so." Juliet tries to laugh.

"You are open to it so maybe it will come by again. It is like the rich. If you make one of them poor, they just get rich again because they know how. Well, see yourself like that. See life like that and then everyone you meet has potential."

"Is there a jury present for this summary?" Juliet digs at Michelle's profession.

"I mean it, Jules. I sometimes think I'm all shrivelled and dry inside. I would love to be back watching that medallion-encrusted barman dance on the table again because this time I would understand what he was saying, be up there with him and seize the moment!"

"And seize him?" Juliet laughs.

"Too right! Everyone has potential, even Mr Medallion Man."

"Michelle, you are doing me the world of good. Do you fancy coming over for Christmas? We'll find you another medallion man." The cat jumps up on her knee. "Hello Aaman. I haven't seen you for a while."

"Is he back?"

"No, no it is the cat. I thought it was about time he got a name. His lady cat has had kittens."

"Let me guess. She is called Saabira and what have you called the kittens?"

"No, she is called Juliet."

"I'm not sure if that isn't a bit sick."

They agree the dates over Christmas that Michelle will visit and they both get excited and giggly. They finally say a protracted goodbye, before Juliet wanders, Aaman on her shoulder, into his room. She has not been in it since he moved in. The door no longer squeaks. It vaguely smells of him. He has changed the sheets and everything is neat. There is a book of Greek verbs by his bed, the one she bought when she returned to England after her first trip to Greece. She opens the built-in cupboard. It is empty, the board at the back not quite in straight. She saw him once, when he had left the door ajar, using it as a place to hide his money. She takes a five euro note from her back pocket and slips it behind the board. *For Aaman*. The cat jumps off Juliet and onto the bed. He sniffs and settles down to sleep.

Juliet wanders through the sitting room and kitchen to the back door. The garden looks beautiful. She makes a decision to get a bench to go under the pergola. No, better still, a hammock. Actually what would be really nice would be a pond, a natural, overgrown-looking pond next to the pergola, and behind maybe a summer house. It could be her office, way in the back corner behind the vines, looking back at the house.

The tools are all lined up on his homemade shelves, his thick gloves on top. Juliet strokes the gloves. She picks them up and slips her hands inside and hugs them to her face. The gloves dangling on her small hands, she meanders to the vegetable plot. It needs weeding. She bends and pulls some of the weeds. They come out easily. She sits in a squat like Aaman would do and weeds the row. It is a pleasant job. With the sun on her back, time becomes irrelevant, the afternoon passes and the vegetable plot looks better for the attention. Juliet drops the gloves on the ground, but thinks better of it and picks them up and returns them to his shelves.

The gravel drive needs a bit of a weeding too but she feels she has done enough for today. She trips over the kittens battling in the doorway. The wine opens with a worthy pop and glugs loudly into her glass.

Aaman finds the aeroplane a little bit frightening, and it takes a long time to get to Lahore. They serve food on little plastic trays with knives and forks in plastic bags. Aaman feels like he is in a film. He looks about to see if the other passengers are equally impressed with their individual portions, but most are asleep, others are reading, no-one shows much interest in the food offered.

Aaman carefully unwraps the food and lays it on the ingenious drop-down table in front of him, which he raises and lowers several times for the joy of it. However, he is soon disappointed by the food as it does not taste of anything. Pushing it to one side, he takes comfort in being surrounded by people mostly speaking his mother tongue and he rests his head back, catching familiar conversations here and there. He closes his eyes for the landing.

The open space inside the airport building at Lahore impresses Aaman even more than the one in Athens, but here the ceiling is lower, supporting it are strong hexagonal pillars at regular intervals. The other difference, which helps Aaman feel he is home, are the people sitting on the floor everywhere he looks. Family clusters, groups of businessmen, people waiting in line for boarding passes. It is natural, it is acceptable to use the floor here.

There is a mix-up at the airport with the bags and the weary travellers move three times to different places to await their luggage.

The last time Aaman was in Lahore, he was overwhelmed by all he saw and the pace of life. He longed for his village, the open spaces, the wandering animals. This time it doesn't occur to him he is in a city. It is just part of his journey.

He feels a pang of loneliness as the other passengers are greeted with hugs and handshakes from waiting friends and relatives. Maybe he should have told them he was coming? He catches a bus into town and walks to the hotel he has booked online at Juliet's. It will cost him six euros a night.

The hotel looks a lot like the immigration centre where he was detained, but without the fence. Concrete, square, encompassing a courtyard of cars. It is very central, which is most important for the many interviews he has lined up.

There is noise all night. People shouting and banging doors. The city doesn't sleep. He is reminded of his days on the streets in Athens and takes pleasure in the width of the bed and plumps the pillows, smiling into them.

The next morning, he dresses carefully and arrives at his first appointment half an hour early. He waits in a glass hall on an aging leather sofa. He runs through in his head the questions they may ask and is startled when his name is called.

He is offered this job with a hearty handshake. The man declares that it isn't often international programmers apply for jobs with his company and that his English employers spoke very highly of him and how travelled he must be to have worked for a British company in Greece. Aaman momentarily wonders if the man has him confused with someone else but when he mentions Greece and A.J. Software House he feels his cheeks colour. The man chats on, switching from Urdu to English in the same sentence and Aaman realises that, despite his dual tongue, his view of the world is confined to Lahore. Aaman thanks him for the offer, tells him he feels very honoured to be given such a chance but would he mind if he takes a day or two to think about it. The

272

man laughs heartily, shakes his hand again and tells him to take all the time he needs.

In the following days, he goes to all of the interviews he and Juliet have pre-arranged to see what the different places are like. Many times he is greeted in the same way as the first interview. As the offers of jobs grow so does Aaman's confidence. Some ask if he would keep in touch as all positions are currently filled but they would be very interested in him in the future.

Near the end of the week, Aaman is sitting in his hotel room trying to decide which job he will take when he thinks of his family. They are still some distance away. It is a three-hour bus ride to Sialkot alone and then farther to the village. If he takes any of these jobs in Lahore, he will not be able to return to his family home at the weekends.

He takes Juliet's laptop down to reception where he is able to access the Internet and sets about emailing software houses in Sialkot. There are five that he finds online. One replies immediately and offers him an interview the following day.

As he cannot afford any of the hotels with Internet access in Sialkot he briefly wonders if he has made a rash decision whilst on the bus that takes him there that evening.

On arrival, he finds his budget room is next door to a shiny, glass-doored five-star hotel. He books into his hotel and then sits on the wall outside, his laptop under his arm and watches the porter at the hotel next door. The porter opens the door for a lady who is being led by a small dog. The dog takes her onto the immaculate narrow lawn that slopes down to the road. Once it has finished its business, it takes the lady back inside. A man draws up in a car and jumps out. He hands his keys to the doorman without even looking at him. The doorman times the opening of the door so the guest does not miss a step. A young man appears and takes the keys from the porter and drives the car around the back of the hotel. Someone comes out. They too do not acknowledge the doorman.

Aaman smooths his hair and walks purposefully along the road to the entrance of the five-star palace. He strides up to the door as if he intends to walk straight through the glass. The doorman's timing is perfect and Aaman continues on to reception, where he asks where he might wait for his colleague. The lounge through an arch is indicated.

The chairs are deeply padded, and Aaman thinks he might sink through to the floor. He was right. There is Internet access here. Two more emails have arrived, both offering interviews the next day. Aaman juggles his times and arranges to see them all in one day.

That night he doesn't sleep despite the comparative quiet. He wonders if he has been rash to turn away from the job offers in Lahore. Dawn comes, and Aaman's eyes refuse to open. Consequently, he is late for his first interview.

The pay is slightly less, but the cost of living in Sialkot is lower than in Lahore. The work is fascinating in all three of the offers he receives. The last interview, in Urdu alone, culminates in him being taken around every department and introduced as the international programmer who will be coming to work for them. Workers stand to shake his hand. Aaman feels a fraud but also enjoys his status. It is a long way from how he felt as an illegal immigrant.

He takes the second job offer of the day. The people seem most interested in their work, and there is a feeling of excitement that he too feels about programming. He begins work the next day and the following evening he finds a flat where he can live during the week and maybe, if she still wants to be near him, his wife, Saabira, can join him. He hopes his decisions would please Juliet.

He finds working in an office more difficult than he had even considered. There is much he does not understand and he makes some mistakes. One involves the changes he made in a programme on one website going live, but he forgot to close down all the other connections that he opened to the database on his computer, and it caused many problems. The site has to be taken off the Internet for some hours to fix it. This is the worst mistake. But the boss declares there isn't a person in the office who hasn't done this at some point and tells him not to worry. Nevertheless, he does worry. He has learnt from this, and it will never happen again.

His flat is not far from work, and his days consist of work, food, and sleeping. At the end of the second week, his days take on a routine, and this gives room for him to think about Juliet and Saabira and his family. Saabira feels so far away. He feels like Juliet is with him. He tries to involve himself in the life around him. Tea with his colleagues, cinema with his boss one time. He throws himself into this integration the same way he dedicated himself to programming, single-mindedly. The result, after a month, is that he is very popular at work and is known by his name at the places he visits. His confidence soars.

But he knows he has to complete his journey by returning home. In a way it would be easier not to. But he longs to see his Ma and the oxen.

Chapter 20

September, for Juliet, brings some relief as the temperature drops. The Greek cogs begin to turn and tourism dwindles. It is more noticeable in the town, but the village seems to continue on its perennial path, methods of a hundred years past still holding strong. The goats still taken out to pasture, left to roam along the hillsides, and brought home to be milked and fed and bedded down. Their protective dogs unleashed and allowed the free run of the village in their time off. The shepherds tend to the goats in their makeshift shacks, on land that is unusable for anything else. Too rocky, too sloping, too out of the way.

Juliet gets a trickle of work through the British Council and she secures the deal to translate the book. She feels excited about the book. She keeps her working hours to the mornings and early afternoons as she has finally learnt that she is more productive for the routine. As the heat of the day passes, she dons Aaman's gardening gloves and potters about in the garden, most of the time not knowing what she is doing but learning gradually. Evenings are hard. What words of wisdom did she pass onto Michelle?

Just adjustment, nothing bad is happening. It does not feel like that.

For a time, Juliet waits to hear from Aaman but as the weeks turn into months, she stops waiting. Hope remains, silent, unspoken, and unsought, occasionally popping up to tear open the wound.

October is glorious, warm but not hot, with gentle rain cooling the earth. Droplets hit the parched soil with an audible sigh, bringing confused kittens in wet coats inside. The vines that grew at an incredible speed during the spring and produced tiny buds of grapes in the early summer, now hang weighted down with clusters of tight-skinned, white-dusted, purple balloons.

Juliet discovers a small vine, which Aaman encouraged up one of the supports of the pergola. Each white, seedless grape is no bigger than her fingernail, and yet each is packed with the flavour of a whole bunch. The passion flower has grown at a phenomenal rate and produced flower upon flower and, as they faded and died, new flowers came, hidden pockets of intense colour amongst its trailing thin leaves.

November has Juliet unearthing her lighter jumpers and wondering what to get her boys for Christmas. The big celebration in Greece is Easter, but some indication of Christmas shows here and there in the shops. In the village shop, Marina has a four-inch tall silver Christmas tree for sale on the top shelf by the bottled wine. Juliet has long since discovered that the local wine, in unmarked plastic bottles at an eighth of the price, is just as good as the labelled glass bottles, but lighter, less hangover.

"Tzuliet! Hello! Isn't it a relief to have the temperature drop just a little? I can move now." And as if to prove it, she stands up and pushes her crate footstool around the front of the counter to the door where she begins to fill it, one by one, with empty beer bottles lined like soldiers against the wall. "There! I have been meaning to do that for a while. Now! What can I get you?"

"I was just wondering if you could tell me what I do with the vines once the fruit is all gone? I know they will need pruning, but when is the best time to prune and whereabouts do you cut them? Is there a rule, near a nodule? I haven't a clue."

"Ha! Neither have I. Best go to Mitsos. Ask him."

"Mitsos?"

"Yes, you know, with one arm?" Juliet shakes her head, not recalling seeing anyone in the village with one arm. Marina goes to the window and points.

"Go down to the taverna here, the little street that goes up the side there." Her pointing is indiscriminate. "Before the road turns, you'll see, not even a few yards, there is Mitsos. He has a shop for medicines for the farmers. I think he is open on Saturdays. Pesticides, that sort of thing. He will know. He went to school with my husband. Always getting into trouble, the two of them." She crosses herself looking serious for a moment before her face lights with a thought. "So have you any plans for Christmas? Will you be going home?"

"Marina, this is my home now. Besides, why would I want to leave here?"

"For your family of course. Which reminds me. Guess what?"

"What?" Juliet cannot help but smile at Marina.

"They are getting married at Christmas! Can you believe it? Suddenly. Bam!" She clashes her hands together like cymbals, her housecoat across her bosom shimmies in response. "I was always sure about him, such a nice family. She has not chosen the dress, or a definite date, but you must come. Everyone must come!"

"I would love to. So right by the taverna?"

"Yes, you cannot miss it. Mr Mitsos." She adds on the prefix in the traditional Greek way for someone who is older, but not quite old enough to rank as a *Papous*, a grandfather.

Mitsos is not there, but his younger brother Stavros is very helpful, his young wife sitting with him in the shop, enormous with child.

Juliet walks home wiser but feeling a little alone. She misses the boys. She misses company. She knows, but does not want to even give space to it in her thoughts, that she misses Aaman.

At home, the kittens are everywhere, one on each of the director's chairs outside, two on the sofa. The mother on one of the kitchen chairs and Aaman curled up on Aaman's bed. *Appropriate.*

Juliet takes up one of the sofa kittens, the stripy one. It droops boneless, and she plops it on her knee and picks up the phone. Thomas sounds happy, but he is talking very quietly, he has a hangover.

"Ah, celebrating, but not just any old common or garden celebration. A very special celebration, I was going to call you today."

"Sounds interesting. Another promotion? Finally learnt your seven times tables? Bought a new tie?"

"Ha ha, Mother dearest. Now, are you ready for this? I asked Cheri to marry me!"

"Oh darling, I'm so happy for you. That's wonderful."

Thomas sounds so excited but points out that the honeymoon (Cheri wants to go to Scotland) and general cost will push back the time he will be able to afford to come and visit Juliet. Juliet's momentary disappointment is replaced with inspiration and she offers them an engagement present of Christmas in Greece, flights, the lot. Cheri squeals in the background, picks up an extension phone and the three of them lay down the outline plan.

They say their goodbyes, Thomas and Cheri clearly excited. Juliet pops the stripy kitten on the floor and makes a cup of tea before returning to use the phone. No sooner has Terrance answered than he interrupts her to ask if she has heard about Thomas and Cheri. Juliet tells him she has offered them a Christmas in Greece and asks him what he thinks. The conversation gets twisted as they both talk from their own viewpoints, Terrance not understanding she is offering to pay for him too, Juliet not understanding his reluctance to join them to celebrate. Eventually they see each other's view and talk over each other with sorries and explanations, until Terrance pulls the conversation to an end with, "Yes! Brilliant. Thanks, Mum. That's fantastic. Yes!"

Juliet suggests he get in touch with Thomas and she promises to ring when dates and tickets are final, and they hang up, both happier for having spoken.

Tiger leaps onto his sister next to Juliet on the sofa and they play fight in a ball. Juliet strokes the writhing mass and gets a scratch for her troubles. Smiling, Juliet goes in the kitchen and rummages through drawers, counting cutlery and crockery. The crockery is a mismatched affair, mostly in white, which prompts Juliet to start a list headed with 'Red Table Cloth', to which she quickly adds 'Christmas Tree' and 'Crackers'. She spends a pleasant day planning and making lists, but as the evening draws in, the familiar, uncomfortable feeling of being alone creeps in with the shadows, and Juliet gets fidgety.

Terrance, the last to arrive, thinks they are terribly childish and resorts to lying on the rug in front of the fire dozing most of the first day he is there. However, Cheri encourages the kittens to lick cream from her fingers, Thomas puts a blob of cream on Terrance's nose. The kittens, lined up by Thomas, run up Terrance's chest, and with their paws on Terrance's chin, two of them manage to be the cats that get the cream. Thomas howls, Cheri cries with laughter, and

Terrance wakes to two little furry faces with big eyes on the end of his nose. Juliet makes the boys take the ensuing food fight into the garden.

The days merge into nights and no-one keeps track of time. Michelle declares she needs a serious holiday, not just a two-week break, and Juliet gives her the key to the spare room and says she has to watch that she isn't deported.

Cheri declares she is going to move in and sleep with the kittens. Juliet tells her that traditionally in Greece the daughter-in-law spends her wedding night in the bed of her mother-in-law to show her subservience and after that it is her duty to keep the mother-in-law's goats for her, so therefore it would be very apt for her to move in with the kittens.

Michelle jumps up and goes into the garden, returning with an armful of pomegranates. She splits them open on the table, the juice squirting at the inquisitive Terrance. Once they are split, she encourages everyone to eat. Terrance, of course is the one to ask why.

"You don't know your Greek myths, do you?" Cheri admits she doesn't and that she is in the mood for a good story. "Well, there was this goddess called Persephone, daughter of Zeus, I think. Anyway Hades, king of the underworld, falls in love with her but obviously Zeus is not into the idea of his daughter living in the underworld. Nor does he want to upset Hades, as you wouldn't!" Michelle hands out pomegranates, and Cheri gets herself a plate. "Anyway, one day Persephone is sitting by a lake and Hades kidnaps her and takes her to the underworld to marry her. Her mum is worried sick and, being a goddess, decides none of the plants should grow, and people and animals start to die because there is no food." Michelle eats a few pomegranate seeds and holds her glass out to be refilled.

"Is that it?" Cheri asks.

"No." Michelle takes a drink. "The mum, as I said, was not too pleased and all the crops are dying and it's a bit of a disaster. So Zeus demands that Persephone should be freed. Hades can't argue with Zeus, but he tricks Persephone and gives her a pomegranate to eat, and lets her go."

Thomas cheers.

"But," Michelle continues, "The law of the Underworld says that if you eat anything while you are down there you have to stay. Anyway, after a bit of a fuss it's decided that she can live on the earth for nine months of the year but has to go to Hades for three, so in those three months, her mum, I forget her name, makes sure nothing grows, that is, it's winter." Michelle drains her glass and takes a bite of seeds. "So, the moral of this story is that if we eat pomegranates whilst we are here, we will have to come back at least once a year."

"Aaman loved pomegranates," Juliet says. Everyone goes silent until she opens another bottle of wine and declares she is not slurring sufficiently.

284

They all go to the church to see Marina's daughter married in time for Christmas. Marina shocks everyone by not wearing her housecoat, turning up instead in a very sophisticated dress. She looks like she has lost weight and is stunning with her hair loose. Juliet hears a few locals remarking what a beauty she was back in her day. Juliet takes offence as they are about the same age and she reckons her 'day' is now.

Christmas day feels like they are in England, with chestnuts by the fire, mince pies and the traditional dinner. They all bundle up to go for a walk after eating so much, to be surprised at how mild it is outside. They strip down to thin jumpers and march off over the hills, greeting a goat herder eating feta and olives in the sunshine, which he offers to share. Later, they meet some children who are excitedly anticipating New Year's Day, the traditional Greek day for exchanging presents. They arrive back as it is turning dark and cold. Thomas and Terrance bring wood in for the fire. Juliet thinks of Aaman and his brother.

The days pass swiftly. It is Thomas who brings about the first reality check as he announces that his and Cheri's flight is the following day. Terrance's flight is the day after, giving Juliet and Michelle a little time to catch up and sober up before Michelle's flight back to the rat race the day after that.

Michelle raises a glass to Juliet. "It's been a brilliant Christmas. Thanks."

"Anytime." Their glasses chink.

"Can you do that then, make Christmas happen anytime?"

"That's easy. You should see what I can do with Easter."

"So how clever are you? Can you borrow Lent?"

"Only if you will draw me up a contract with terms and conditions."

Juliet chuckles as she holds the phone and stands and looks out of the glass in the kitchen door to the garden.

"Funny how it is easy to sort out other peoples' lives, but not your own."

"You're thinking of Aaman?"

"Yes."

Juliet opens the door and steps into the cool night. His old gardening shoes are under the shelves he made for the tools. She hasn't noticed before. Michelle stands beside her. The sky looks vast. There are no street or town lights to dull the hood of bright stars. Stars beyond stars. The more Juliet looks the more she sees. Michelle hangs an arm around her, hand dangling. They look up to the myriad of scintillating pinpricks in the galaxy. Distance and time at its mercy, the enormity crashing everything into perspective.

"I don't think we should leave it twenty-two years before we see each other again," Juliet says.

"Absolutely not!"

"Want to come out again at Easter?"

"Sod that. Easter's in March. I thought I might take a two-week holiday beginning of February. I might manage to work that long. Besides, that company owes me so much overtime, I could come out for a year and still be in the black."

"Seriously, when do you want to come back?"

"Seriously, I don't want to go, but seeing as I have to, I mean it, I can be back in February if I am invited."

"Do you need to ask?"

"Well I didn't even dare ask for—"

"Twenty-two years," Juliet and Michelle say in unison, laughing, walking farther into the garden.

"Juliet?"

"Yes."

"Who owns that disused barn next door?"

"Yiannis the taxi driver. Why? Oh, what are you thinking? Are you thinking what I think you're thinking?"

"Just playing with the idea. What do you think?"

"I think it would be brilliant, and if you have to stay in England and work, I could holiday let it for you. An extra little earner for you."

"And you."

"Why me?"

"Friendship is friendship, but business is business."

"No, I think I owe you."

"Will you look into it for me? See if he wants to sell, how much, if we can convert it and so on. Let's see if it's feasible first."

287

"Sure. You would become my neighbour from hell, building works day and night. I would have to sue you, you know."

"I understand your best friend is a lawyer so it wouldn't cost you much." Michelle laughs.

"Is that even technically possible, to represent someone who is suing you, sue yourself, as it were?"

"I understand in Greece anything is possible. It is the land of myths and dreams," Michelle says in a terrible Greek accent.

Chapter 21

Juliet sits outside in some rare warm sun.

January was fine, but cloudy. At the beginning of February, Michelle popped over for a week with promises of returning at Easter to talk to Yiannis some more about the barn. The winter was passing quickly. But by March, Juliet is becoming impatient for the summer sun.

The countryside bursts with wild flowers and colour. Banks of yellow flowers flank the road to the town. Women in black collect edible weeds in the fields, under trees, on hillsides. Purple flowers crack through the cemented lane. The sky is cloudless, but a pale blue, not the deep dark blue of the height of summer. It looks warmer than it is. There is still a nip to the air and there is a steady breeze. But tucked on the front patio, Juliet can enjoy the sun and is free of drafts. The bougainvillea the neighbour gave her is popping with buds, and spikes are hidden with tender green leaves, a pink flower here and there promising a cascade for the summer.

The remaining pomegranates hang low under the leaves, cracked and gnarled, bloated and split by the rain. The orange trees are bare as Juliet has plucked and eaten all the fruit, freshly squeezing them for breakfast, snacking midmorning and using them as afternoon refreshers. The kale is still producing its curly compact leaves, but Juliet replanted most of the vegetable plot at the beginning of January, and it is currently growing deliriously along with the weeds. It thrills Juliet to see, bringing the promise of fresh food and summer around the corner.

One of the kittens, now more cat than kitten, is on the roof of the barn next door. The orange tree rustles against the barn with the breeze, and the cat turns sharply, crouching instinctively in response, before continuing its way. The gate buffets a little against its chain. Juliet makes a mental note to get the old lock mended, although she knows that she really will not get around to it. The lavender by the gate is doing well and the climbing rose, which she hopes will grow in an arch over the gate, looks sturdy now, after a thin and hesitant start.

Another layer of gravel would help, but keeping up with the weeding on the drive is a job for which Juliet can never find enough time. The wall behind the pomegranate trees could do with a fresh coat of white paint, and the lane also needs weeding. Juliet cannot quite manage it all as everything grows so furiously.

She puts her feet up on the chair opposite. A cat jumps on her knee, but Juliet's eyes are closed, her head thrown back to face the sun. She feels and guesses which one it is. Possibly Tiger, definitely not Aaman. She has not seen Juliet, the mother cat, for some weeks now and suspects she has deserted

Aaman for another. She opens her eyes to nothing but blue sky, a trail of a long gone jet frilling out at distant heights.

If she sits much longer, she will break her habit of working in the morning. She knows herself well enough to spot the slippery slope. She looks down. It is Tiger. She lifts him as she stands and puts him back on the warmed seat. He purrs.

She wanders into the house. Two of the kittens are on the bed in the guest room play fighting, the sheets twisting beneath them. Juliet shoos them out, straightens the bed and closes the door which has begun to squeak again.

Today Juliet decides to work at her desk in the bedroom. She sits down and opens her new laptop, presses return and waits for everything to appear. Looking out the window, she still thinks it would be nice to have a pond by the pergola, something natural looking with a few rocks behind, all overgrown with ground-covering plants.

She opens her email account and starts to delete unsolicited emails from the top, working down. She reads ones that are work related and answers them. There is one from Michelle. She puts it in the 'Michelle' file for later. There's one email address she does not recognise. Her heart beats quicker. It's from a Pakistani email address.

She opens it, and her stomach turns over, her pulse doubles, and she momentarily feels dizzy.

Dear Juliet,

It is nearly six months since I left you. I thought it best to leave some time before writing to you. It has helped me. I hope it has helped you.

I am sure much will have happened in your life since I have left. Much has happened in mine.

The aeroplane was a little bit frightening and took a long time to get to Lahore.

I attended the interviews that we had arranged. I received offers of work but I then took a courageous move. I hope you do not think this was ungrateful of me but I did not take the jobs offered. I looked for jobs in Sialkot. I found several software houses and applied to them, printing out the email that you wrote. I hope you don't mind?

It was a great success and I was offered a job that would have been my boyhood dream.

I stayed in Sialkot for a month before I returned home. I did this because I wanted to be sure that I had the job and that I was not going to be sacked for not being good enough. I also did this because each day that I worked I could feel my confidence growing and I wanted to go home a confident man, not a man who had last been seen as an illegal immigrant. I also needed some time on my own to be back in Pakistan.

When I decided I could go back to my village I felt very nervous. Many things could have happened. I feared my grandparents could have died, or my mother could be unwell. Many things I thought as I took the bus to near our village. The last part must be walked and so I entered the village on foot.

The first person Aaman sees is his grandfather. He looks like he is walking along the street for no reason. He looks up at Aaman from a distance and squints at him. It takes him a full minute to recognise Aaman. Aaman savours the sight, then his grandfather drops his stick and tries to run. Aaman runs too and catches grandfather as his legs wobble. They hug, grandfather's hands patting Aaman's back. Aaman has tears running down his cheeks, grandfather is talking so quickly he is making no sense. They pull away and look at each other and hug again.

"I thought I would never see you again," is the only thing Aaman can hear him say clearly. But Aaman is making noise too, he is laughing and asking how grandma is, how Ma is, how Father is, are the oxen OK, has anything changed?

They are such a noise that grandmother and Ma come out of the house to see what all the fuss is. Ma drops the bowl she is drying and runs to Aaman, her soft, brightly coloured clothes fluttering. She cries and hugs Aaman so tightly he cannot breathe. She kisses him all over his face and head and hands.

"I thought you were dead!" she wails, new tears upon old. Aaman strokes her hair and makes calming noises. His grandma has hold of his other hand, she is kissing it and rubbing it against her soft, chestnut skin.

"Where's father?" Aaman finally asks.

"He's in the corner field, I will go and get him."
Grandfather sets off, swinging his stick, a bounce in
his step.

The women hug him some more until Aaman
asks, "Where is Saabira?"

He looks to the house and sees her peering from
the door. He puts his hand out to her. She hesitates
and then comes running into his arms.

"I was afraid that you did not want me anymore."

He takes her face in his hands and looks into her
eyes for a long time.

"Hello, Saabira, I have come back to you." Aaman
pulls her to him as she sobs.

Whilst Aaman hugs Saabira, a neighbour comes
out to see what the fuss is and screams when she sees
Aaman. That causes several other faces to appear and
soon people are flocking from all directions, slapping
him on the back, asking him questions about Iran,
Greece, Italy, and Spain.

There is such a great commotion that Aaman does
not find space to tell his family about his job in
Sialkot. His father comes next and barges through
everyone to greet Aaman. He hugs him so tightly,
Aaman is impressed by his strength for his age.

The sun is beating down on them, and Aaman's
mother herds them all into the house. The room
quickly fills as more and more people hear of his
return and come to wish him welcome.

The questions never stop. Neighbours bring food,
and the welcome becomes a party. No one asks about

the money for the harvester, they are all just pleased to see him home.

The whole weekend involves much talking and telling of the tales of his journey to Greece and back. Children stand wide eyed, gasping at the dangerous parts and cheering at his accomplishments. Saabira sits by his side, never losing physical contact.

By Sunday evening, Aaman is exhausted, but people still come to visit and everyone is still very excited. He tells his family that he must go to bed early as he must leave very early in the morning. This produces looks of horror from his mother and Saabira who cling to him all the more.

The room is still full of visiting neighbours and there is so much noise that his Ma and Saabira cannot hear him. Aaman stands up and quietens the room. He then announces to everyone that he has a job at Sialkot as a programmer which is received in a deathly hush as no one quite understands. He, Aaman, is a farm boy. Aaman then tells the tale of Juliet; it becomes unreal in the telling. Before he reaches the end of the tale, more neighbours arrive and want to hear from the beginning. The younger ones ask him to tell it again as well, they enjoyed it so much the first time. So Aaman starts the tale again, and Juliet disappears from reality into the word of folklore.

Not a sound is made as he tells his tale. When it culminates with the offer of several jobs in Lahore, and then him taking one in Sialkot, his mother screams and cries tears of happiness afresh, and his father and grandfather can be seen to grow a few inches, their heads are held so high. Saabira glows with pride. One of the younger boys cheers. This is followed by someone else who cheers and claps, and without design, the party starts all over again and sleep is forgotten. Aaman feels so happy to bring such joy to his family.

Aaman goes back to Sialkot for the week and returns the following weekend. His mother says it is like a show where you get all the story in pieces. But that next weekend, he tells everything. When he tells them he has made the money for the harvester, his father runs to tell their neighbours. Before the afternoon is finished, the whole village is in Aaman's family house again talking about how soon they could get the machine. Every time Aaman speaks now, the room hushes, his words hung on to like beans during a famine. Aaman points out that harvest is over for the year, and it would be better for the money to stay in the bank to earn interest than having a machine sit idle for long months. If they all put their money together into one account they would raise enough interest between them to buy a slightly newer harvester than the one they had set their sights on.

His mother declares him to be the cleverest man in the world, and his father slaps him on the back. They are so proud. Aaman stands tall like a man. He wishes Juliet could have been there.

Juliet wipes away a tear and reads on.

296

Now I will tell you about Saabira. She was shy like when we first were married but I knew I had to deal with my fear of hurting her. So I was bold, Juliet. I tried to sweep her off her feet. But I hesitated and often forgot where I was and some of my thoughts I am not proud of. Saabira is my wife and my thoughts are only for her. But I had spent so long apart from her, she was not foremost in my mind, and I drifted to what was a more familiar vision for me. I believe you can understand all this.

But time has healed us and the greatest news I have yet to tell you. Saabira is pregnant. We live in Sialkot during the week and I have good doctors checking her regularly so I feel confident that all will be well.

When she realised she was pregnant, we became closer and I have told her all about you. I have told her about your kindness and your care and she has asked me to send to you her very greatest regards. She respects you highly.

I have come to realise that ours is not a relationship that is to pass, Juliet. I want to know you for the rest of my life in some capacity. I trust I have your permission to write to you often now I have settled where I am.

I nearly forgot to say Saabira is adamant, she wants to call our baby Juliet. I trust this is acceptable to you.

With Warmest Good Wishes
Aaman

Juliet pulls another tissue from the box and wipes her nose. She looks over the garden and can see Aaman vividly at every job. But the Aaman in her mind gives her only happiness.

297

Dear Aaman,

I am delighted by your hero's return. It is no more than you deserve. I think what you have done and achieved is extraordinary and I applaud you.

I think I would like Saabira. Please pass my warmest regards back to her. I would be honoured if you named your child after me.

I hope your harvester makes your father's life easier and brings prosperity to your village.

You have brought me nothing but happiness. I too feel that ours is a relationship that will not pass and I too wish to know you the rest of my days.

Maybe when the baby is born, I could come to Pakistan, stay in an hotel in Sialkot and visit you.

Your Loving Friend
Juliet

Juliet wipes her eyes on her tissue and looks out of the window. The grass needs cutting. Her thoughts are still with Aaman, and she rises from her desk and wanders through the kitchen and out into the garden. She picks up his gardening gloves and holds them to her face as she walks amongst the trees. Nearing the vegetable plot, she puts the gloves on and bends to pull a weed or two. She is disturbed by an odd noise. She looks up. It is coming from behind the orange tree by the gate. It stops, and she continues. The noise is there again, a hollow wooden sound. She takes the gloves off and straightens. It is a rhythmic tapping sound. She walks around the orange tree. A man stands by the gate. He stops tapping it with the stick he holds. Juliet walks up to him.

"Hello, Madam. My name is Harpeet. I am looking for work."

Good reviews are important to a novel's success and will help others find The Illegal Gardener. If you enjoyed it, please be kind and leave a review wherever you purchased the book.

I'm always delighted to receive email from readers, and I welcome new friends on Facebook.

https://www.facebook.com/authorsaraalexi
saraalexi@me.com

Happy reading,

Sara Alexi

Also by Sara Alexi

Black Butterflies
The Explosive Nature of Friendship
The Gypsy's Dream
The Art of Becoming Homeless
In the Shade of the Monkey Puzzle Tree
A Handful of Pebbles